KEEPER VS. REAPER

JENNIFER MALONE WRIGHT

KEEPER VS. REAPER

GRAVEYARD GUARDIANS

ISBN-13: 978-1500745875
ISBN-10: 1500745871

Visit the website of Jennifer Malone Wright at
www.jennifermalonewright.com

ACKNOWLEDGMENTS

I would like to thank my good friends Rose and Kym for helping with every step during the process of bringing this story into the world.

Thank you to *We Got You Covered* for the amazing cover and interior design.

Thank you to my editor at *Ink Slasher Editing*.

I want to thank my amazing team leader and friend Jeni for absolutely everything that you do. You have been a life saver so many times over the last couple of years.

A shout out here for Willow and Cheree because you guys are a huge part of this as well.

I love you all.

Finally, thank you to my husband, for his continued support and encouragement of my writing. Thank you, Honey. I love you.

ALSO BY JENNIFER MALONE WRIGHT

Keeper vs. Reaper (Graveyard Guardians #1)

Keeper of the Peace (Graveyard Guardians #2)

BearyTales

Savior (A Higher Collective Novel)

Once Upon a Zombie Apocalypse – Jade

Once Upon a Zombie Apocalypse: Episode 2

The Vampire Hunter's Daughter Part 1

The Vampire Hunter's Daughter: Part 2

The Vampire Hunter's Daughter Part 3

The Vampire Hunter's Daughter: Part 4

The Vampire Hunter's Daughter: Part 5

The Vampire Hunter's Daughter: Part 6

The Vampire Hunter's Daughter: The Complete Collection

Love & War (The Arcadia Falls Chronicles 1)

Taking Talon (The Arcadia Falls Chronicles 2)

Vampire Apocalypse (The Arcadia Falls Chronicles 3)

Blood Warrior (The Arcadia Falls Chronicles 4)

Winds of Fire (The Arcadia Falls Chronicles 5)

Innocence and Evil (The Arcadia Falls Chronicles 6)

Origins and Impulse (The Arcadia Falls Chronicles 7)

Mortals and Magic (The Arcadia Falls Chronicles 8)

Sound of Sirens (The Arcadia Falls Chronicles 9)

Heart of the Hurricane (The Arcadia Falls Chronicles 10)

Broken Souls (Runes Universe)

HE WAS A REAPER
AND
SHE WAS A KEEPER

JACK

1

Jackson Walker peeled open his eyes when the morning sun came streaming through his bedroom window.

"Fuck." He ripped the black cotton sheet away from his naked body and staggered toward the windows. Once he maneuvered past the maze of clothing on the floor, he grasped the heavy drapes and yanked them shut.

With a groan, he detoured to the kitchen instead of going back to bed. "Fucking cheap ass beer," he muttered under his breath as his feet hit the cold tile of the kitchen floor. The tiny little house actually had a decent kitchen in it, not that it mattered to him, since he hated cooking and avoided any sort of kitchen activity … unless it involved a blonde with nice rack. Then, activities in the kitchen were acceptable.

At the ancient porcelain sink he reached up and grabbed the bottle of aspirin off the window sill. He poured three into his hand and popped them into his mouth, following up by chugging a gigantic tumbler of water.

"Hey, baby."

He heard the sugary voice of the woman behind him and wished he had sent her home the night before.

The awkward business of sending them home the next day was one of those things Jack never looked forward to. Not that he really cared about their feelings. It was more of an inconvenience than anything.

He turned around and leaned against the sink, giving her full view of his nakedness. She stood in the doorway to the kitchen, his white cotton tee shirt covering her more than amazing upper body. He noticed she had also slipped the tiny wisp of black fabric she called panties back on. Briefly he wondered how they were even still in one piece after the night before.

"What are you looking at?" he asked her, knowing full well exactly where her eyes had gone. The glossy look of lust that Jack was more than familiar with appeared in her eyes as she ran her gaze from his eyes, down over his taut muscles, and finally settling below his midsection. She licked her bottom lip and bit down on it gently before gliding toward him.

Jack felt the sudden rush of blood as he grew hard, knowing that Janet ... or Janice, was ready for another round. He waited for her to come to him. She crossed the kitchen, tossing her long dark hair behind her shoulder just before she pushed herself up against him.

"Let's go back to bed," she whispered, rubbing her tee shirt covered breasts against his naked chest.

Jack groaned as his erection pushed against her panties. "Right here seems fine with me," he whispered in her ear, bending down to grasp her legs and lift her up so that he could more efficiently grind himself against her.

She wrapped her arms around his neck and tilted her head back with a moan. Jack could feel her panties almost dripping with want for him already. Any man would have a hard time turning that down. With ease, he spun around and set her tiny ass on the edge of the counter, yanking her legs forward so that his erection pushed hard between her thighs.

Reaching down, she lifted his tee shirt up over her enormous breasts. Jack knew they were fake, but they were still down right amazing. Over the head with the shirt and onto the floor, leaving Janet ... or Janice, God why wasn't he better with names, in only her tiny black panties. Deciding instantly that she wasn't going home with those intact, he ran his finger across the inside, grazing her sweet spot. With a sudden gasp she arched her back, thrusting herself toward him. At that moment he curled his finger around the fabric and yanked. The string of lace at the hip popped loose and he pulled them all the way down her leg and over the toe where the ruined panties joined the discarded shirt.

Before he went any further, he felt around below the edge of the counter, searching for the handle of the drawer he filled with junk from his pockets. He knew there was a condom in there somewhere. If not, he was going to have to take her back to the bedroom because there was no way he was fucking anyone without a condom. He didn't have a clue where most of the women he was with had been, and furthermore, the very last thing he needed was to knock someone up.

Better safe than sorry.

His hand shuffled around and then, bingo. As quick as he could he brought the square package to his lips and ripped it open with his teeth. He had the thing on pretty much instantaneously. If putting a condom on in record time was ever made into a sport, he was likely to be voted the fucking MVP.

Up against her again, he pulled her close with one large hand and let the other find its way into her hair, grasping a handful and pulling back.

"Now," she moaned. "Right now."

With no further invitation needed, he pushed into her and his lips found hers. Her moans were muffled against his lips and tongue with each thrust. He felt her orgasm building, until finally she erupted, thighs clenching around his waist and her body thrashing

3

against him.

At the exact same moment of his own climax, he grasped her head with both hands to prevent her from moving away. Keeping his mouth crushed against hers, he felt her soul release from its encasing tomb of a body and flow up through her chest and throat. The blue mist of her soul that he could not see was transferred into him. Souls had no taste, but filled him the same as food would satisfy a ravenous hunger.

His body lurched again with another orgasm in response to the soul entering him. He felt the woman's body begin to weaken as her grasp on him loosened. He ripped his mouth away from hers, breaking the seal of the transfer for the soul.

Carefully, he pulled her against him. Her head lolled to the side and her limbs sagged.

"Shit." He silently chastised himself for taking too much. With some of the living he found that he could take a little of their soul and they would never even know because they were dying inside already. Mostly this type of person was found in the depressed, alcoholics, hookers, and the like. The living soul provided so much more for him than the dead souls did, not to mention that they were still alive. He may be a self-admitted asshole, but there was something about taking a soul and preventing it from crossing over that didn't sit right with him. He preferred to know that he wasn't a murderer and taking the souls of the dead was on the same level for him.

Most of the women he took from never had a clue anything was wrong. It was masked by their orgasm, and usually some sort of booze.

With a sigh he scooped her up, letting her limp legs hang over one arm, her head and arms dangling over the other, and carried her into the bedroom where he deposited her onto the bed. As he set her down onto the soft bedding, her dark eyes fluttered open and she looked up at him with confusion. "Damn it," she croaked. "I must still be a little drunk. I think I passed out." She pushed herself up onto her hands so that she was sitting up and then used one of her hands to brush the brunette locks away from her eyes. "I'm so sorry."

Jack rose up and stood over her, looking down at the beautiful woman who would never be for him. He ate souls to live, and she was a single woman who didn't think she was worth anything. Life had beaten her into submission so badly that she no longer lived for herself, but merely to survive. He just couldn't be with any woman who was half dead inside because he would end up killing her himself.

Sadly, this was the problem he encountered with most women.

"No worries," he told her, turning away. "I'm going to go get in the shower. I have an appointment in about an hour, so…"

"You want me to leave?"

He nodded. "Nothing personal." He spread his hands. "This was fun, but I can't let you stay here while I'm gone."

She turned her head away to avoid his eyes and self-consciously covered her breasts with one hand while pulling the sheet over her midsection with the other. "I'll get my things together in just a minute. I'm still feeling a little bit dizzy."

Jack smiled, flashing her his perfect set of white teeth. "Take your time."

She looked up at him like he was the biggest asshole on the face of the earth, because even she knew that 'take your time' was read as 'get the fuck out.'

Still naked, he sauntered through the door to the connecting bathroom. Once inside, he leaned over the ancient clawfoot tub and turned on the hot water. The tub had a circular curtain around it and a shower head had been added to the original fixtures. After making sure he had a towel on the rack for afterward, he stepped into the shower and let the hot water wash over him.

The wicked headache from the cheap beer he had

downed the night before still plagued him, despite the aspirin and sex. Bending over he turned the water on as hot as he could take it, and then grabbed up his trusty bar of Irish Spring and began the ritual of scrubbing the sweat and sex away from his body.

He didn't really have an appointment to get to, and he stayed in the shower purposely longer than he would have normally showered to give Janet … or Janice, time to get her clothes on and leave.

When the water heater finally gave out and the water began to run cold he turned the faucet off and stepped out onto the cushy blue bath mat to dry off. After drying his body, he wrapped the towel around his waist and stepped up to the sink. He used the hand towel to wipe away a spot on the mirror so that he could see his reflection.

His hair was getting a bit longer than he usually wore it. The wet charcoal locks fell down over his green eyes, scraping against his long black lashes that most women would kill for. He hadn't shaved for a couple of days, except to trim it up. He turned his face from side to side in the mirror, inspecting his facial hair and tossing around the idea of growing a goatee.

After deciding against the goatee and simply tidied up the hair that was already there with his electric trimmer, he brushed his teeth and then made his way back to the bedroom where he slipped on a pair of jeans and a plain black tee shirt.

The serene silence of the old house was abruptly interrupted by his phone ringing. He recognized the ring he had set for his mother and hurried over to the nightstand where he had left his phone the night before.

"Hey Mom."

"Jackson." Her response was cold, as it always was.

"How are things going at home? Everyone all right? Dad?"

"Everything here is fine, your father is doing well … for now. The Florida heat wears on him though, we are considering a move to a more regulated climate."

"I'm glad he's all right."

A short silence took place before his mother continued to speak. "Have you found the new Keeper?"

"No Mom, I just got here."

He heard her sigh over the line and he could picture her sitting in one of the uncomfortably straight dining room chairs in their uncomfortably fancy dining room, shaking her head at his incompetence. "Jackson, you have had ample time to get used to your accommodations. What have you been doing with your time?"

He glanced over at the rumpled sheets strewn across his bed and grinned. "Just getting to know my way around town."

Another sigh. "Which means you have been whoring yourself around, I take it."

Jack didn't respond. Camille Walker was one he learned early on not to argue with.

"Jackson, you have to understand that your freedom with your sexual endeavors does reflect on the family. I just don't understand why you have to go around giving yourself to every money hungry slut on two feet. There are plenty of women of our kind who would be more than happy to be with a man such as yourself."

It was Jack's turn to sigh. "It's not about that mom."

"Well what it is about then, please enlighten me." Even though he sensed her anger, her voice didn't change one octave. She had been that way ever since he could remember. Camille didn't have to raise her voice. She was unnervingly calm all the time.

"Just let it go, please. I'll slow it down," Jack lied.

"You will get your head in the game, Son. You have one job and one job only. The Estmond Keeper needs to die and it needs to be soon."

"I know, I know … because she could be the one the legend speaks of."

"Sass me again, Jackson. I will have the guard there by tonight to drag your ass back home."

"Get the job done and call me when it's accomplished."

"Yes, Mother."

"Goodbye, Jackson." Camille hung up the phone without waiting for Jack to bid her goodbye as well.

Jack clicked off his phone and chucked it onto the bed. "Fuck," he muttered to himself. Stupid fucking orders. The Reaper Council had plenty of Reapers out there to do jobs like this. But no, it had to be him because he was Camille and Ephraim Walker's son. He couldn't even count how many times in his life he had wished that he wasn't their son.

The Reaper society came with a hierarchy, and his parents were at the top of that chain. Only the High Elder of The Reaper Council sat above his parents, which left him next in the line of Walkers to take his father's place, and that looked like it was going to be sooner rather than later if his father's health kept deteriorating.

He had no interest in killing the Estmond Keeper, or even going into her graveyard. He would have been happy just to hang out in Summer Hollow for a month or so and then go back home, or find another place to chill for a while. But, apparently, the orders were something that the Council was not going to ignore and he was going to have to get the job done.

He sat on the edge of the bed, grabbed his boots and shoved his feet into them. He would have to wait until nightfall to head over to the graveyard, so first things first. Time to chase the lingering hangover with some caffeine and a nice greasy breakfast at the diner.

Jack headed out the door, not bothering to lock it behind him, and headed straight for his black Ford truck parked in the gravel driveway. Once behind the wheel, he started the engine and looked through the windshield at the scenery surrounding his rented place. Oak trees were gathered around the house, with a few pines stuck in between them. A crescent shaped pond lay at the bottom of the slope on the west side of the house. On that same side of the house was a porch with an expanse of lawn, a fire pit, and a few pieces of outdoor furniture.

This was a nice place, cozy and peaceful. Nothing like the cold, harsh home and décor he had grown up with. This was exactly the kind of place he could actually think about settling down for a while.

Although, after killing the Keeper he would have to disappear and let the Reaper Council do what they do best and cover it up. Settling down any time soon simply was not in the cards for Jack Walker.

ℒUCY
2

Inch by painstaking inch, the casket sank lower into the freshly churned earth.

The scent of lilacs floated on the breeze along with the heavy stench of perfume and cologne, reminding Lucy of the fragrance aisle in a department store.

Lucy stood beside the grave, dressed in a modest royal blue sundress. She had chosen it specifically because her father always said the color looked the best against her hair, which was a mix of reddish brown that shone burgundy in the sunlight.

Tilting her head up, Lucy looked through the canopy of the aging oak trees that were scattered throughout the cemetery. The breeze shifted the branches, causing a few of the leaves to pull free and flutter off into the wind. There were almost no clouds in sky, allowing the sun to shine down over the funeral.

Her brothers and sisters surrounded the open grave opposite of her. All six of them also wore something fitting for a funeral, but nothing depressing enough to send their father into a rage in his afterlife.

Smiling, Lucy remembered the argument she and her father had during his last moments. "Lucy!" he had shouted at her. "Don't you dare let them bury me in a suit. I am not going to spend eternity in a stuffy ass business suit. Make sure I'm wearing my khaki shorts and a Hawaiian shirt because I'm going on the vacation of a lifetime."

That was toward the end, when the cancer was so bad that her dad spent most of his time in bed, moaning about how he should be up and about doing something. They both knew that the end was near, but Lucy had cried only in private. Her father wanted her to be happy he was moving on to the next life, but she couldn't understand in what way, shape or form that his dying was a good thing.

So she shed her tears alone in her room until there were no more left to cry.

The fog of the memory lifted from Lucy's mind and she looked across the grave at her brothers and sisters. The entire brood of Estmond siblings had the same color hair that Lucy had been blessed with. Each of them, as well as Lucy and Ethan, held a white rose in one hand. Later, before the grave was sealed, they would each take a turn throwing one down onto the casket, as a symbol of their wish for their father's peaceful journey into the afterlife.

Just behind her brothers and sisters stood the mourners who came to pay their last respects. Most of them were townspeople whom they had grown up with, except for one group who stood close together, most of them around her father's age. These were the Keepers her family had been closest to over the years. She could see Gloria and Edward White, the Keepers from one of the Napa Valley graveyards, standing solemnly beside Ellen and Stanly Evans, who worked in the hospital in Santa Rosa. There were several other Keepers surrounding them who she recognized and made a note to speak to them later.

Beyond them, further out into the trees, the spirits began to show themselves. They appeared in the form of their human bodies, a bit transparent, but solid for the most part. It was harder to see in the daylight, but their misty blue auras swirled around them, helping form the solidity of their bodies.

The spirits were fascinated by funerals. When Lucy was little, she used to think that they wanted to say goodbye to someone, but really it was because there wasn't much else to do in a graveyard except talk to each other and attend burials.

Pastor Brown spoke solemnly, saying kind words and telling her father's life story. Inwardly, Lucy cursed her father for choosing Pastor Brown, a man who had not known her father, and she was sure he didn't give a flying fuck about him either. Her father hadn't set foot in church since he was a child. Not because he didn't believe in God, he just didn't believe in organized religion.

Sensing her tension, Ethan squeezed her hand reassuringly. Turning to her left, she looked up and met her best friend's eyes through the tint of his sunglasses. Even through the dark lenses she could see the sorrow in his eyes. He had loved her father too, just as much as any one of the Estmond clan. In response, she squeezed his hand back and then turned to stare at the grave again.

"And now, Lucy Mae, Gregory's youngest child, will say a few words about her father." The preacher cleared his throat, signaling to Lucy that it was time.

Lucy had no tears staining her face. She had cried all those tears long before the day of the funeral. Again, Ethan gave her hand a gentle squeeze and then released her so that she could reach down and withdraw the folded piece of yellow legal paper out of her miniscule handbag.

As Lucy unfolded the paper she felt like it was taking an eternity.

This day is never going to end.

Finally, the paper was open in front of her and she began.

"I know that this speech is going to sound like the speeches given for so many others who have passed on. But, when someone we love dies, we all feel pretty much the same way … so here it goes. My father, Gregory Estmond, was the best person I've ever known. Today, we stand here, not to mourn him, but to celebrate him. He didn't want any one of us to be sad that he was gone. Because … he isn't gone. He will always be with us. For those of us who spent each day with him, his teachings and his love will always be with us. He taught us love, he taught us respect, he taught us of our family heritage, and he taught us how to *live*.

"For those who are acquaintances of my father, you may have met him only once and you are here because he impacted you in some way."

A few nods came from the crowd.

Lucy continued. "He had that effect on people because he had a genuine love and respect for human life. Which is not something all of us can say we have. He treated everyone the same, with kindness.

"Because my father had cancer, he knew that this day was coming and he had time to prepare for it. We had many discussions and the one thing he consistently told me was to embrace life. He didn't say this because he was dying, it was his mantra. This man lived every day of his life like it may be his last. He didn't wait until he was dying to find the beauty in this world or the people in it. He was always this way.

"Remember my father, not with sadness, but with the memories he left behind. Remember him with love, with laughter, and knowing that he is exactly where he wants to be."

Lucy stepped back, reaching out for Ethan to grasp her hand once again. She eyed her siblings. None of them were crying either. Daniel, the second oldest son, reached into his gray trench coat and pulled out a silver flask. Lucy sighed and watched as her brother didn't even try to hide it as he took a long pull of the whiskey she knew was inside.

Sadly, as inappropriate as her brother was being, she couldn't help but wish she could take a giant swig off

13

that flask too.

It's almost over.

"Would anyone else like to say a few words?" Pastor Brown offered.

Sheriff Davis stepped forward, he had his Stetson clutched in one hand and hitched up his gun belt with the other. As always he was wearing his uniform. The sheriff and her father had been pretty close ... well, as close as a Keeper can get to someone without that someone thinking that they are out of their mind.

"I'd like to, if that's all right." The sheriff looked down into the grave before his eyes swept across the crowd of mourners. Finally his eyes met Lucy's and she flashed him a smile meant to encourage him to proceed.

"Greg was my friend ... and an old grump like me doesn't have many friends. Greg knew a lot of people in this town, but I feel damn sorry for anyone who lives here and never had the chance to meet him. No one, aside from my own wife, Darcy, could make me laugh like Greg could. He was loyal and respectful, even if he was a bullshitter. Good grief that man liked to tell stories. Also, any man who can raise a brood of children by himself and manage to keep them all out of jail is a good man in my book."

Lucy could have sworn that she heard Principal Robertson blow air between his lips like he was blowing a raspberry. A few people looked his way and then back at Sheriff Davis.

"That is all I got." Sheriff Davis stepped back into the crowd.

Evelynn Andrews, the librarian at the Summer Hollow library, raised her hand slightly. She was about seventy years old, but didn't look a day over fifty-five. Lucy hoped she would age that well as the years progressed.

Evelynn pushed her glasses up her nose and closed her eyes for a moment before she began to speak. "I don't think I can say much more about how wonderful

14

Gregory was, but I wanted to make sure to pay my respects by voicing them. I've known the Estmond family all the way back to when Kathleen was still alive, as far back as when she and Greg were high school sweethearts. No one could have been a better father to these children. Sure, they have caused a fair amount of ruckus over the years, but he did it all on his own and they are educated, mostly well-behaved."

She paused to glance at Daniel, who had decided that moment would be appropriate for another pull from his flask. "And above all, Greg gave these children a sense of loyalty. Anyone who knows these kids knows that if you mess with one, you get the whole bunch of them."

A few people giggled, even Lucy, knowing how true that statement really was.

"This may not seem like a good thing in retrospect, but a family who stays together so closely is a rare thing these days. It is to be cherished. Greg gave them this sense of family and that is something to be proud of." As she finished, she closed her eyes again and then looked to Pastor Brown.

"Would anyone else like to speak?" Pastor Brown addressed the crowd of mourners.

Unexpectedly, Ethan released Lucy's hand and raised it up a little bit. "I need to say something."

Pastor Brown nodded and held his hand out beside him. Ethan moved over to the other side of Lucy beside the pastor. "There are very few people here who don't know who I am," Ethan began. "Gregory Estmond took me under his wing a long time ago, when Lucy and I were both very little. My parents, who have moved away now…"

He paused and took a breath, pondering if he should let out the deep, dark family secrets. Well, secrets that the whole town knew anyway. That was how small towns worked.

"They were drug addicts and alcoholics who barely took care of me. Greg came by the house one day to see

15

my parents for some reason, and what he found was a little boy locked in his room with no food or water, his parents passed out in their bedroom surrounded by drugs and trash. The story is a long one. A long sad story. But it ended with Greg and the rest of the Estmonds making sure I always had a place to go, that I always had food. Greg even went so far as to pay me for making good grades, just to give me incentive to do well in school."

Lucy grimaced as he told the story, hating Ethan's parents for what they did to him. Ethan had conveniently left out the part about how her father had beat the ever living snot out of Ethan's dad that day he found him locked up in his room half-starved. It was hard to believe Ethan's parents came from a Keeper line, but sadly, not all Keepers were immune to addiction. Keepers were human, just like everyone else.

Ethan scanned the crowd through his glasses. "No one, except for maybe the Estmond kids, owes more, or loves that man more than I do. He saved me and I will *never* forget that. I hope that none of you ever forget that either."

Ethan lowered his head and hurried back to Lucy. She immediately took his hand again, knowing how hard it must have been for him to say all that in front of everyone. He *never* spoke about his parents. They moved away when he was fourteen and left him alone in the house. After that, he came to live with the Estmonds for good. She and Ethan were friends long before the incident at Ethan's house, but after he came to live with them, they were inseparable.

Pastor Brown closed up the ceremony with a prayer and then the bagpipes started on Amazing Grace. Lucy stepped forward with Ethan's hand firmly in her grasp and looked down into the dark, deep hole where her father's body would spend eternity. Luckily, she knew better than most that his soul would not remain in that body.

She held the white rose firmly over the grave. "I wish you peaceful passage." She released the rose and it drifted down into the depths of the hole. "I love you, Daddy."

Ethan mimicked her actions, familiar with the meaning of the ceremony from the many deaths of Keepers past. Her siblings had moved into a line directly behind her and Ethan, tossing their roses in as well.

The other mourners milled about, giving Lucy and the family some time before they headed over to her house for the wake. She caught sight of Gloria and Ellen chatting beside the giant wreath of flowers with her father's picture inside. She wandered over to say hello. "Gloria, Ellen, it's been so long since I've seen you."

Gloria smiled, as did Ellen. "Yes dear," Gloria greeted her. "It has been some time. I'm sorry we couldn't make it sooner."

"Or under better circumstances," Ellen added.

Lucy nodded. "Well, I'm just glad that you could make it. I'm sure my father would be happy that you are here now."

Gloria and Ellen nodded, they made a bit more small talk and then Ethan appeared beside her. "I think we had better get over to the house now," he whispered just loudly enough for the older ladies to hear.

"Oh," Lucy checked her watch deliberately. "You are absolutely right. I'm sorry ladies, I need to get some things ready over at the house."

Gloria smiled again, a loving gentle smile of someone she had known her entire life. "You go on dear, we will see you over there."

With a quick 'see you later,' Lucy backed away and then turned to join hands with Ethan again. "Thanks for saving me. I didn't really want to talk to them, but I had to make sure to say hello to them."

"You doing all right?" Ethan asked, rubbing the back of her hand with his thumb.

Lucy nodded. "I'm fine." She turned her head to try and see his eyes through the dark tint of his glasses. "How 'bout you? Are you all right?"

He twisted his lip up a little, and she knew he was giving a slight eye roll. "I'll survive. I just miss him, and all this," he gestured to the crowd, "actually makes it harder."

She nodded again. "I know what you mean. I feel the same way." Her gaze strayed from the grave and focused on her house. Their home sat on the edge of the cemetery, separated from the dead by a white picket fence and about thirty yards of grass. The yellow farmhouse had been in their family for several generations, and now it was hers, as was the family business.

"Let's head over."

She nodded. Of course they had to get to the house. But, it wouldn't be for relaxing. There was food to get out and serve. People would come up to her and tell her how sorry they were for her loss, or how much her father meant to them, or some awesome memory they had of him. It was going to be a very long afternoon.

Almost over, she told herself again. *Almost over.*

JACK
3

Jack pulled open the single glass door of Brandy's café. The bells attached to the handle jingled merrily, announcing his arrival to everyone inside. He let the door swing shut behind him as he stepped inside and took a look around the tiny restaurant.

The place was almost full and immediately Jack regretted choosing it over the larger café. Sadly, the choice establishments to get a good breakfast in Summer Hollow were rather limited. There were only two restaurants in town, a pizza place and a deli slash grocery store. It was a sad situation. This tiny ass town didn't even have a decent hotel, which was why he was living in a house. At least in a hotel of his class he could order room service ... well, not in this town.

Reaching up, he removed his sunglasses so he could see the interior better. There were six booths lined up back to back by the windows. They were made of vinyl and were a god-awful brown color that was almost, but not quite, a burgundy. All of the booths were taken and the tables situated in the center of the place were also full. Looked like he was going to have to sit at the bar instead of a table.

Shit.

He would have preferred not to have to socialize

with anyone. A table would have allowed him more privacy.

All the patrons sat eating their breakfasts, drinking their coffee, and staring at him with curiosity as he strode over to the bar and pulled out the only open stool. He ignored the stares, but did notice that his stool was in between an older man with graying hair and a younger woman with blonde hair and an extremely sexy pair of legs. His gaze slid from the woman's high heeled foot, up her calf, to the thigh where it met with a business type skirt. Yanking his eyes up even further he realized she was also wearing a blazer.

"Mind if I sit here?" he asked, shifting his eyes back and forth between her and the old man.

The old man looked up from his biscuits and gravy. "It's all yours, Son."

"Go ahead," the woman mumbled without looking up from her newspaper that was spread out in front of her.

Jack turned the stool a bit and then plopped his ass down onto it. He had no sooner turned the chair back around to face forward when the waitress appeared, holding a pot of thick looking coffee in one hand. "Hey there!" She tilted the corners of her mouth into a smile. "Are you going to have breakfast this morning, or just coffee?"

He grinned back at her, lowering his gaze from her bright blue eyes down to the breast of her tan button up blouse, where her name tag was snuggled above the pocket. The white plastic tag told him her name was Lisa. "I think I'm going to have both," he told her and flipped over the coffee cup sitting on a napkin in front of him.

Damn, he thought. For such a small town, Summer Hollow sure was full of hot chicks.

"Great." She poured the coffee and then handed him a single sheet of laminated paper. "Here's your menu. Let me know when you decide what you want." She winked at him and took off down the bar, checking to see if anyone needed refills or anything.

Before he paid any real attention to the menu he took a giant swig of the steaming black coffee. It was hot going down, so hot that it burned his tongue and throat, but he didn't care. He savored the bitterness of the liquid and hoped it would help kick back the lingering headache that still plagued him.

He held up the laminated menu and checked out the selection. Breakfast was available all day, and there was far more breakfast choices than there were lunch or dinner items. This was not surprising for a little café.

"Have you decided yet?" Lisa appeared in front of him, holding an order pad in her hand.

"Yeah," I think I'll have the Summer Hollow Special."

"You want sausage or bacon?"

"Can I have both?"

"For an extra buck fifty you can."

He nodded. "Done."

"How do you want your eggs?"

"Over easy."

"White, wheat, French, sourdough or multigrain."

"Sourdough."

"Anything to drink besides coffee?"

"You have beer this early?"

She looked up from her order pad and raised her eyebrows with disapproval. "We don't serve beer at all, but if we did the answer would be no."

He met her eyes and rewarded her with a little grin. "Well, I'll just have an orange juice then." He held the menu out to her.

She took it and shoved it under the counter. "All right, coming right up." She ripped the order sheet off the pad and headed down the bar again. He watched her ass as she rounded the corner into the kitchen and let out a breath. Judging from how those hips swung back and forth, she was probably fucking awesome in bed.

He leaned back in his chair and took another swig off his coffee. The blonde with the sexy legs closed her newspaper and he spotted the large photo of an elderly man taking up an eighth of the page. He leaned forward a little bit so that he could get a better look. The head line above the photo read. "Gregory Estmond Funeral on Saturday."

Jack did a small calculation of the days in his head and realized that it was indeed, Saturday. Shit. The entire brood of Estmond Keepers were going to be hanging around the graveyard, plus all the Keepers that had traveled over to attend the funeral. The last thing he wanted was to fuck with the entire lot of them. Trying to kill the Keeper would be more of a suicide mission than the job it was intended to be.

Looked like he was going to have to wait a few days for the Keepers to thin out and go home before he could continue with his assignment. He let out a deep sigh as he envisioned his mother's face and the condescending tone of her voice when she found out. She was going to be pissed. Really pissed. When she wanted something, she wanted it done right then, no fucking around.

Lisa arrived with his breakfast in one hand and a tall glass of orange juice in the other. "Here you are," she announced as she set them down in front of him. "You want any ketchup or anything?"

"You have any tabasco?"

She reached under the counter and withdrew the spicy sauce, setting it in front of him as an answer.

"Thanks. This looks awesome."

Lisa topped off his coffee without his having to ask. "It is awesome," she told him with a tiny smile. "Enjoy your breakfast."

While Lisa was gliding away, the old man next to him got up and threw some money on the counter. "Lisa, I'm leaving. Money is on the counter." He eyeballed Jack as if to let Jack know that he was letting her know the money was there so that Jack didn't steal it.

Jack merely smiled in response and dumped a bunch of tabasco on his food.

Lisa appeared around the corner from the kitchen again. "Are you heading over to the Estmonds?"

The old man grunted as he pushed in his stool. "Yeah. I think everyone in town is gonna be there or at the wake."

Lisa nodded. "I'm going to try to get to the wake. I don't get done here until two."

"Maybe I'll see you later then." He lifted his hand in a weak wave and headed for the door.

Lisa came back over near him. "Jess, are you going over to Mr. Estmond's funeral?"

The blonde with sexy legs next to him lifted her head. "I'm leaving in just a minute to go over there."

Lisa frowned. "I feel like everyone is going but me. It's going to be so dead in here with everyone over there."

Jess nodded. "Yeah, I don't know why Dave didn't just close the place down for a couple of hours. I mean, he's going, so his employees should be able to go too." She shrugged. "Just my opinion though."

Lisa laughed a little. "Well, it's my opinion too."

Jack watched the conversation between the two women with interest, scraping food into his mouth without really looking at it.

Jess ran her shiny French tips over the photo of Gregory Estmond. "I'm going to miss him."

Lisa nodded. "You and everyone else. He was certainly one of a kind."

Good lord. Fucking Keepers. Gregory Estmond wasn't the only Keeper to have a reputation like that. You would never catch anyone talking about him, or any other Reaper for that matter, with such adoration. Most Reapers were assholes. In his case, at least he was a good looking asshole. It worked more in his favor with the ladies.

Jess folded her newspaper and left after she and Lisa had a few more minutes of discussion about how wonderful that old Keeper was. She offered Jack a tiny smile and headed out with her newspaper tucked into her handbag.

He finished up and paid for his breakfast, throwing Lisa a nice tip in addition to the cost of the food and then left the café, not sure of what he was going to do with the rest of the day, since he couldn't exactly proceed with his assignment anymore.

Half an hour later, Jack pulled his truck into the parking area alongside the road outside the cemetery. "Fucking finally," he muttered to himself as he parallel parked his truck into a spot between a beat up old station wagon and a brand new Prius. It had taken him forever to find a spot to park.

He had been driving along the back roads aimlessly, exploring and getting to know the town when he'd decided what the hell, why not go over and check out the funeral? None of the Keepers were ballsy enough to do anything to him while surrounded by a crap ton of people anyway.

After finally getting his truck wedged into the spot, he sat there and looked out over the headstones, through the trees at the crowd gathered around the plot. He recognized the pastor because he held a bible in his hands. Beside the pastor he saw several heads of dark red hair and knew those must be the Estmond Keepers.

Beyond the Estmonds, the crowd stood silently in the midday sunlight. Even farther, out in the cover of the trees, the souls were gathering to watch the procession. Jack felt his body tingle and his heart beat picked up a few notches.

He wanted to devour those souls.

It had been a long time since he'd had an entire soul. The little bits he took from the women were just enough to sustain him. The souls of the dead were far better to consume. Their energy lasted longer, kept him healthy longer, and all in all, just made him feel better.

The mist of the dead glittered and swirled among the shadows of the trees. It was all he could do not to get out of the truck and proceed to massacre those beautiful auras. He closed his eyes and took a deep breath, his fingers tightening on the steering wheel, trying desperately to maintain control.

Dammit. He was a fucking soul addict.

But he couldn't help it, right? *This* was what he was. A Reaper. A *soul* Reaper. Reapers had to consume souls to live.

Right, like that kind of thinking made this shit any better. He was still a junkie.

"Son of a bitch," he muttered out loud and then slammed his fist into the steering wheel. Without giving himself much more time to even consider getting out of the truck, he rammed the vehicle into drive and shoved his foot down onto the gas pedal.

He peeled out of the parking spot, spraying up gravel and sped off down the crowded back road. The entire funeral procession probably turned to see what the commotion was, but he didn't give a rat's ass what anyone thought. At the moment, he just needed to get away from that fucking funeral.

As he drove, he took long, deep breaths and gripped the wheel so tight his knuckles turned white. He kept his eyes on the road, trying not to think of how amazing that blue, misty energy would feel absorbing into his body.

He didn't want to go back to the house. He was far too worked up to go back there and just sit around doing nothing. He passed the city limits, but kept on driving. As long as he kept going, he would get control of himself.

He slowed the truck considerably as the highway began to slope upward and the turns got tighter. The little creek that ran alongside Summer Hollow could not be seen from the high altitude, but the oaks and pines grew even thicker.

He followed the twisty pavement for miles and miles

until the trees began to thin and vineyards took over the view. As he drove, he felt his body begin to relax and the hunger slowly dissipate. When he reached the crest of the mountain, he pulled over onto one of scenic viewpoints to take it all in. He gazed out at the land before him, awed by its silent power. He wasn't anywhere very special, but there was still something extremely calming about being so high up, staring down at acres and acres of grapes.

Beyond the grapes he could see the structures of the wineries. Some were old and antique in appearance. Others were more contemporary, having been built more recently. Farther out, he spotted large homes that were set against the hills.

Well … now that he was feeling better, maybe he should go do some wine tasting.

On second thought, nah. He still had to drive back to Summer Hollow, and he didn't really care for wine all that much anyway.

With nowhere to go and not caring to go anywhere in particular, he opened the door and jumped down from the driver seat. He grabbed a pack of cigarettes that he rarely touched from behind the seat and crawled up onto the hood.

Lighting a smoke, he settled back against the windshield and puffed on his cigarette as he stared down at the beauty below him. He knew full well that the beauty of nature was about the only thing that he would come close to loving in his pathetic life.

LUCY
4

E than let go of her hand and they strode quickly
across the short expanse to the farmhouse. Lucy
heard movement in the house as they stepped up
on the porch. She hurried to the front door and flung it
open to find all of her brothers and sisters had gotten
to the house before her and Ethan. The entire brood
of adult children were scurrying about in the kitchen
uncovering the food and making coffee.

"Hey Luce!" Her oldest brother, Gregory Jr., set a
tray of blueberry muffins on the counter and embraced
her. "How ya doin'?"

"I'm all right." She gave Greg a squeeze and then
wiggled out of his arms. "Just want this day to be over,
mostly."

"Well, we're almost there."

Thank God.

Lucy knew his intention was to reassure her, but she
saw that his eyes were the ones holding back sadness.

Lucy knew Greg well enough to know he was
regretting that he hadn't been around as much the
last few years. Well, longer than that really. Greg was
thirty-five years old and lived in San Francisco, which
was about four hours away from home. He had been
called over to become Keeper for one of the Bay Area

graveyards. The family who had been Keeping it had no living heirs to take over. Before that he had assisted her father at home in Summer Hollow, like all the children did.

Greg smiled, "Ethan, how 'bout you man, you good?" He held his hand out for a shake.

Ethan returned the smile, but his was weak. Lucy knew he was happy to see Greg, but he missed Gregory Sr. Ethan grasped Greg's hand. "I've been better, for sure."

"Son of a ..." James yelled from in front of the open oven. His sharp yell was immediately followed by the ear assaulting clang of metal muffin tin against tile kitchen floor. "Shit! I burned my fingers." He stuck two of his fingers between his lips.

Lucy and Stephanie both hurried over and fell to their knees to try and save the muffins. "Use an oven mitt, dumbass! Look at what you did," Steph screamed at him from the floor.

"Are you serious? Fuck the muffins, I *burnt* myself, Steph."

"Well you wouldn't have if you had used a fucking oven mitt." Steph's voice escalated and she stood up to face him.

James stood a full foot taller than Steph, but she stared up at him and fearlessly balled her fists at her side. Their identical dark brown eyes met and then he flipped her the middle finger as a silent challenge. Lucy stood up from the mess to intervene but Hannah slid in between them.

"Let me look at it, J." She put her arm around James and gently led him away. The impending fight would have likely been an embarrassing scene had they been left to go at it. Sadly, it wouldn't have been the first time the public had witnessed an Estmond family brawl.

"You got lucky!" Steph called as they headed toward the bathroom. "God, I can't believe he is twenty-four years old and hasn't learned to use the freaking oven mitts."

Lucy sighed, trying to push her frustration with her sister aside. Stephanie and James were fraternal twins and one of the closer pairs out of the clan. They were the youngest, aside from Lucy.

Since birth the twins had fought a lot, but anyone who dared pick a fight with either Steph or James had to deal with the other half of the pair. "Leave him alone, at least for today," Lucy whispered to her sister.

Steph rolled her eyes, insinuating a 'yeah right, like that's gonna happen,' and then bent back down to the floor. She gathered the remnants of the crumbled muffin mess and tossed it in the metal trash can at the end of the counter.

Across the kitchen, Olivia had her hair pulled up into a messy bun to keep any renegade strands from getting in the food. She whipped away from the Formica countertop with a tray of cookies and hurried toward Lucy. "Get this stuff out in the family room. I can see people starting to come over from the cemetery."

Lucy frowned at her sister. "I don't understand why we have to do this shit," she muttered as Olivia shoved the tray into her hands.

Olivia sighed. "Because we are it. There isn't anyone else." She pointed at the door leading to the family room. "Now get your ass in there."

Lucy clutched the tray and stalked out of the room, hearing her sister giving orders to everyone else. About thirty seconds after she set the tray on one of the folding tables they had set up in the room, the kitchen door swung open and the rest of her family marched out, each holding an item for the folding table. Ethan trailed behind them with a giant silver coffee pot.

"Open the door, Lucy," Olivia demanded. "Ethan, put that on the buffet and plug it in."

Lucy shook her head. Olivia had always been this way. It wasn't just the stress of the funeral. She was a complete control freak. Lucy could only be grateful that she didn't have to share a room with her growing up. She had to share with Stephanie, which was entirely on the other side of the spectrum since Steph was carefree and extremely messy.

A quick peek out the curtain before she opened the front door for the guests had her looking back at her family. "Man, we made all these snacks and every single person out there has a freaking casserole or something."

"Lucy! Just let them in, for crying out loud."

"All right, bossy." She swung the front door open and then propped open the screen door so that everyone could wander in and out freely.

"Hi, Mrs. Bradley." She waved as the elderly woman navigated the steps with a casserole dish covered in aluminum foil.

"Hello Dear." Mrs. Bradley smiled as she stepped up onto the porch. The smile added a few more creases to her age wrinkled face. "I brought you my special recipe, homemade mac 'n' cheese."

Lucy reached out to take the dish from her. "Oh, this is wonderful. I can't wait to dig in to it. Thank you, Mrs. Bradley."

In truth, she could wait. Mrs. Bradley brought her homemade mac 'n' cheese to every public event involving food, and it tasted like what Lucy imagined a burnt piece of rubber might taste like. Whatever the special ingredient was, it did not help the recipe at all. But somehow, every place she took that darn mac 'n' cheese, she took the dish back home empty.

Lucy stood there while Mrs. Bradley nodded, apparently approving of Lucy's comment about the mac 'n' cheese and then she reached out, placing her liver spotted hand on Lucy's shoulder, "I'm so sorry for your loss, honey."

Here it comes.

"Your daddy was a darn fine man."

"Thank you again, Mrs. Bradley."

Mrs. Bradley withdrew her hand and left Lucy

standing on the porch as she wandered into the house muttering "Yes, darn fine man."

While the rest of the crowd began their ascent up the steps onto the porch, Lucy hurried into the house after her. Depositing the mac 'n' cheese on the folding table without even bothering to uncover it, she caught Ethan's eye across the room and made a face. Ethan was just as familiar with Mrs. Bradley's special mac 'n' cheese as she was, so he gave her a smile and rolled his eyes.

The chatter of voices escalated as more people poured into the house. Lucy tried her best to be cordial as each person appeared in front of her, expressing their condolences for her loss. Each time she glanced up, one of her siblings was also engaged in conversation with someone. Even Ethan was being sought out by the mourners.

The walls of the house began to feel confining, too small and crowded. Lucy grabbed a mug, filled it with black coffee and stepped out onto the porch. Her hopes for a few minutes of alone time were crushed when she found several people out on the porch chatting with each other.

With no other option, she glanced out at the graveyard and quietly slipped off the porch. Once she had crossed the lawn and passed the fence, she found herself in the peaceful silence of the dead. Just what she needed.

Wandering slowly up one of the gravel pathways with her mug in hand, Lucy stared at the strips of sunlight filtering through the trees. The shadows from the branches moved back and forth with the gentle breeze. She found one of the old iron benches that were scattered along the trails and sat down to stare out at the tombstones. The graveyard had always been one of the places she liked to go to think. This time, she found herself pondering why it bothered her so much that everyone had something great to say about her father.

People sure did love him. She tried so hard to be a good person like he was, but it came easy for him. For her, it was much harder to live up to his standard of goodness, she had too much intolerance for stupidity. She also didn't like being around people that much, so kindness just didn't come that easily.

"Just be yourself, Lucy Mae," her father always said to her on the many long talks in the graveyard. "You don't have to be like. I am me and you are you. Besides, do you honestly think that I never get fed up with the idiots we come into contact with on a daily basis? We all have our moments, Lucy Mae. It doesn't make us any less caring and it sure as hell doesn't make you any less of a person. It's human nature baby girl."

God, she missed him so much already.

"It was a nice speech." She heard the familiar voice behind her. "A bit generic, but still a nice one."

Lucy's fingers loosened from their grasp on the coffee mug. It slipped from her hands and fell with tiny clink onto the gravel. She swung around quickly to prove to herself that she wasn't just hearing things. "Dad?"

There he was. The blue mist swirled intensely, trying to hold the form of her father's human body. "It's me, baby girl."

"Dad! What are you doing here? You were supposed to have crossed over."

His ghostly form reached up and adjusted the collar of his tacky vacation shirt. "I had business to take care of. Why else would I be here?"

"But … but I thought that we took care of all that. Dammit Dad, you were supposed to have taken care of it so you didn't have to be stuck here!"

"Lucy Mae, don't you dare raise your voice to me. We have some business to discuss and when it's all over, then I can cross over."

Lucy began to pace back and forth in front of her father. "I can't fucking believe this." She shook her head. "Dad, *why*?" She hadn't known that she was crying until she reached up in frustration and placed a hand on each side of her face and felt the tears that had escaped the corners of her eyes. "What could be so important that you couldn't take care of it when you were alive? Holy shit. Fuck."

"Lucy Mae, watch your language."

"Dad! This makes it so much harder, you have no idea."

Greg grinned and shook his head slightly. She remembered him doing the same thing when she was a child and did something naughty but too cute to be punished for. "Honey, we have to talk."

She threw her hands in the air. "We should have talked about whatever it is before you died."

"I couldn't tell you then, because then, I was in charge of the Graveyard. I was the Keeper."

"We are all Keepers."

He reached out to touch her and his transparent hand slid right through her solid one. Lucy turned away and wiped more tears from her cheeks.

"But now you are in charge, honey. This is your graveyard. Your brothers and sisters will help you. Everyone takes shifts just like always, but this is your turf to protect from the Reapers."

She sniffed. "And that's the information that you thought was so important you had to avoid crossing over to tell me?"

He shook his head again. "No, it's not."

"Well don't be so cryptic Dad! Out with it." She crossed her arms over her chest and waited.

Her father gestured to the bench, "Sit down."

"No."

"Fine then." He spread his arms out. "Honey, you are a legend. Up in the attic, in Grandma's trunk, you will find the proof of what I am about to tell you."

Greg paused to let her react, but Lucy simply waited for him to continue his explanation.

"The legend says that the seventh child, from one of

the original seven lines of Keepers, born on the seventh day of the seventh month, is the chosen Keeper who will bring forth an end to the Reapers."

Lucy, arms still crossed at her chest, raised an eyebrow. "Really?"

Her father said nothing as he allowed her to process the information.

With a rather large sigh, Lucy bent over to retrieve her mug from the gravel and then sat down on the bench where she lapsed into silence. "So ... I'm really not understanding why this was something that you kept from me while you were alive."

Greg moved to stand beside where she sat. "What kind of life would you have lived if you had known that you were the Chosen One, knowing your destiny would be something so vital to our world? I wanted you to live a normal life for as long as you could."

"We are Keepers for crying out loud!" Lucy blurted. "Our family has always been anything but normal. Unless you think going out to patrol a graveyard and kill Reapers since you were just a little kid is normal."

"It was my decision. Right or wrong, it was mine to make."

Lucy pushed her hair out of her face and looked up at her dad. "You should have *told* me. You should have made sure this was taken care of and you wouldn't be stuck here. Now, who knows how long it will be until you can cross over."

Her father's voice was soft. "I was worried about you."

"Well I'm more worried about you now," she countered.

The blue mist around him began to shimmer and fade a little bit. "I think it's time to go. I'm still new to being on this side of things." Greg gestured to his body and the misty aura it was made up of. "I'm fading out."

Lucy stood and locked her eyes on her fathers. "I love you Daddy."

He reached out to touch her and once again his body slid through hers. "Promise me you will go find the trunk in the attic."

Lucy nodded and felt tears begin to well up in the corner of her eyes again. "I promise."

"I love you too, baby girl. I'll be here when I figure out how to recharge my batteries." He gave her one final smile and then she watched as her father's body slowly dissolved and then disappeared.

Once he was gone, she lifted her head to the sky and breathed out some of her frustration. "Just fucking great. Way to go, Dad."

On her way back to the house, coffee mug in hand, she wondered how in the hell she was supposed to tell her brothers and sisters that their dad was out there. That their father, the Keeper, was now one of the souls they would have to protect from the Reapers. Furthermore, she had to go tell them all she was some kind of Chosen One from an ancient legend. Wonderful.

Back at the farmhouse the wake was still in full swing. The mourners stuck around for hours. It simply amazed her how much people could talk and eat and visit at a wake. Didn't they understand that she just wanted them to go home so she could take the torture devices off of her feet and head up to the attic to look through antique trunks for some info on the legend?

With a sigh, Lucy mentally kicked herself. These people were here because they loved and missed her father, she should stop being so selfish and have some respect for other people. Although, with the townspeople of Summer Hollow, this was more easily said than done.

Greg Jr. and Ethan saw her enter the house and hurried over. "Where were you?" her brother asked at the same time as Ethan asked her if she was all right.

She waved them off, trying to get them out of her personal space. "I'm fine, I'm fine … really. I just needed some air and went out to the graveyard for a while."

She must have really looked messed up because both Greg and Ethan eyeballed her as if they didn't believe one word that came out of her mouth.

"Seriously you guys. I'm fine and I'll explain later. I just needed some space. Now go away."

It was seven p.m. before the house was clear of everyone but the Estmond clan and Ethan. Lucy shut the door softly behind the last mourner to leave and then let out a long, tired sigh of relief. Finally, it was over.

Ethan swung the kitchen door open and strode across the family room. "Well, it's over now."

Lucy looked up into his piercing blue eyes. "Finally, now I just need to get these shoes off and I'll be even better." She bent down and slid the sling back pumps off of her aching feet one at a time and chucked them across the family room. Running shoes or flat soled boots were more her style. Pretty much anything was more comfortable than those freaking alien shoes. God only knew how women wore those things all the time when she could barely get through one day in them.

Ethan reached for her hand, pulling her away from the door and leading her toward the couch. "You want me to stay with you for patrol tonight?"

Lucy shook her head. "Nah, I'm pretty sure Greg is staying over. He can help out." She plopped down onto the couch.

"Is anyone else staying with you?"

"Damn, Ethan. I'm not that fragile. I'm totally fine so stop worrying. And no, everyone else is going back to their houses."

The rest of the clan, with the exception of Greg, lived in their own homes in town. Lucy was the one at home, so Lucy inherited the business. That was how it worked unless you got assigned elsewhere.

"Lucy!" Olivia called from the Kitchen. "Get in here and help us or we are going home and leaving the mess for you!"

"Screw off!" Lucy screamed back at her.

"Get in here!"

"No. Just leave it and I'll take care of it tomorrow."

Ethan shook his head and pulled Lucy of the couch. "We're coming, Liv."

"I hate you so much," Lucy moaned as Ethan dragged her into the kitchen to help clean up. Once they were in the kitchen, Lucy decided that it was probably the best time to tell them about their father and the legend since they were all together in one place. It was better than having to repeat it over and over again.

Letting go of Ethan, she wandered to the counter and picked up some paper plates to put in the trash. "So, I saw Dad in the graveyard today."

The chatter stopped, the air went static and she felt every head in the room turn her way. For a full minute the silence enveloped the room. Then, abruptly, it started again. Everyone asking the same questions that she had asked her father and Lucy doing her best to answer them.

"It gets even better you guys."

Greg raised an eyebrow. "I'm dying to hear this."

Lucy leaned on the counter, facing her family. "So, apparently Dad couldn't cross over because he had to tell me that I'm the Chosen One to bring an end to the Reapers. It's some kind of legend."

James snorted. "What! Of all the awesomeness in this family you are the one who got chosen. Seriously?"

Olivia glared at James and responded, "That's *all* you got from what she just told us?"

"Well, it's true," he mumbled.

Lucy shook her head and looked to her siblings who appeared skeptical. "Dad says there is proof in the attic in Grandma's trunk."

Ethan sat down in a kitchen chair. "Well isn't that original. The old family legend is hidden in the trunk of an ancestor in the attic of the really old house."

Steph laughed. "My God, that's so true!"

Greg caught Lucy's eye. "Well, let's go up to the attic then."

"You guys go on," Olivia waved them on. "We are going to stay down here and clean up. You can bring it all down when you find it since we won't all fit up there anyway. The ceiling would probably cave in with all the weight."

Daniel, who was lounging against the counter, drained his flask and stuck it back inside his trench coat. "Well, I'm not hanging around to find out how special any of you are. Catch y'all later."

"Dan," Lucy reached out and grasped the sleeve of his coat. "Don't go. You can't drive like this."

He yanked his arm from her grip. "I'm fine."

"You're not fine." Dan reached into his pocket, pulled out his keys and tossed them on the table. "It's not worth fighting with you guys," he sneered. "I'll fucking walk." With that, Lucy and the rest of her family watched him stagger out the back door and into the darkness.

Lucy shook her head in frustration and worry. Dan was becoming progressively worse since their dad died. "I can't go up there right now. I have to go patrol in a little while."

James waved at her. "Steph and I can go patrol while you're up there. You can take over whenever you're done."

Lucy looked to Greg and he shrugged. "We should probably go now, while we're all here."

"Yeah, that seems most logical."

Ethan stood up and moved to her side. "I'm coming up with you."

Looking from her brother to Ethan, Lucy took a deep breath and let it out slowly. "All right then, let's go see what kind of legend I am supposed to be."

JACK
5

J ack sat on the mountain until nightfall. He had lounged on the hood of his truck and watched the sun go down in a glorious picture of orange, red and pink. It was perfect, but was all too soon replaced with darkness as the curtain of night drew itself over the earth.

It was lonely as fuck.

Reluctantly he began his trip back over the mountain. After about ten minutes, he figured he should probably get the call to his mother over with before she started with the harassing phone calls.

He plugged his Bluetooth into his ear and poked at the image of his mother on the front of his phone. The phone rang so long he thought for a moment that it would dump into voicemail and he would have to leave her a message about the Keepers.

Eventually she answered. "Jackson."

"Hey Mom."

"Is it done?"

"That's actually why I called. I can't take care of it tonight."

A long sigh escaped from his mother and he could just see her sitting in her uncomfortable fucking straight-back chair she loved so much, shaking her head in disgust at her incompetent son. Surrounded by all the delicate perfection that their home was made of, he knew she was wondering how in the hell their son turned out so imperfect.

"And why exactly would that be?" she questioned.

"The old man Keeper, his funeral was today. The whole town is crawling with Keepers." He paused, waiting for a response from her. When she said nothing, he continued. "It would be a suicide mission to attempt it tonight."

Finally she answered him, her voice cold and unfeeling. "Very well, tomorrow then."

God, this woman was exasperating. "Mom, trust me. I'll get the job done, but I will take care of it when I feel the time is right to do it."

"I said very well. Do not disappoint me, Jackson."

For fucks sake.

"Love you too mom. I'll talk to you later." He punched the end call button and ripped the Bluetooth out of his ear. His mom was a bitch. His dad was a dick. And they wondered why he was such a fuck up … um, kettle … black. Yeah.

The rest of the drive was spent speeding over the mountain, taking the corners way too fast and not giving a shit if he flipped his truck and died a horrendous, bloody death.

Later, the truck tires crunched over the loose gravel driveway leading to his little house and he wished that there were some kind of light illuminating it. He had also left all the house and porch lights off, so the whole place was completely enveloped in darkness. He set the truck into park and sat there for a few minutes staring at the dark shadow of a house and then, in a spur of the moment decision, he shifted to reverse. "Fuck this," he muttered and carefully backed out of the driveway.

The streets of town were pretty crowded because it was a Saturday night and everyone except the church goers could sleep in the next day. There were no spaces at the curb in front of the bar, so he drove around back and found a spot in the dirt lot that was located on the backside of Knight's Bar.

He parked, locked the truck with the little button on his key chain and headed inside. He chose to walk around to the front even though he could have gone in the back door. Before he even reached the door he could hear AC/DC hollering about dirty deeds done dirt cheap and people yelling to be heard over the music. He pushed open the swinging metal door and found that the bar was packed pretty close to what he imagined legal capacity was for the little hole in the wall.

The bar was your typical hick town bar. Nothing fancy. The bar itself was scratched and dull. There were only about six tables in the whole joint, and the walls were covered in historical pictures of the town.

He maneuvered through the initial crowd by the door and then squeezed into a place at the bar between a large man and a skinny guy who looked like a junkie. Looking behind the bar he finally spotted the bartender and signaled to her.

The curvy brunette caught his gaze and nodded to him. She finished pouring some shots of tequila for a group of giggling housewives at the end of the bar and then hurried over to him. "You again? You want to stick with MGD?"

Jack propped his elbows against the bar and leaned forward so he could hear her better. "Like I have any other choice," he responded.

Reese, the bartender, straightened her shoulders and took a pint beer glass out from beneath the bar. "Well, you know what we have so suck it up, buttercup." She held the glass under the tap, filled it up and then handed it to him.

"Yeah, I'll live, but drinking this shit is just asking for a hangover."

"What kind of beer do you prefer, Mr. Fancy Pants?"

Jack examined the light golden liquid underneath

the thin layer of foam and then looked back up at Reese. "Dark, very dark. I'm more of a Guinness man."

She shrugged. "Why don't you have whiskey instead, the good stuff is better than cheap beer."

Jack shook his head. "I'm trying to stay away from hard alcohol." Truth of the matter was that he had to stay away from the hard stuff or lose what little control he actually had over himself. The last time he'd gone on a bender he almost killed some chick after fucking her in the back seat of his truck. Soul reaping from the living was a very delicate matter and that situation was one that he did not want to relive anytime soon.

"Suit yourself." Reese threw her dark curls over her shoulder. "You know you could get your own beer at the grocery store, right?"

Jack took a long pull from his glass. "But then I wouldn't have the pleasure of your company, now would I?"

His wit was rewarded with an eye roll that clearly said, "Not a chance, asshole."

"What's it take to get a fucking beer over here?" some jerk shouted from the end of the bar opposite of the gaggle of housewives.

"Shut your trap, Larry! I'm coming!" She sighed with exasperation, then turned and yanked open the large fridge behind her. Without even really looking, she reached in and extracted a bottle of Bud Light. After popping off the cap, she headed over to give Larry the loudmouth his beer.

Jack smiled. He liked Reese. He had met her the night before when he had picked up Janet, or Janice, whatever her name was. Reese owned the bar. She was pretty cool and probably awesome in the sack, but something inside him told him not to go there.

He turned around to check out what was going on around him. The tiny bar had one pool table, which was currently occupied by two old men who looked like they were about eighty years old. There was an extremely tiny space clear of tables or anything else.

He assumed that was supposed to be a dance floor. An ancient juke box sat in the corner, all lit up and waiting for people to pick their music. And just beyond the dance floor, was a little platform for when the bar hosted live music.

Over by the restroom, which was unisex, a blonde in a pair of tight jeans was bent over with her foot propped up on a chair. She appeared to be adjusting the strap on her high heel. Jack took in the view with pleasure, as did several other men in the establishment.

Bingo.

As she straightened, she moved the wave of straight blonde hair over her shoulders. It hung down her back, just shy of touching the waistline of her jeans. Seeming to sense that he was staring at her, she suddenly turned and met his eyes. Only, his eyes couldn't help but move south.

Holy shit, she had a fucking rack on her that any man would have killed to bury his face in. Her upper half was adorned in a tiny, black camisole tank, and she must have been wearing a push up bra because the top of her breasts were prominently exposed for his enjoyment.

The blonde snatched up her purse off the chair that her foot had vacated and began her fuck me strut in his direction.

Jack continued to lean against the bar. He polished off the last of his beer in one long drink while he watched her make her way over to him. He turned without taking his eyes off her and set the empty on the bar.

"Want another one, Casanova?" Reese's voice came from behind him.

"Hit me," he called over the music, just as the blonde arrived in front of him.

"So, if you're going to look at me like I'm already naked, you should at least buy me a drink," she told him, with no introduction at all.

"Well, that shirt doesn't exactly scream out that

you're saving yourself for marriage"

She smirked. "Well, what does it say to you, then?"

He pretended to think a little bit. "It says that you are a woman who wants to be touched. That you are a woman who is comfortable with her own body ... and that body craves a man's hands."

She took a step closer to him and touched a fingertip to his leather jacket. "That, is exactly what this shirt says."

"Here's your beer, Jack."

He turned away from blondie just long enough to wrap his fingers around his beer glass and catch Reese's eye. She shook her head at him and he cocked his head back at her in confusion. Reese shook her head again and then glanced over his shoulders at the blonde. "Slut," she mouthed to him.

The fact that Reese was trying to warn him about a slutty chick was pretty comical since he was usually the slutty one. Well, he still was.

"Good," he mouthed back to her.

"Ugh." Reese waved him off and wiped the bar with a white towel. "Go get herpes if you want. I really don't give a crap, but don't say I didn't warn you."

"No worries, Mom. I've got this." He turned away from Reese and back to the girl. "I'm Jack. Who might you be?" he asked her.

She opened her purse and pulled out a cigarette. "Sadie. My name's Sadie."

Jack nodded. "What would you like to drink, Sadie?"

She laughed. "Well, ironically, I would love a Jack and coke."

"You hear that Reese."

"Already on it," he heard her somewhat disgusted voice say from behind him. "Here you go."

Jack turned and took the plastic cup from her and handed it to Sadie. "So, should we go out back and have a smoke?" He gestured to her cigarette. Reese had set up a fenced in smoking area right outside the back door since it was illegal to smoke in any establishments in California. She was smart, knowing that if people couldn't smoke while they drank that they would just stay home and drink there.

Sadie took a big gulp from her cup and grinned. "Yeah, let's do that."

Suddenly the door burst open and man in a gray trench coat staggered in. He had dark red hair and brown, bloodshot eyes. He also carried a light silvery mist of an aura around him. The aura of a Keeper.

"Shit," Reese muttered from behind him.

"What is it?" Jack asked. He honestly wanted to know what she was worried about, but he was also worried about the fact that not only could he see the Keeper's aura and know who he is, but that Keeper would see his red misty aura and know that he was a Reaper. Not a good situation at all, especially since this Keeper appeared to be snockered already. Usually, in public it was a given rule between the Keepers and the Reapers to leave each other alone, but it was best to just avoid the confrontations all together.

"It's Daniel Estmond. He's drunk again. Today was his dad's funeral, but it's been a hard time for him ever since his girlfriend was murdered."

"Damn."

"Yeah. It's shitty. I'm just tired of seeing him coming in here and ruining his life."

Jack reached out and took hold of Sadie's shoulder. "You know what? Why don't we get out of here instead?"

Sadie giggled and swayed a little bit. "Okay."

Jack kept his eyes on Daniel, hoping that the guy would be too distracted to see him. Yeah. Not so lucky. Daniel's eyes shifted around the bar, most likely looking for Reese, and that is when he spotted Jack.

Suddenly the Keeper was charging toward him and shouting. "I will fucking kill you."

Jack had seriously expected the Keeper to just pass him by and he would leave the bar and everything would be fine. But, this dude fucking jumped him.

The next thing he knew Daniel's fist was connecting with his cheekbone.

"Shit!" he heard Reese shout from behind him at the same time as Sadie squealed and jumped out of the way.

"Damn it!" Jack cursed. Instinctively, he reared back and returned fire on Daniel. He didn't even realize that he had hit him until he felt his knuckles connect with the Keeper's jaw. Daniel staggered backward, recovered his footing and then lunged again, but Reese jumped over the bar, baseball bat in hand and shoved it into Daniel's chest. "Fucking stop it, Daniel, you're drunk again." She looked up at Jack. "Time for you to go, man. I've got to take care of this."

Jack nodded. "I don't even know this guy." He wanted her to know that, even though she probably didn't give a flying fuck.

"I know. Just go now please."

He turned to Sadie. "You coming?"

For a moment, she looked like she might back out, but then she nodded. "Yeah, I'm coming."

Yeah, she was going to be coming, all right.

God, why was he such an asshole.

"Let's go." He reached out for her to take his hand and they both hurried out of the bar.

The warm summer air carried a slight breeze, which hit him right in the face as he opened the door of the bar and ushered Sadie out onto the sidewalk. The streets weren't as busy as when he'd come in, but there were still a few people milling about on the sidewalks.

"I'm parked around back." He grabbed Sadie's hand and led her around the building to the dirt parking lot. "This is me." He gestured to his big black truck.

"Nice ride," she commented as he disengaged the locks.

"Well, hop in," he told her.

Jack didn't want to take her back to his place and have a replay of that morning all over again. Asking them to leave was always an awkward business that

46

he would rather not have to deal with. So, once they were settled in the truck, he backed out of the dirt lot and headed a few blocks down and then made a left. He was headed for the old stone bridge that he had found on his earlier exploration of Summer Hollow.

Before he had even pulled out of the parking lot, Sadie had scooted over into the center of the bench seat and pressed herself up against him. "I hope you're ready for a real fun ride, cowboy," she whispered into his ear. He felt her lips graze his lobe and then move a bit lower to his neck.

Why was it that these slutty chicks always said pretty much the same thing? Was there some sort of handbook with a script, like 'Sex Lines for Dummies'?

Before he could respond he felt her hand on his thigh, moving up slowly until she was cupping his cock.

Holy shit.

As he pulled over into one of the two spots beside the bridge, his dick was pressing hard against his jeans and was more than ready for her. He slammed the truck into park and turned to the side, taking Sadie down onto the bench seat of his Ford.

His mouth found hers at the same time as his fingers moved the camisole top down and his thumb grazed her nipple. She moaned and arched her back. He took the signal and pushed his hips forward, grinding himself fully clothed against her.

"Please ... please." He heard her begging for him and that was all the signal he needed. He lifted his weight off of her, letting her unbutton her jeans and wiggle out of them. While she did that he reached over and unlatched the glove box, letting it fall open. Reaching in, he fumbled around until he came into contact with one of the condoms he had thrown in there. Then he worked on his own jeans, only bothering to undo his belt, unzip and let them fall to his knees.

"Wow."

He looked down at her and saw that she was staring

at his erection with wide eyes. "I can't fucking wait to have you in me."

It wasn't the first time he'd heard a woman in awe of his size, but it still sent him over the edge. He had the rubber on in a flash, pulled her silky red panties to the side and pushed himself all the way inside of her.

"Oh. My. God," she screamed out upon first entry. He gave her a second to adjust to the intrusion of him inside her and then he began pumping his hips. He grabbed her legs and pulled them up so that he could get even deeper. His hips slammed against her again and again until she called out that she was close to climax.

He leaned over her as he felt her hot core clenching around him. His lips took hers and for the second time that day, he pulled a soul from a woman's body. She rocked against him, moaning into his mouth as her soul slid from her body into his.

Suddenly, his own orgasm hit hard as his body absorbed the energy. He arched his back and released her mouth, letting out a slight moan of pleasure.

When it was over, he pulled out of her and turned away so that he could take care of the condom. Turning back toward her, he yanked his pants up. She lay there across the seat with her legs spread wide open and her bare sex glistening. He wanted to roll his eyes because it appeared that she didn't plan on moving any time soon.

"That ... was amazing," she said between breaths.

He had to wonder why the fuck she was out of breath. He was the one who did all the work. All she had to do was lay there.

He smiled and reached out to help her sit up. "It was amazing. Fucking awesome." He leaned over gave her a kiss and then set her pants on her lap. "Here's your pants, honey."

She looked slightly confused, as if any man would be crazy not to have her sitting half naked in his truck. "Oh, ah, thank you."

"You going home or back to the bar?" He turned the key in the ignition and fired up the engine.

Now she was really getting the clue that she had just been used. Guess she was normally the user, not the other way around. "Um, home, I guess." Her voice was barely above a whisper and a solemn expression crossed her face as she gave Jack directions to her house.

Jack lit a smoke and handed it to her then lit one for himself. After taking a long drag, he pulled out onto the bridge and crossed over it. Oddly enough, Sadie lived up Cemetery Road so he had to drive by the graveyard on the way to her house.

He peered out his window as they passed by and he saw nothing but the soft glow of the street lamps that had been placed by the benches on some of the trails through the plots. There were no glowing blue souls to chase after, for the moment.

A few miles later, he found himself pulling into a short dirt driveway and coming to a stop in front of a double wide trailer house.

Sadie flicked her ash out the window and then tossed the entire cigarette out into her driveway. "Do you want to come in for a while?" Her voice was hopeful.

No way in hell.

Jack shook his head and smiled charmingly at her. "Nah, I've got to get home and get some sleep." He noticed how her face fell and added. "I've got a long day ahead of me tomorrow. Lots of work."

She seemed happier with a response that sounded valid. "Oh, all right. Well, let me give you my number just in case you want to get ahold of me later." She opened her purse and took out a little piece of paper and a pen, scribbled her digits onto the paper and shoved it into his hand." With one last look at him she opened the door and hopped down into her driveway. "Thanks for the ride." She clutched her purse, wobbled over the gravelly driveway and into her house.

Jack backed out of the driveway as soon as he saw that Sadie was safely inside her house. On his way out of the driveway he opened up the glove box again and added Sadie's number to the rest of the little bits of paper and business cards he kept in there.

He drove down Cemetery Road in the thick darkness, but as he approached the graveyard, he clearly saw misty blue shimmers cutting through the night. Not too far from the blue, he spotted the silver auras of the Keepers. There were at least three of them out there in the graveyard with the souls.

The darkness was anything but camouflage for a Keeper, a Reaper, or even the souls. Briefly the thought crossed his mind to just go in there and take care of all of them and be done with this godforsaken town, but then reality kicked in. There were far too many Keepers here for him to attempt anything tonight. He was pretty damn strong, but going up against three or more well-trained Keepers wasn't ever a good idea.

Fatigue suddenly hit hard. He slammed his foot into the accelerator and heard the engine roar as he sped off into the night.

LUCY
6

Lucy and Ethan followed Greg Jr. up the narrow stairwell leading into the attic. Greg stopped at the second to last stair and reached for the door knob. "Eeeek!" he squealed like a girl and swiped both his hands blindly in front of him.

Lucy and Ethan burst into laughter as Greg lurched backward, almost teetering off of the stair he was standing on. Ethan reached out and pushed on Greg's back to keep him from tumbling off the stair and taking both of them with him.

"Fucking spider webs!" Greg mumbled under his breath after he had regained his balance. "Didn't you and Dad ever clean up here, Lucy?"

Lucy shook her head. "No, Greg, the two of us cleaned this whole house and after Dad got sick it was just me, so pardon me if I didn't get to the attic."

"Well these webs are everywhere."

Lucy rolled her eyes even though her brother couldn't see her. "So sorry, I'll just have the cleaning lady get right to that. She is scheduled to come when I win the fucking lottery. Now shut up and open the door."

After girlishly waving away more spider webs, Greg managed to get the door open and they all filed into the dusty, dark attic. Greg found the light switch to the right side of the room and flipped it on. A single, dim bulb illuminated the large room and the three of them all sighed in unison. "Well, it looks like the search for Grandma's trunk is the name of the game," Ethan whispered.

Lucy looked around at the crap that was piled everywhere and wondered where in the hell they accumulated all of it. Trunks galore were stacked all over the place, boxes and filing cabinets were pushed into every nook and cranny, there was furniture covered with sheets, and even a freaking piano had been shoved into one corner.

She wandered through the maze of antiques and memorabilia, running a fingertip through the years of dust that had settled on top of everything. "Well," she said turning to the guys, "this could take forever. There is so much stuff up here."

Ethan looked around the room with an expression on his face that was a cross between awe and frustration. "Yeah, this could take a while."

She shrugged and wiped her finger on her dress before wandering over to a stack of ancient looking trunks. "I guess we better get moving then, help me unstack these."

Greg and Ethan each grabbed hold of a handle of the top trunk, lifted it down and then did the same with the middle one. Dust, which had lain undisturbed for so long, billowed up around them in a large cloud. Once the trunks were down, each of them opened one and began to inspect the contents.

Finding nothing in the those, the three of them searched the attic, finding several more trunks before Lucy finally spotted one over in the corner that, while appearing the same as all the other trunks, had an emblem on the front that wasn't on the others.

Lucy abandoned the open trunk before her, drawn in the direction of the trunk in the corner. The leather was a dark, stained brown. Wide straps spanned the circumference of the giant chest, holding it together with antique buckles. The emblem on the front was a two inch circle, made of bronze and engraved with the letter J.

Her grandmother's name was Josephine.

She knelt down onto her knees in front of the trunk and ran her fingertip across the bronze emblem. This had to be the one.

Looking over her shoulder, she saw that Greg and Ethan were busy sifting through the masses of junk lying around in the attic. She turned back to the trunk and blew out a long breath, sending the thick layer of dust up into a tiny storm as it flew up and away from the trunk. Slowly, she unlatched the buckles holding the trunk together.

Before opening the lid, she paused and reflected for a moment. This old chest could possibly hold the proof that she was some kind of prophecy. Her life, from this point on was probably going to change. She didn't know how, but she was sure that there was no way it could remain the same.

She lifted the lid of the trunk.

The hinges creaked with age and lack of use as she slowly lifted the top and looked inside. The first thing she saw was a very, very old crossbow lying on top of a white silk cloth. The cloth covered the rest of the contents in the trunk, keeping it from sight until someone got around to removing it.

With a trembling hand, Lucy reached out and lifted the bow. It was so old she felt that it would crumble in her hands when she picked it up. But, when her fingers wrapped around the metal and wood of the weapon, she knew that it was made for her.

Gently, she lifted the crossbow from the trunk and turned it over in her hands. It was old, but she was sure it was sturdy and reliable. Her eyes caught something engraved into the side of the handle, and she turned it so that the light shone more directly on the weapon.

There, carved into the metal, was a circle with the

number seven inside of it. At the top of the circle, above the seven, was her family name, Estmond. Below the seven, at the bottom of the circle, was the word 'Guardian.'

"Guys," Lucy called out, not taking her eyes off of the weapon. "Hey guys, I found it."

She heard shuffling behind her and knew that Greg and Ethan were on their way over. "Wow, nice crossbow," she heard Ethan say as he and Greg settled down on their knees on either side of her.

"Yeah. It is," she mumbled, more to herself than anyone. "Look at this." She pointed to the engraving on the side.

"That's awesome," Greg told her, holding his hands out for the weapon.

Reluctantly, Lucy handed it over so that he could inspect it. Since she now had her hands free, she looked down into the trunk and then carefully removed the silk to see what other treasures were nestled inside.

The first thing she saw was the arrows, six of them. Lifting one, she examined it and was sure that it was made of solid silver. Silver was a Reapers weakness. They could die like humans, but they were naturally just stronger and more powerful than regular humans were. The silver weakened them, slowing them down and harnessing them so that the Keeper could kill them … or give the soul they were saving time to get away.

"Look," Ethan whispered from beside her. She looked away from the arrow and set it aside to see what Ethan was looking at. He had reached into the trunk and was extracting a large, leather bound book that looked far older than the Keeper lines themselves.

Carved into the leather on the front of the book was the same symbol of a seven with their family name that was on the crossbow. Ethan set the book carefully on his lap and opened it. Lucy leaned over so she could get a better view. The pages of the thick book were yellowed and brittle with age. Ethan flipped through the first section with a delicate touch. Peering over, Lucy could see that the first entries inked into the book were in a foreign language.

Boy, I hope the whole book isn't like that.

The history and lineage of the Keepers was a topic that Lucy had been fascinated with since she was a small child, which was one of the reasons she was so pissed that she didn't know about this legend of the Chosen Keeper crap.

"Lucy." Greg had set the bow down beside him and had his hands in the trunk. "Check this out." He lifted out a piece of parchment, rolled up snug and tied with a bit of red ribbon. Greg's eyes flicked to Lucy in question and she gave him a nod. Guess it didn't really matter who opened it, even if she was supposed to be the Chosen One and all.

He nodded back at her and then gave the ribbon a tug with his forefinger and thumb. The ribbon came loose from the parchment with ease and Greg set it aside on the dusty attic floor. With both hands steady, he gently unrolled the parchment, holding it open so he could read it.

"God, I hope it's in English," Lucy whispered.

"It is," Greg told her as he scanned over the antique document.

Ethan leaned over Lucy, trying to get a look. "Well, what's it say?"

Lucy swatted at Ethan. "Get off me."

Ethan rolled his eyes and set the book he was holding back in the trunk. Then he got up and went around to lean over Greg's shoulder.

Greg cleared his throat a little bit and began to read.

"My name is Anabel Estmond. I am the daughter of Keepers, Samuel and Mary Winward. I am the wife of Jonathan Estmond."

"Our great-grandmother," Lucy murmured.

"Yeah, now keep quiet so I can read," Greg shushed her and then continued to read. "The Estmond bloodline stems from the original Keepers. There were only seven bloodlines in the beginning, and Abraham Estmond was of the very first.

"I write this today as witness and to record.

"Not long ago, I met an oracle. A true oracle. We happened to meet on the street. I went to town to put a letter in the post. As I was leaving the post, I dropped my coin purse and bent to pick up the scattered coins. As I bent, my arm grazed a woman passerby. This woman, she was normal. There was no strange aura, no odd feeling, she gave no sign of being someone who would have known that I was a Keeper.

"She paused as I gathered my coins and then bent to help me. But, really she wanted to whisper something upon my ears.

"'You are a Keeper, yes?'

"My hands began to tremble. I knew not if she was dangerous since I could not see any aura from her.

"'Fear not,' she told me. 'I mean you no harm.' Her hand rested gently upon mine. 'I have seen what the future brings for the blood of your blood.'

"My coins were gathered so we stood. Her hand grasped mine even more firmly once we stood face to face. We appeared to any passersby as merely ladies speaking quietly amongst each other.

"'Your offspring are of the original Keeper lines. It is a long told prophecy that the seventh child, of one of the seven original Keepers, will be born on the seventh day of the seventh month. This child will bring forth an end to the Reapers who plague the earth. I have seen that this child will be of your own bloodline.'

"I could not speak. How could this woman know such things? However, if Keepers and Reapers and other such beings existed, why shan't a seer of the future exist as well.

"'Will it be my child?' I asked her.

"'That much I cannot see,' she whispered, 'only that the child will come from your blood.' She released my hand and I looked into her beautiful blue eyes and saw truth. 'I must go,' she told me. 'I apologize for the intrusion. You have a wonderful day.' With those last words, she left me standing there in confusion.

"My days afterward were spent searching. There had to be a record of a prophecy of such importance somewhere in the Keeper records. I contacted the other original bloodlines and asked to search any documentation that they might have. I did everything I possibly could to find proof, for no one would ever believe the word of a woman I'd met on the street who claimed to see the future.

"Finally, the day came when I found it.

"In the vast library of an original Keeper bloodline, I found a very, very old book. Written in a language I did not know. I knew that this book was old, and even the possibility that there could be information about the prophecy drove me to do something I'd never done ever before.

"I stole it.

"I hid the book among my belongings and left the Keepers mansion after thanking them for allowing me to use their library. Afterward, I found someone who could translate the first entries in the book and discovered that the language was Gaelic, the language of our origins. And there, in this book, I'd finally found the proof I'd been looking for. The written word of another had been told by a seer of the future, the very same thing which I had been told.

"This document is record of my experience. I have added it to the book as well, so that it may become a part of history. This document, however, is for my family, to stay within our blooded relations should the book ever go missing. If the book disappears, I do not want the proof of our destiny to fade along with it."

Greg took a deep breath and rolled the parchment back up. "That's it."

"This has to be the book she was talking about." Ethan held up the book he was holding.

Lucy nodded. "I totally agree. It has to be. Only thing I want to know is why our family name is on it if she found it in another family's library."

Greg shrugged as he tried to get the ribbon tied back onto the parchment. "Maybe it was added later. Maybe it was just lost among the masses of documentation that are floating around." He held up the rolled parchment that he still couldn't get the ribbon on. "Our lines go back so far in history, there has to be a ton of it that has been lost over time."

He was right.

Ethan nudged her. "Don't you even care that all of this," he gestured to the trunk and the book, "is actually true. You are part of a prophecy, Luce."

Seriously, it sounded like something huge, but what difference did it really make. All she could do was just go on with her life and wait for the chips to fall into place. There was nothing that she could do that would make the prophecy come true any faster.

Wearily, she nodded. "Yeah, I care. I just don't know what I'm supposed to do."

Greg put the scroll aside and looked down further into the trunk. "Nothing you can do, Sis, except wait it out."

Her thoughts exactly.

Greg extracted a jewelry box from the trunk. It was wooden box with no decoration to clutter the simplicity of it. He handed it over to Lucy. "Do you want this, or should we leave it in the trunk."

Lucy shrugged. "We should probably just take the whole trunk downstairs, that way we can keep everything together. Except the crossbow. I'm totally using the crossbow." Her hand crept to the side and grasped the weapon as she claimed it. She couldn't explain it, but when she had held the crossbow, it felt right, like she hadn't been quite complete without it.

Ethan chuckled. "I'm so not surprised to hear that come out of your mouth."

"Me either." Greg shook his head and picked himself up off the dusty floor. "Come on you guys, let's get this big ass trunk down stairs. All this dust is getting to me."

They repacked everything back into the trunk and then hauled it all down to the main floor. Olivia and Hannah were lounging about in the living room while they waited for Lucy, Greg and Ethan to come down out of the attic. Steph and James were still out on patrol and Daniel had gone off somewhere, probably to drown himself in booze.

I have to get out there, she thought. Even though Steph and James most likely had it more than covered, she still felt the need to go out. It was the nature of the Keeper. Also, living off of a few hours of sleep per night, if that, was apparently the nature of the Keeper as well.

After depositing the trunk in the living room, Lucy turned to find her sisters staring at her. "What?"

Hannah spread her hands out and shot an exasperated look at Lucy. "Well? What happened?"

Yay. I'm prophesized. Whoot, whoot.

"It's true. The info is in there. We found a book that we will have to get translated, but yeah, I'm the one who is supposed to um … bring forth an end to the Reapers." Lucy used air quotes to emphasize her sarcasm.

Olivia got up and went over to get a look at the trunk. "Lucy, this is huge."

"I know. That thing weighs a fucking ton too."

"Shut up, you know that's not what I mean."

Lucy shrugged and flopped down onto the couch. "All right, all right. I know what you mean, but in all honesty how in the hell does it really change anything?" She waited for someone … anyone to answer.

No one did.

"See what I mean. I go about my life, do the same things I always do and hope that I'm fulfilling the prophecy." She stood back up. "Now if you guys don't mind. I need to change my clothes so I can go out for patrol." She lifted the lid of the trunk and extracted her crossbow. "At least I get to use my new toy."

AIDEN
7

Aiden marched up the large stone staircase. The Empress had called upon him and he was fairly sure as to why. Her son ... his best friend, was on an important mission right now, and Jack usually fucked shit up when it came to doing things for the Reaper Council. Which meant, as usual, that Aiden was going to be sent to clean up his mess.

The mansion's double doors opened as soon as his boots hit the landing.

"Welcome, sir." The elderly butler bowed slightly as he opened the way into the grand house.

"Thanks, Winston."

"It is my pleasure, sir. The Empress is taking in the evening sun at the south pool. Shall I take you there?"

Aiden waved him off. "No worries. I know the way."

"Very well. Do you require a refreshment?"

"I think I could tolerate a beer."

Winston bowed again. "I shall pour you a Guinness." Aiden smiled at how much the old butler loved doing his job. "You are a life saver."

"I am nothing of the sort." The old man cracked a grin and waved Aiden off in the direction of the south pool. "You should be on your way or the Empress will wonder where you are." With that, Winston shuffled off toward the kitchen.

After navigating his way through the marble hallways that he knew so well, Aiden opened the back doors that led to the south wing patio. The warm Florida breeze lifted off the palms and brushed his blond hair up off his ears.

The whole estate was in comparison to the major hotels in the area. This was one of the three pools that graced the mansions grounds. Everything around him was beautiful and delicate, from the many kinds of flowers that covered the grounds, to the prissy ass lawn furniture that was anything but comfortable.

The lush green lawns were bordered by a stone wall that was about eight feet in height. He knew that the wall was also covered in security cameras every few feet, ensuring the safety of the royal family.

"Aiden, there you are."

Beside the glowing, aqua waters of the pool, sat his Empress. As always, she was dressed in a feminine business suit. Today, the fabric was a soft cream color, and her high heels were the exact same shade of cream as the suit. Her charcoal hair had been styled into a bobbed hairdo that sat just underneath her diamond clad ears.

Aiden fought the urge to shake his head. He knew this woman not only as his Empress, but also as his best friend's mother. She was always stern, never, ever showing any signs of weakness by displaying any form of love or emotion to anyone.

She was a straight up bitch.

"My Empress." He bent to kiss her extended hand and then returned to his position of attention "I rushed right over as soon as I received your call."

"Sit." She gestured to the chair across the table from hers.

He sat in the uncomfortably petite chair.

"Aiden," She took hold of her tiny tea cup and lifted it to her lips, "I trust you. As a member of the Reaper Guard and one who has grown up close to our family,

I have to once again send you to correct my own son."

He fought an eye roll. "What has he done now?"

"I have sent Jackson to the small town of Summer Hollow, California. One of the Keepers from the Estmond bloodline has died. He leaves behind seven children, one of which was born on the seventh day of the seventh month."

"The prophecy?"

Camille nodded. "Unfortunately, yes. I sent Jackson to take care of the young Keeper. If she is the Chosen One, she must be eliminated."

Aiden merely shook his head. He was shocked that Jack wouldn't be doing his job when it came to something this serious. "Anything you need, Empress. I am at your service."

"Good. I need you to go to this, Summer Hollow, and dispose of the Keeper." She took a delicate sip of her tea. "Jackson tells me that there are many Keepers there. He insists that to attempt the extermination would be a suicide mission. So, I am sending you as reinforcement. You will help him accomplish the mission."

"Of course. I will leave immediately."

Winston arrived at that moment with his Guinness, poured into a chilled glass and sitting on a silver tray. "Your beverage, sir."

Aiden accepted the dark beer and figured he better at least drink it so he didn't offend the butler who had gone through the trouble of getting it for him. "Thank you, Winston." He plucked the beer off the tray.

His Empress set her tea cup onto the tiny table. "No need to leave right this second. Please, sit with me and finish your beer."

"Thank you, Empress. It would be my pleasure."

She waved him off. "Besides, it will give us a moment to go over the details." She examined one of her scarlet fingernails and then caught his gaze. "I trust that your friendship with my son will have no merit when it comes to accomplishing your task."

Beer. Thank the lord for beer.

"You should never worry. I love Jack like a brother, but my life service is to the Reaper Council." Yeah, that was what she wanted to hear. He could tell by the way her mouth curled up into a wicked little smile.

"How is our Emperor, if it does not offend for me to ask?" He was expected to ask, as a member of the Guard and a close family friend.

"So kind of you to inquire. He is hanging on. He can no longer go out to reap the souls he needs to survive, so we must bring the souls to him. It's a messy business, having to deal with that in the home, but it is necessary."

Another swig of beer. Almost gone.

Camille looked away, breaking her gaze from Aiden's green eyes. "The doctor doesn't expect him to last much longer. We are in the midst of preparations for his passing." She released a long sigh. "I wish my son was a more capable member of the Council. It shames me that he is the only heir available to take my husband's place."

Aiden did shake his head this time. "With all due respect, Empress. Do not underestimate your son. Jack is a very capable and very lethal man. He has learned well from you and your husband."

She raised a sarcastic eyebrow. "You mean to tell me that you think my son would do well as a leader."

What the hell was he doing? He should know by now when to keep his damn mouth shut. "Yes, Empress, I do."

She leaned back and let out a little cackle. Or maybe the cackling was just him imagining the evil queen from a fairy tale. "Well, Aiden, perhaps when he takes over, you will become his advisor. Thus far I've found you to be far wiser with your decisions in life."

Good God, if she only knew. The only difference between himself and her son was that he knew how to keep his mouth shut and his endeavors quiet, while Jack made a show of the whole matter just to spite his parents.

He polished off his beer and set the glass on the small table for Winston to pick up later. "I shall take my leave now, with your permission. I need to prepare for my trip."

She nodded. "I understand. I do so enjoy your company though."

He stood and bent to kiss her hand. "And I yours."

She extended the jewel laden fingers to him and let him press his lips to the back of her hand. "I am sure you will report to me with a positive outcome."

"Of course," he responded with certainty.

"I have already arranged your airline tickets and rental car. You need only to check in at the airport. Your flight will land in San Francisco and you will have to drive the rest of the way. You can stay wherever Jack is staying." She shook her head. "He rented a house. Apparently there are no appropriate hotels in the area."

Aiden turned to go. He was anxious to call his friend and find out what the hell was going on. Son of a bitch. The fucking legend of the Keepers bringing an end to the Reapers was happening, and he was procrastinating the kill. Oh, hell no.

Aiden bowed just a tiny bit. "Thank you, Empress."

It was all he could do not to hit those marble floors at a dead run. Fucking Jack. Damn him.

As soon as he was back in his car he had his cell phone out and hit Jacks number on the speed dial. It went over into voicemail. Of course, Jack wasn't answering the phone. He was probably fucking everything on two legs.

Fine. He would just surprise him. It would be better if Jack didn't know he was coming till he was actually there, anyhow.

Back at his houseboat, which was actually more of a yacht, he made the few preparations to close up the boat for a few days. After he had settled arrangements for the caretaker and the housekeeper, he went to his bedroom and opened his closet. He looked over his weapons collection and frowned. It was a shame that he was flying and wouldn't be able to bring any of his favorites with him. He was going to have to acquire others when he arrived in Summer Hollow. Not that he really needed any weapons. He could fight and he could take their souls. That was all he needed.

Killing a Keeper by taking their soul was not easy. Sure, they could die just like any other human. Most of the time if they had to kill a Keeper it was straight up murder and a bloody mess. Occasionally though, it came down to the soul sucking.

Because of the way a Reaper and a Keeper were created, their chemistry did not mix. It was usually quite painful to touch each other, so to suck their souls was extremely difficult. But, the soul of a Keeper also gave them more energy and life force than your average run of the mill soul did.

For the most part, the Reapers just tried to avoid the Keepers. It was more trouble than it was worth to have to worry about disposing of the bodies. The Keepers did pretty much the same thing. The normal scenario went a little something like … Reaper goes hunting for souls in the graveyard and, if you were lucky, you got one before a Keeper spots you. If the Keeper spots you then there would typically be a fight in which you both get really tired and one of you ends up injured and retreats. Hardly ever did killing occur between the two.

Murdering each other had serious consequences in the human world. Just because one was a Reaper or a Keeper did not mean that you were magically spared the death penalty.

Both the Reapers and the Keepers had families, lives in which they would be missed, and a murder of one or the other would always make its way into the human world. Neither side wanted the law prying into their business.

But this Keeper was different. This one had to die.

He had always thought it was just a story. Just another old wives tale that had been spun over the years. It was on the same level as the world ending because the Mayan calendar didn't go any further than 2012.

This tale was turning out to be true though, and he wasn't going to take any chances. Everyone he cared about was a Reaper, his servitude was to the royal family and the Reaper Council, and he wasn't about to let one little Keeper get in the way of any of that.

The Empress was right to call him. Jack did have a habit of screwing everything up when it came to anything that had to do with his parents or the Council. He was going to go to Jack and they were going to take care of this together.

And then ... he was going to give Jack the credit with the Empress.

He was going to make Jack the Emperor of Reapers so that they could lead together when that bitch mother of his finally kicked the bucket.

Without giving much thought to his wardrobe choices, he shoved all the things he was going to need into one small duffle bag and headed up to the deck. Once he had locked all the doors and windows he hopped onto the dock and gave his house boat one final look before he pulled out his phone and called a cab to the airport.

It was going to be a long couple of days. That was the one thing he was sure of.

LUCY
8

The next morning Lucy woke to her screaming alarm clock. Not even close to ready to get out of bed, she reached over and blindly beat at the bedside table until her palm came into contact with the snooze button. She opened her eyes just enough to see what time it was, and then let out a groan when she realized that she set her alarm for two hours earlier than she needed to get up. Turning over, she curled up on her side with the fluffy white comforter drawn over her head until the alarm clock went off again ten short minutes later.

Sleep was something a Keeper learned early on in life to do without.

The alarm went off again and this time Lucy threw the covers aside and sat up. "Ugh! Fine, I'm up," she muttered to the empty room. She turned off the alarm for good this time and then shuffled to the bathroom so that she could do her business and wash her face.

In the bathroom, she splashed cool water onto her face in hopes that it would help wash away some of the fatigue. After she had coffee she would shower and that would help, but first she needed to caffeinate herself. She reached out for the fluffy blue towel hanging by the sink and dried her face and hands with it. As she turned to hang it back up on the hook she noticed a pretty good size bruise on her upper arm by the shoulder. Well, it looked like she wouldn't be wearing any tank tops for a few days.

The bruises were something *she* was used to, but if people saw you covered in bruises more than a few times they started to get curious, which would lead to them poking around in your business. None of the Keepers wanted anyone messing around in their business. So, even though bumps and bruises were a way of life, it was something they tried to keep hidden if possible.

With a frustrated sigh, Lucy slipped her black terry cloth robe on over her night shirt and headed down to the kitchen.

The strong scent of coffee wafted its way through the house, letting her know that Greg had already made a pot for them. Her brother had probably been up for hours already. He had always been a morning person, just like their dad.

She shuffled into the kitchen and, as she suspected, she found Greg sitting at the table with a steaming mug of coffee and a paperback book. He looked up from his reading when she entered. "Hey Luce, you sleep all right?"

Even though she felt like she could crawl back into bed and sleep for hours, she nodded. "Yeah, I'm fine." She poured herself a cup of black coffee and then added French vanilla creamer to it. "I just wish I didn't have class today, I'd rather stay home." She sat down at the table across from her brother.

"How is school going anyway?"

She shrugged. "It's good." She stirred her coffee and then took a testing sip. "I'm passing all my classes, so that's good."

Her brother set his paperback on the table. Curious as to what it was, she leaned over so that she could get a good look at the title. As soon as she saw the author she burst into laughter. "I never pegged you

69

for a Sookie Stackhouse fan, Greg!"

Greg quickly swiped at the table, picking up his book and hugging it to his body. "Leave me alone. I happen to like vampires, all right."

Lucy covered her mouth with both hands and tried to suppress her laughter. "I'm sorry. I'm sorry," she breathed out when she had calmed down enough to speak. "I just … that seems like chick stuff. I thought you were a too manly for that kind of reading."

He straightened his spine and looked her in the eye. "It is not chick stuff. Guys can read it too. Plus, I like the show."

"The show is totally different than the books."

He raised an eyebrow. "So, you've read them?"

"Yeah, I've read them. I like the show better."

"Well, they aren't just for girls, and I can read whatever I want."

Lucy shrugged and took another sip of her coffee. "Are you headed back to San Francisco today?"

"Yeah," Greg nodded. "I have to get back. Are you going to be all right here?"

"Of course I will. It was just me and Dad for a long time anyway. Besides, it's not like everyone else isn't just around the corner. You are the one who lives far away."

Greg lowered his head at that. "It's not like I wanted to be that far away. I had to go there."

Dammit Lucy, she inwardly chastised herself.

"I'm sorry. I know that you feel bad for leaving us. But, it's not that bad, Greg. You got out of here and that's all right. The graveyard here is my responsibility. Everyone else helps me out with patrol."

"This is our home though, and I don't like being away from you guys."

Not sure what to say to that, Lucy simply nodded. There was nothing they could do about it. Greg had only accepted the job because, between the Estmond siblings, there were more than enough Keepers in Summer Hollow. As a Keeper, he felt obligated to take the job, but as an Estmond, he felt obligated to stay with the family.

Greg ran his hand through his dark red hair. "It just feels wrong not to be here, especially with all the stuff we found out last night."

"I told you. There is nothing I can do about it except go on with my life as I normally do." She took a swig of coffee. "Speaking of which, I'd better go get ready for class." Lucy pushed out her chair and stood. "We are fine here. Trust me." Leaving Greg with those final words, she took her coffee cup with her and headed back up to her room.

About an hour later, dressed in a pair of jeans and a tight red tee shirt that had a black skull and crossbones on it, she was ready to leave for class. Grabbing her backpack, she hurried downstairs and found Greg waiting for her in the living room. She saw his bag resting on the bench by the door and realized that he was leaving. "You heading out already?"

He nodded, a solemn expression still on his face. Lucy hated seeing her brother like that, but the whole family had been sort of in the dumps since Dad died.

"Yeah, it's time to get back."

"I wish you could stay." She ran over to him and threw her arms around him. "We miss you when you're not here."

Greg finally cracked a smile. "Yeah right. Lucy Mae, you know as well as I do that you are a terrible liar."

It was true. She had one of those faces that told exactly what she was thinking. But, this time she was sincere, he had to have misread her expression.

"But, we do miss you."

"You just got done telling me how well you have things under control here."

She pulled away from him and their matching eyes met gazes. "That will never, ever mean that I don't miss you and you know it. Estmond power, man."

Greg smiled at the little family saying that their father had made them say when they did things as a family or when the kids fought and were forced into making up. It may have not seemed like a big thing to anyone else, but those two words had loyalty and love behind them.

She punched him in the arm and grabbed his bag for him. "Now get out of here and go back to the big city."

He smiled and hugged her again. "I wish I could have seen Dad with you."

Unwilling to let the goodbye get any mushier than it already was, she hugged him back and then wiggled out of his arms. "Me too."

"Make sure you tell him that I love him if you see him again."

Lucy sighed, knowing it was pretty much a given that she was going to see her dad out there once he learned to stay solid. "He knows, Greg, but I will tell him anyway."

He opened the front door and stepped out onto the porch. "Thanks."

"Drive carefully." Lucy eyed Greg's piece of shit Ford Escort and hoped the elderly vehicle would make it back to San Francisco. He picked up on her concern and threw his bag over his shoulder. "I'll be fine. Don't worry."

And then he was in his car and pulling out of the driveway, while she stood on the porch waving goodbye.

School was something that Lucy loved. She was a sponge when it came to learning, especially about things that interested her. And she was interested in the paranormal. Being a part of the family she was in, she didn't really have a lot of career options, so paranormal studies was what she had decided to go to school for. The problem with that was there wasn't even one college in the United States that offered a degree in paranormal studies.

After a bit of research she learned that a physics degree offered a majority of the same classes that she would have needed for the paranormal studies degree, although she still wasn't sure exactly what she was going to do with the degree. It wasn't like she wanted to be a freaking ghost hunter or anything. She would probably be an active Keeper until she died. School was just one of those things you did to better yourself, and learning about stuff you're interested in is a lot more fun than stuff you're *not* interested in.

On this particular day though, she just couldn't get into paying attention in class. There were only a few students in the room because it was summer and most people took the summers off to go on vacation or be with their families. The instructor stood in front of a giant whiteboard attempting to explain vibrations and waves to a class that was half asleep.

Her mind kept wandering to the vision and the prophecy. How could someone like her possibly be the one that would bring an end to the Reapers? On one hand, that was her life's mission, the thing that had been driven into her head since she was born. On the other hand, there was nothing special about her that would justify her being a "Chosen One."

"Hey, Estmond," she heard a whisper from behind her. Quickly, she turned around to see who was trying to get her attention and saw that it was Adam. Inwardly, she fought to remember his last name and couldn't. He lived on campus and she had more than one class with him.

Adam was one of those students who were good at everything. He excelled in all his classes and he participated in sports as well as extracurricular activities, like the debate team and the school newspaper.

"What?" Lucy hissed back, not wanting to be loud and interrupt the instructor.

He leaned forward so she could hear him better. "A bunch of us are going to the coast this weekend. I was wondering if you wanted to come with."

Shocked, Lucy shook her head involuntarily. No one ever asked her to do anything. Probably because she just came to class and that was it. She was too busy to do anything fun, what with classes and homework, martial arts training and patrol, she barely had time left for anything else, much less going out with friends.

"We have a group camp out every year. I thought you might want to join us."

You barely know him, Lucy. Say no.

"Uh ... I can't. I have some family stuff to take care of."

He smiled and Lucy noticed for the first time how good looking he was. He was clean cut with short, dark blond hair, and had a build which made it completely clear that he worked out. He shoved a piece of paper with a number scratched onto it across his desk, "Here, in case you change your mind."

Lucy took the paper from him a bit hesitantly and tucked it into her pocket. "Thanks. I'll let you know." She turned back around to face the instructor. She knew she would never call him. It was almost impossible for her to go out with anyone who wasn't involved in their world. It would be too hard to hide it from any potential dates, and would mostly likely end up with the guy thinking she was crazy.

It was exactly this kind of encounter, one with a hot guy, which caused resentment toward the family business. She loved pretty much everything about her family and the life she was born into, but the thought that she might be alone for the rest of her life was one that haunted her often.

She thought of Ethan. She knew he felt more toward her than she felt for him. Sure, they were best friends and always would be, but there just wasn't any spark there on her part. During the times when she was feeling down about her love life, or lack of, she wished that she could love Ethan like he loved her.

Sure, she and Ethan took each other's virginity. She smiled as she doodled on her notebook paper. It had been more of an experiment than anything, both of them complaining that they felt like they were both going to be virgins forever. She had known even then that Ethan loved her, but when you're young you don't realize the repercussions of having sex with someone who likes you more than you like them.

The first time was awful. She was pretty sure it was more awful for her than it was for him, but they went ahead and tried a second time, then a third. After that Steph had learned what was going on with them and told her that she shouldn't lead Ethan on in that way.

Ethan would do anything for her and she knew it. But, he was that way about the entire Estmond clan and they felt the same for him. The fact that she and Ethan were able to stay friends, best friends, after having a sexual relationship was one thing she would be forever grateful for. Life would really suck ass without her best friend.

Her class ended and the instructor released them with directions for the homework assignment due at the end of the week. She hurried to shove her textbook and notes into her bag and headed for the door with thoughts of her nonexistent sex life, and how she was going to caffeinate herself, heavy on her mind.

"Make sure to call me sometime, Estmond," Adam called from his seat, where he was also gathering his things.

"I'll try." Ugh, what a lame response. She regretted it the moment it came out of her mouth.

Inside, she was shaking her head at herself. She didn't want to make him think she was actually going to call, but at the same time she didn't want to be rude either.

Adam didn't seem to think anything of it. He certainly wasn't struggling with it as much as she was. He simply flashed her a smile and threw his backpack over his shoulder as he passed by her.

Once he was out the door she went back to craving her coffee and hurried out to her car. She drove a simple gray Honda Civic that looked like everyone else's Honda Civic. It had been her dad's car, so now it was hers. At least it wasn't a beater like Greg's car. Most of her siblings drove shitty cars because lack of money was another problem associated with being a Keeper.

It was about an hour's drive back from Santa Rosa to Summer Hollow, so she grabbed a triple shot latte from a drive through coffee hut for the road. She took the twisty turns of the Saint Helena Mountain faster than the speed limit recommended, having driven this road most of her life she could probably do it with her eyes closed.

Back in Summer Hollow, the first thing she did was head over to her sister's shop. Olivia started her own business before she even left home. She loved cooking and baking, plus she was extremely good at it, so it made perfect sense for her to start her own bakery.

Personally, Lucy couldn't believe that she got up at three a.m. every fucking morning to bake ten tons of food for everyone else. But, she made a decent income and she enjoyed it, so that made it worth it. It also made Lucy happy that her sister was happy. She wasn't oblivious to the fact that Olivia seemed to be the only one of the Estmond siblings who was tempted to get out of the family business. So, if Liv wanted to bake shit, then by God, she should bake shit.

She parked out on the street and stared up at the sign for her sister's bakery. There was a dark blue awning over the door and two tiny iron tables with matching chairs outside the door. They were occupied by people Lucy didn't know, so they were probably tourists.

With a smile for the tourists, she pushed open the glass door and waved at her sister who was behind the counter boxing up enough cupcakes to feed an army.

"Who ordered that many cupcakes?" Lucy asked.

Liv wore an apron over her jeans and polo shirt to keep her outfit from getting messed up, but there wasn't even one stain on the apron that Lucy could see. She had her dark red hair bound up into a bun, as she always did when working, so that none of it would fall into the food.

"It's not that many, and it's for Tabatha Jenson."

Lucy made a face, expressing her disgust. "Really? She actually ordered from you?"

Liv smiled and shrugged. "I know, right. I think it's more to spite me than anything, though. You know, to show off how much money she has. This…" she gestured to the cupcakes, "is for her son's second birthday party."

Lucy opened the glass case that held a variety of baked goods and helped herself to an éclair. "Well, she may have married into money, but she is still just as much of a bitch as she always was."

"Don't forget to write down that you took that," Liv told her.

Lucy rolled her eyes as she poured a cup of coffee to go with her éclair. "Don't worry, I won't."

Liv put the last cupcake in the one of the boxes and gently placed a lid on top. "There. All done. And, no, Tabatha will never change, she is even worse now that she married Jeremy and his money."

"You want me to kick her ass?" Lucy asked as she deposited her coffee and éclair to table and pulled out a chair.

Liv shot her an incredulous look. "Why? She didn't do anything but order a ton of cupcakes for her kid's birthday party."

Lucy made a face and shrugged. "I don't know, because it would be fun and she deserves it for harassing you all those years. I don't know why *you* never kicked her ass."

Liv sighed. "Because, unlike you, I don't think that violence is the answer to everything."

Tabatha was older than Lucy, but she still would have loved to punch her in the face. She let it go, knowing that the last thing Liv wanted to do was talk about her life-long bully. "So, what's going on today? Anything exciting?"

Liv placed the boxes in the walk-in to keep them cool and answered just as she was closing the heavy door behind her. "Well, Dan took his drunk ass to the bar last night and tried to start a fight with some guy."

Lucy had just shoved the last of her éclair into her mouth. "What?" She managed to say around the pastry. "Who was it? How do you know?" She choked down the rest of the éclair and took a desperate swig of coffee to wash it down.

"I don't know who it was and the only reason I know about this is because Reese was here this morning." Liv poured herself a cup of coffee and joined Lucy at the table since there were no customers. "I'm not surprised, he has been on a permanent bender since Dad got sick."

Lucy felt her chest tighten. "I wish I knew how to help him." And she was serious. Family was everything to her. Seeing her brother hurting was killing her inside.

Liv looked just as sad as she felt. "There is nothing we can do until he wants to help himself.

Just then, the door swung open. Lucy and Liv both turned to see who the customer was. A jean clad, motorcycle booted, black haired beauty of a man stepped over the threshold into the shop.

Lucy might have swooned right there if it hadn't been for the misty red aura of a Reaper swirling around the sexiest guy she had ever seen.

JACK 9

Jack pulled open the door of the bakery and found himself face to face with two of the Estmond Keepers.

"Holy shit!"

Fuck, did he actually say that out loud.

When he'd left the house to find something to eat for breakfast, the last thing he thought he would encounter was a Keeper and surely not two of them in the same place.

Both girls were on their feet in the same instant, taking their fighting stances automatically, as if it were second nature to them. Although ... it was probably more like first nature to them.

The sisters were both what he would consider beautiful and he almost never thought that about any woman. But, the younger one ... she was straight up fucking hot! It wasn't just her looks either. She wore a defiant look that told him without words that she would kick his ass if he made even one wrong move.

Surprised to see the light silvery mist swirling around the two girls, he halted just inside the door so abruptly the handle thumped him on the ass as the door swung shut behind him.

The older red head stepped up beside her sister.

"You shouldn't be here," she told him in a low voice. "Get out." She pointed at the door.

Jack, who had fully been prepared to turn around and walk right back out the way he had come, suddenly decided that he would go when he fucking felt like it. His eyes flicked over the taller older sister, and then the younger one. God, what he would do to her if she wasn't a Keeper.

"You heard her, get the hell out!"

Jack held up his hands. "Whoa, calm down, I just wanted a fucking doughnut."

The young Keeper lifted her chin and rewarded him with the sexiest glare he had ever seen on a woman. "Get your damn doughnut somewhere else. You need to get the hell out of here and out of Summer Hollow too."

He should have turned around. Confrontations with Keepers in public were never a good thing, like what happened the night before in the bar. It got people talking, and that was even worse. But, for some reason, he could not force himself to turn around and walk back out that door. He could barely force himself to take his eyes off the younger Keeper.

But, he did, his gaze moved to the older one again and a thought occurred to him. "Are you the Estmonds?"

"None of your damn business who we are!" shot back the smaller one. "You have literally three seconds to take your ass out of here."

"Ah," he nodded, "so you are."

"One!"

"I still need my doughnut."

"Two!"

"Do you have any with lemon filling?"

"Three!" The younger Keeper charged him.

He took his fighting stance as she flew toward him. He was ready for her. She pulled back her arm, preparing to nail him in the face. He raised his guard, ready to deflect, but at the last second she went low, sweeping out her leg.

Jack felt her leg connect with his and suddenly his body was headed for the floor. "Shit!" The curse expelled from his lips just as the side of his body connected with the spotless white tile of the bakery floor.

He turned and kicked out, hoping to make contact with her. No chance, before he could twist away she was on top of him, straddling his body and driving her arm into his jugular. "I told you to leave."

"Lucy, there are people outside," came a soft warning from her sister.

"Shut it, Liv. Like anyone in this town hasn't seen my temper."

A long sigh from the sister. "They're tourists, Lucy."

The distraction from her sister gave him just enough of an opening. He reached up and grabbed her arms, tossing her aside and then threw his leg over the top of her, reversing their positions. Now, he sat on top of her, holding down her midsection with his body weight.

God, he really hoped he didn't get hard. The fact that she was struggling beneath him wasn't helping matters any either.

"Get off me asshole!"

"Not a chance."

"Just fucking go, why are you trying to make this worse for yourself?"

He drove his arm harder into her neck. "It doesn't look like I'm the one in a bad position here. You're the one who attacked me and now look where you got yourself."

As if he sensed it was coming, he turned his head slightly just in time to catch Liv's running shoe in the face. The force of her kick was so much that he flipped over onto the floor beside Lucy.

His cheek felt like someone had slapped him with a brick. Time to get the hell out of here. He had almost no chance against two Keepers. But, he did have a mission, lest he forget. Seriously though, what was he going to do, kill her in the town bakery with a ton of people right outside? No, that wasn't even an option. Besides … he didn't know if the young Keeper was even the one he was looking for.

He could just hear his mother now. 'Well, the answer is simple Jackson, kill them all.'

Yeah … he wasn't doing that. Having to off one of them was more than enough for him.

He stayed on the floor so he didn't appear a threat. Lucy had scrambled to her feet and both girls towered over him, Liv had her fists raised just in case he breathed or some shit.

"Look, I'll leave. Okay? Just let me get up." He rubbed his neck where Lucy had held it and realized something. There had been no burn when she touched him.

His head snapped up and his gaze found Lucy, she mirrored his reaction. Her fingers were softly touching her throat where the bare skin of his arm had made contact. Her eyes were wide and staring at him as if he had the answer.

That's it. "I'm outta here." No way was he going to sit here on the floor like a little bitch who does what he's told one second longer. He pushed himself into a standing position, smoothed down his black tee shirt, shot Lucy one last look and headed for the door while mumbling, "Fuck this shit."

Later, while he was holed up in his little house with some nasty doughnuts he'd acquired from the grocery store, he flipped through the channels on the TV and wondered how in the hell a badass like himself had just gotten beat by a couple of chicks.

He bit into a chocolate glazed that tasted like someone had drizzled chocolate over dog shit and called it a pastry. Damn. He wished that he'd been able to wrangle some real baked goods out of those Keepers.

Thinking about the doughnut only got him thinking

about the young Keeper, Lucy. Boy, she was just a ball of fire all around. From her red hair to her attitude, she was the whole package. Why there was no burning when they touched was still a mystery. He would sure like to know why that was.

Normally, when the Reapers made physical contact with a Keeper, it was painful. Mere brushes of skin usually felt like when you shock yourself from static electricity build up, but when the contact was more intense, like a grab, it felt like skin under flame.

Apparently neither of them had felt any of that.

Bang, Bang, Bang. A sudden pounding at the door had him off his feet in an instant. He hurried over to the table and snatched up the .45 that he had set there when he'd returned home from his failed breakfast outing.

"Open the door, asshole!"

Jack smiled and rested the gun back onto the table top. He hurried over to the front door and flung it open. "Aiden." He greeted his best friend with far less enthusiasm than he actually felt. "Get your ass in here."

Aiden lifted his bag and crossed the threshold into Jacks rental house.

Taking note of the bag, Jack raised an eyebrow. "You staying a while?"

Aiden dropped the duffle on the floor. "You know exactly why I'm here."

Jack shook his head and sighed. "My mother."

"Damn straight," Aiden confirmed. "She wants this Keeper dead … like yesterday."

Jack turned away, headed for the kitchen and the meager stock of cheap beer in the fridge. Aiden followed him. "What the hell, Jack? It's one Keeper. One! I know you don't like having to do stuff like this but it's a matter of survival. We can't fuck with the Reaper Council."

Jack pulled open the fridge and extracted a bottle of Sierra Nevada. "I've been fucking with the Council all my life." He popped the top off his beer with the bottle opener and leaned against the counter as he took the first pull.

"Jack, dude, it's like eleven in the morning."

"Oh, I'm sorry, did you want one."

Aiden shook his head, then stepped up beside Jack and opened the fridge. After taking stock of the lack of food within the contents, he shrugged and pulled himself out a beer as well.

With a smirk, Jack handed him the bottle opener.

"Asshole," Aiden muttered.

Jack loved his best friend. They had grown up together, but at this particular moment, he knew that Aiden being here wasn't a good thing. He was going to make Jack kill that Keeper or do it himself.

"So, mom sent you over to make sure I was getting my chores done, eh?"

Aiden finished taking a swig of his beer and nodded. "Yeah. She is pissed, man. Really fucking pissed. She's even talking about how you won't make a good leader when they're gone and all that bull shit."

Jack rolled his eyes. "I've never wanted to be a leader. I don't even like most of the people on the Council, including my mom and dad. Why in the hell would I want to lead the entire species? Fuck that."

Aiden set his beer on the counter and grabbed Jack by the shoulders. "No. Not fuck that. You have a chance to lead, Jack. To change things. You don't like the way your parents have led our people, so now is your chance to change that. If you do this one little thing, you will finally have some favor on your mother's side and when she goes, you will be Emperor."

"I don't want to be Emperor and that 'one little thing' you are talking about is called murder, Aiden."

Aiden didn't blink an eye. "We are going to do this. I will do it for you if I have to, and you are going to come home with me to report it to the Empress. When she asks if it's done, we tell her that you did it."

He thought of Lucy, her red hair, her dark eyes, her

fierceness. "What if we don't do it?"

"Do you really want to chance not killing the Keeper who might be the Chosen One? The Chosen One who is supposed to bring forth an end to the Reapers?"

Jack knew that Aiden would do whatever the Empress ordered him to do. He may be Jacks best friend, but he had been raised to obey the Council, especially orders from the Empress. Through their life-long friendship, Jack had never asked him to choose between his loyalty to the Council and himself, and he never would.

Why was he even considering not doing this in the first place?

"Fine." He nodded. "Let's do it. We'll go tonight."

Aiden held up his beer, "That's what I'm talkin' about."

"Yeah, tonight should be good. Their father passed away a few days ago and they had a funeral, so the whole crew of Keepers were here. The place was crawling with them."

"How many are at the house?"

Jack shrugged. "Should be just, Lu ... just one, the rest of them live in their own places around town. They do go out and help her in the graveyard sometimes though."

"Good." Aiden nodded approval. "At least you've been doing your homework."

Jack turned away and rolled his eyes. "Yeah, you know me."

Aiden laughed. "That's the thing, I do know you, Jack, and I know that you do everything you possibly can *not* to do your homework. So, tell me what you have been up to in this shithole of a town."

Well, first I fucked a chick and fed on her soul, and then I went to the bar and got punched by a Keeper, *and then* I fucked another chick and fed on her soul. "Nothing much, I've gone to the bar a couple of times, but mostly I hang out here."

"In this shack."

Jack shrugged. "I'm offended, I like it here. It's quiet."

"And rustic."

"Shut up, it's better than their shitty bank of rooms they call a hotel."

Aiden wandered into the living room and flopped down onto the couch. "I get why you like it here. Hidden away from life with your mom and dad."

Jack had followed him into the living room and sat down beside him. Aiden knew him well. He understood that Jack hated life with the Reapers. Mostly, he disliked it because of his mother and father trying to raise him to be the next ruler. If there were any way that Jack could leave and not live under the radar of the Reaper Council, he would probably do it. He tipped his beer and finished the last of it. "After we take care of this tonight, we leave right away and never come back here. I don't care what you tell my parents, but I am going to find a way out."

"Out?" Aiden raised an eyebrow.

"Yeah, out. It's not so much having rules or doing the things, like this, that I don't want to do. I want out of the Reaper society because I'm tired of living someone else's life. Everything I do is what someone else thinks I should do to become the person that they think I should be. I have no goals, no skills, nothing that will help me out in the real world because I've been raised in a fucking mansion with people waiting on me hand and foot. I want to live my own life."

Oh fuck, cry me a fucking river. Jack couldn't believe what had just come out of his own mouth. Next thing you know he'd have a carton of Ben & Jerry's and a box of tissues while watching a chick flick on the tube.

At first, Aiden didn't respond. Jack leaned back into the cushions and closed his eyes wishing he hadn't spilled his lady guts to his best friend. Dudes just didn't do that, there was a code for that, a bro code, he was sure of it.

"I'll help you," he heard Aiden's voice after a

moment. "I'll help you get out."

His lids snapped open. "You will?"

His best friend nodded and brushed his blond hair back with his fingertips. "Yeah, I will. This last mission is something that needs to be done, though. I know you don't like it, but we are talking about the Chosen One here. We can't risk our entire race being wiped out because you didn't do the job."

At risk of continuing to sound like a little bitch, he opted for keeping his mouth shut. He had to do it. "Like I said, after tonight I'm done."

Aiden nodded, signaling that he understood. "Deal." He worked his way out of the couch cushions and stood up. "I'm going to shower and take a nap so I'll be good to go tonight. You got a place where I can crash here?"

"Bed's in there." He pointed in the direction of the bedroom. "Go ahead and use that, I have to look a few things up on the computer and then pack so we can leave right after it's done."

"Good plan," Aiden called as he strode toward the bedroom. "I'll be in here if you need me for anything."

After the bedroom door clicked shut, Jack hurried over to his laptop and logged in. He googled the Estmond family and Summer Hollow. He needed to find out if Lucy was the seventh child in the family's bloodline. He sincerely hoped that she wasn't the Chosen One.

No such luck. He pulled up the obituary for Gregory Estmond, their father, and found that he was survived by seven children, Lucy being the youngest of the seven.

"Shit."

Time to man the fuck up and do this last job. Aiden said that he would help him get out, and he knew that his friend would keep his word. His mother, on the other hand, would probably fly off the handle and send out the armies in search of him. So, as easy as getting out of the life may sound to some people, it wasn't going to be an easy task at all. He would probably spend the rest of his life in hiding and on the run ... well, the rest of her life anyway.

Or maybe she wouldn't care at all. He didn't know which of the two options was worse.

LUCY
10

L ucy stepped out into the night.

Beyond the white picket fence, sheltered only by the trees and the Keepers, the blue mist of the souls danced among the darkness like the galaxies on a clear night sky. Watching the souls at night was her favorite thing. It was the time when they looked most alive. The time when they shone the brightest.

The summer air was warm enough that she didn't need a hoodie or even a long sleeve shirt. She wore a black tank top with spaghetti straps and a pair of jeans. Her shoes were the ladies combat boots that she always wore when she went out to patrol the graveyard. A knife was tucked into one of her boots, secured by an ankle sheath. In her right hand, she carried the antique bow she'd found in the attic trunk. The silver arrows were fitted into a belted quiver made of hard leather, which she wore at her hip.

Nightly patrol was part of the job, but tonight she was hoping to get to talk with her dad. As mad as she was that he had done what he'd done by not crossing over, she still ached for him. Losing him had been the hardest thing she'd ever been through. Now, she would have to go through losing him all over again when the time came for him to cross over.

She trekked her way across the lawn and onto the cemetery grounds. Even though it was dark, she could see by the dim lamps that were posted along the well groomed trails of the graveyard. Her father had placed the lamp posts there before she was born. However, over time some of lamps had occasionally needed to be replaced. Lucy had gone with her father to the hardware store in Santa Rosa to get the supplies and then helped him replace the posts.

The entire Estmond clan had been responsible for cleaning and upkeep of the graveyard. As the heir to the estate, it was now her sole responsibility. Although it was hers alone to take care of now, none of her brothers and sisters … or even Ethan, had abandoned their responsibilities. All of them still came by and did their jobs with the upkeep. Mr. Dawson, the funeral director, employed the workers who came to dig the graves and work the burial vault, so the family didn't have anything to do with that part of keeping the graveyard.

She made her way along the trails, thinking about those little things and watching the beautiful blue mist of the souls.

"Dad," she called out softly. "I know you're here somewhere."

The souls didn't always learn to solidify themselves into their previous human form. Most souls usually passed on right away. Some of them just didn't have the urge to return to how they had looked when they were alive, but then there were the ones that had an urge to communicate that wouldn't go away, so they learned to make their mist appear as their shell had.

Her dad seemed to have learned how to do it pretty quickly, but apparently it drained his energy and it took a while to rejuvenate it.

"Da…addd."

He didn't appear. Oh well, she knew that he would come to her the moment he could solidify. Continuing her walk, the cemetery trails moved upward into the older part of the cemetery. She liked the older part of the graveyard a lot. Most of the headstones were large and gothic looking, made of aged stone. The modern markers used for graves nowadays were simple plates in the ground. The actual headstones were made of granite or marble. Sure they looked nice, but they all looked the same. The older ones each had a personality all their own, like the person buried beneath them.

"Hi there, Lucy Mae."

She spun, knowing her father's voice instantly. "Dad!"

Her father stood there, the blue mist of his soul still swirling around him in effort to remain solid. He wore the same thing he was buried in, making Lucy want to giggle at the sight of her father's ghostly image in khaki shorts and colorful Hawaiian shirt. He even had the flip flops to top off the whole 'vacation of a lifetime' look.

He gave her a small smile and nodded at the bow in her hand. "I see you found the trunk."

"Yeah, we found it all right," Lucy scoffed. "So, I'm the Chosen One. I am the prophecy. Honestly, I don't think it changes much, Dad."

He nodded. "I figured you would react this way."

"Well how else am I supposed to react? The legend doesn't say *how* the Chosen One is supposed to bring an end to the Reapers, only that they will. No when, no how, no reasonable life changing information whatsoever."

Her father shimmered, his body flickering and making some of the solid parts invisible. "Lucy, fate will show itself in due time. There is no reason for you to change what you do or who you are. This is a destiny that you will eventually fulfill."

Lucy rolled her eyes and shifted her bow to the other hand. "Well, a little more information would have been nice."

"Of course it would have. But, do you honestly think that taking down the Reapers, with whom the Keepers have been fighting for generations, would be a simple task? It is not meant to be known how the Chosen One will accomplish this great feat, only that they will."

This was getting ridiculous. "Well, what's the point of the whole prophecy thing then?"

Her father shook his head. "Lucy Mae, sometimes your common sense concerns me. The point is to give us *hope*. To know that someday all of the fighting, all of the sleepless nights protecting the souls, and all the generations of loss will eventually account for something. That is what the prophecy is meant to do."

Her father's words stopped her. It hadn't occurred to her that there was more to the prophecy than the foresight of the future. "I never really thought about it that way."

"Well, it's time you did start thinking about it like that."

He was right. She was looking at the legend like it was an instruction manual for the Chosen One. A prophecy in itself was mystical, brought forth from someone who could see into the future, so obviously every single detail would not be foreseen.

"Yes," she nodded. "You're right. I'll stop taking things so literally."

"Good girl."

"Dad, you know you didn't have to keep from crossing over because of all this. You could have left a note … or something."

Again, he gave her a soft smile. Even though he was what some would call a ghost, the lift of his lips brightened his eyes and crinkled the creases around them. "Ah, don't you worry so much honey, this isn't so bad."

"But you never know when you will be able to move on. You might be stuck here for a lot longer than you wanted to be."

He waved her off. "I told you before, this was my decision to make. I will move on when the time comes for me to go."

Lucy couldn't bring herself to say it, but she was most afraid of a Reaper somehow getting to her dad. They had lost souls to the Reapers before, but she had never lost one who was close to her.

"I know what you're thinking, Lucy Mae."

She shook her head. "No you don't."

"Don't you doubt your old man. I've known you all your life and I know every expression that pretty little face of yours makes."

Defiantly, Lucy straightened her spine and squared her shoulders. "What was I thinking then?"

"You're worried about the Reapers. You think I'm vulnerable since I am now a soul and not a Keeper."

"You will always be a Keeper. *Always*," Lucy told him in a low voice. "Don't talk like that."

"But, it's true. All of it is," her father insisted.

Lucy wanted to hug him so badly. What she would have given at that moment to throw her arms around him and lay her head against his shoulder. "Don't worry about it," she told him. "I have this taken care of out here. There isn't a chance in hell a Reaper will get ahold of you."

"But, Lucy, they are going to be gunning for you if they find out that I've died."

A flash of that sexy Reaper came back to her. 'Are you the Estmonds?' Were they here already?

"What is it?" Her father's voice washed away the image of the Reaper she and Liv had met.

She shook her head. "It's nothing."

"Damn it, Lucy Mae." His hands were on his hips now. "I told you I know when you're lying."

"Sheesh, fine! Liv and I were at the bakery today and a Reaper came in. He seemed surprised to see us there, but he did ask if we were the Estmonds."

"They *are* after you." Lucy watched her father's cheerful eyes darken. "There is no other reason that a Reaper would ask for you by name."

Lucy agreed. "Yeah, it didn't occur to me until you mentioned it. I guess I'm just used to people knowing who we are."

Her father nodded. "I can see how that could happen. Just be careful, if they're asking for you by name it can't be that long before they try to attack."

"I'll be fine, Dad!"

He didn't look convinced. "You make sure that from now on you have one of your brothers or sisters with you ... or Ethan."

"I can handle myself, you know that."

"Lucy Mae, you listen to me. All the Reapers you have ever defeated were only after souls. These Reapers are after *you*. Do you hear me! They want to get rid of you."

"Dad ..."

"No," he cut her off. "This is not up for debate. You don't patrol alone, got it."

Lucy looked at the ground, knowing that she wouldn't win this one. "Fine. I'll bring someone with me from now on."

"Lucy, you know that this means you need to be prepared to be just as lethal to the Reapers. If they are trying to kill you, you aren't going to be able to just run them off. They will be back. If you kill one, they will probably send more."

"I know Dad."

She understood what this meant, however, it didn't mean she liked the idea of it at all. But, if someone tried to murder her or one of her loved ones, there was no way in hell she was going to let them live to try it again.

"Don't be stubborn, Lucy Mae."

She sighed. "I said I wouldn't come out alone."

He finally appeared convinced enough to let the topic go. "Tell me what's going on with everyone. How are your brothers and sisters?"

Switching the crossbow to her left hand she ran her hand through her hair, pushing it away from her face. "All right I guess. Dan is still drinking like crazy and picking fights at the bar. But, everyone else is just dealing. Losing you was hard ... too hard. Greg hates being away from home, but I think he likes his job over there."

She didn't want to make him feel bad, but she didn't want to lie either. The Estmond clan didn't really make it a habit to lie to each other, they just didn't think there was a need for it. She watched her father's eyes reflect mixed emotions.

"I didn't want to leave you, Lucy Mae."

"Dad, we all know that."

"It was just time to go." He moved his gaze away from her, looking off into the distance beyond the headstones. "But, now ... now I am free of the pain. My body doesn't feel like every move is an accomplishment. I have finally escaped the prison I was living in."

Fucking tears. She wiped her cheeks with her free hand, brushing away the evidence of how much she hated that her father was gone, but how happy she was that he wasn't going through everything that he went through before he died. Cancer is a bastard. Fuck Cancer.

"Don't cry, honey. I'm better now than I have ever been. Even if I am just a shadow of who I once was."

"You are still you," she told him, trying not to choke up. "A soul never changes."

"Well, stop the tears then." He reached out, as if he wanted to wipe them away himself, but then he stopped before he was close enough to make contact. She looked up and saw pain in his eyes and realized that he knew he wouldn't be able to touch her, even though he wanted to so badly.

"It's all right, Dad. I'm okay." She forced the emotions back. No more crying. "Everyone really wants to see you tho..."

"Lucy!" he hissed, his voice barely audible. "Look."

She searched the graveyard in the direction her father was pointing and saw what he was trying to tell her. "Fucking Reapers," she mumbled under her breath when she saw the red flashes out in the trees to her right.

"Lucy!"

"Not the time to reprimand me on my language, Dad."

"There are two of them."

"I know."

"Be careful, honey."

"I will. You know I can do it." She shifted the bow back to her right hand and headed off to a more open area.

Their auras were one of the things between the two factions that were a blessing and a curse at the same time. The red and silver shimmering auras allowed them to identify each other immediately, which was usually a good thing, like earlier in the bakery. However, it was times like this when you wanted stealth and the auras just wouldn't allow it. They were all glowing like beacons in the night.

May as well have been holding a big flashing sign that said 'come and get me mother fucker.'

Once she was in the larger open area, she lifted the crossbow and let it rest against her shoulder. She watched as they crept across the graveyard, trying to stick to the trees. What, were they drunk? Did they actually think that they were hidden and she couldn't see them?

Finally, they were close enough that she aimed the crossbow at the red targets and called out. "I can see you."

One of the Reapers shot off to the left and the other went to the right. Lucy cursed and picked one to shoot at. She should have just taken the shot while they thought they hadn't been seen. It's a lot easier to hit a target that's not moving.

She pulled the trigger and waited. Nothing. "Shit." She must have missed. Quickly, she fitted another arrow into the crossbow and took aim on the same one she had just fired. She had just gotten him within her sights and her finger was tickling the trigger when she heard her father call out.

"Lucy, behind you!"

She was only able to turn slightly when someone, most likely the other Reaper, slammed into her body and took her down onto the soft earth floor. Her crossbow slipped from her fingers and skidded across the dirt, coming to a stop completely out of her reach. "Owww, shit!" She turned and struggled, trying to get out from beneath him.

"Dad, get out of here!" she screamed. "Disappear! Hide!"

She didn't care what he did as long as he got the hell away from these Reapers. But, he was her father and he probably wasn't going to go far.

She turned to the side, hoping to at least get onto her back where she could have a better chance at fighting. With all the force she could muster, she slammed her elbow backward, hoping to make contact with something.

She did.

Unsure of where she hit him, she heard a grunt and then he grabbed her hair, pushing her face downward into the dirt. Again, she elbowed him and then bent her knee and topped it off with a nice kick in the butt.

As he reacted just slightly, she flipped herself, landing on her back. She knew she had to get out of this. She couldn't die here in front of her father, who had chosen not to cross over so that he could help her fulfill the prophecy.

Once she was on her back, the Reaper had fully recovered and came at her again. This was not the Reaper she had met in the bakery earlier in the day. This one had blond hair, dark green eyes, and a look so intense she knew that this man was a stone cold killer.

He was attractive, but not like the other Reaper she'd met.

What the fuck was she thinking! Dammit, Lucy.

You're going to die, snap the fuck out of it!

In an instant he had a giant knife in this hand. She saw the lamplight glint off the steel blade as he lunged at her. Instinctively, she pushed her feet out and her boots connected with his chest. He staggered backward a couple of feet, giving her time to jump into a standing position.

He held the knife at his side. "Don't make this harder on yourself," he told her calmly.

Lucy fought the urge to look around for the other Reaper. She had seen two red auras, so she knew the other was out there somewhere.

The blond Reaper lunged for her. Lucy was already in her fighting stance, her guard up and her foot in front of her. Problem was he had a knife and his reach was longer than hers. Decision made within an instant, she snapped out a kick, making contact with his knife hand. His fingers unclenched, dropping the weapon to the ground. Not giving him even one chance to try and go for the knife, she moved in and threw a right hook, her fist slamming into his jaw. Then an uppercut with the left to his stomach as she simultaneously grabbed his hair and raised her knee, effectively bashing his face into the hard bone of her knee cap.

"Son of a bitch!" the Reaper cried out, grabbing at his face.

Blood leaked out between his fingers from his obviously broken nose.

"Who's got it hard now?" she asked him, shaking her hand where it tingled from the contact with the skin of a Reaper.

"I am going to kill you, bitch!" Then he pulled one of her favorite moves and went low, knocking her to the ground with a sweep of his leg and grabbing his knife with his right hand.

It seemed only a second passed, she saw him coming and went for the only weapon she had available. Reaching down, she slipped one of the silver arrows out of her hip pouch. The next thing she knew the

Reaper had her pinned, his legs pressed into her arms with so much weight it was impossible for her to move them. The blade was at her throat before she could attempt any sort of attack or escape.

Shit, shit, shit. All of her training flew out the window when the cold steel of the blade touched her skin. Her fingers clenched around the arrow, refusing to let go even though she couldn't move her arm to use it. All she had left was to hold still and hope for a miracle. Her chin tilted upward and her eyes closed, she silently prayed that her father was not watching this.

Then suddenly, she heard someone shout, "get the fuck off her!" and she felt the Reaper being lifted away from her body. Her eyes snapped open and she saw the sexy Reaper from the bakery lifting the blond one off of her. His dark eyes were angry and his aura was on fire.

The knife grazed over the tender skin at her throat as the Reaper was pulled away from her body. She knew she was bleeding, but that it wasn't fatal. Without thinking, she swung her right hand over and plunged the arrow into any part of that Reapers body that it would make contact with.

She was so pissed that the silver crossbow arrow plunged into the Reapers calf with so much force it went in a couple inches.

"Mother fucker!" the blond Reaper, still in the clutches of the sexy one, cried out and bent to clutch at his leg. "Jack, you mother fucker! Kill her dammit!"

Her eyes met Jack's and he gave her a slight nod.

At that moment, Lucy knew she had a few options, but her fear gave way to any other method of attack and she ran. She scooped up her crossbow from the ground, ignoring the blood dripping from her neck wound and ran as fast as she could over the earthen covered bodies of the dead and hit the gravel of the pathway, almost falling from the marble like pebbles.

She could see the blue mist of the souls gathering to

99

see what was going on. "Get out of here!" she yelled at them. "Hide!"

She stumbled into the house and grabbed her keys off the side table. Not stopping for anything else, even her purse, she ran to her car and started the thing, then peeled out of her driveway in a spray of dirt and gravel.

She drove for about ten minutes, trying to calm herself. Her heart was still beating extremely fast and she kept feeling the wound at her neck. It was just a scratch, thank God. But ... fuckin' A, someone had just tried to kill her.

She sped into Ethan's driveway and halted the car so quickly that it skidded to the side. Still unable to calm herself she staggered out of the car, leaving the door open and hurried up on to Ethan's porch where she pounded on his door.

JACK
11

"What the fuck!" Aiden stood up and swung at Jack.

Jack stepped back and let his friend's massive fist fly through the air in front of him.

Aiden looked like shit. His nose was bleeding profusely, staining his face and tee shirt with the evidence of the fight. "Let me look at your leg?"

"You get the fuck away from me," Aiden hissed at him. Then, he reached down and clasped his fingers around the sliver arrow protruding from his calf and yanked. The arrow slid out easily and Aiden tossed it on the ground at Jacks feet."

"Aiden …"

"I don't want to hear it," Aiden growled. "We had a deal. I fucking knew you couldn't do it, so I was going to take care of it. Why did you do that? We had her!"

"I don't know." And he didn't know. All he did know was that when he saw Lucy on the ground with Aiden on top of her and his knife at her neck, something came over him and he wanted to rip Aiden limb from limb.

He had seen Lucy's fear, seen her fighting not to give up, and his instinct had taken over. He had barely known what he was doing before he realized that he had grabbed his best friend from the back and tore him away from the young Keeper.

Yeah. What the fuck was wrong with him?

"You don't know." Aiden limped away from Jack, headed for the trail that would take them back down to the road where Jack's truck was parked. "You don't fucking know! Dammit, Jack."

He couldn't explain it to himself, how in the hell was he supposed to explain his irrational behavior to his friend. "I told you, I don't fucking know what happened!" Jack yelled back at him as he followed him out of the graveyard.

Jack opened the door of his truck and slid behind the wheel while Aiden struggled to get himself into the passenger side. Aiden looked over at him out of the corner of his eye and Jack knew he had really fucked up. "You are supposed to always have my back. Always. That is one fucking thing that we have never wavered on."

He was right, he was totally fucking right. Throughout their life Aiden had covered for Jack more times than he could count. He had always been there to help him or protect him, no matter what the situation. He had owed him this one.

"I don't know what to tell you, except what I already did. I. don't. fucking. know."

"You're an asshole, Jack. A big one."

"I know."

"More than big, like fucking huge."

"I know."

Jack wanted to say something more. Instead, he just pulled the truck out into the dark street and headed toward his house.

Aiden kept quiet until they got back to Jack's place. The silver of the arrow was going to weaken him and he would need a little time to recover, so Jack assumed that they would go back to the house and chill. But, as soon as Jack pulled into the driveway and parked, Aiden hopped out of the truck and then stepped up onto the back of the truck and pulled his bag out of the bed.

Jack watched as he swung it over his shoulder and headed for his rented SUV. He opened the door to the back seat and threw the bag inside.

"Where are you going?"

"I'm getting the hell away from you. I tried to give you a chance to make it right with your parents and the Reaper Council and you fucked me over. Maybe the Empress was right. Maybe you aren't capable of leading. You can't even do one fucking thing that could save our entire race."

"I can't murder her," Jack told him softly.

Aiden stepped up into the SUV and sat down on the soft leather interior of the driver seat. "Well, I can." His gaze locked on Jacks. "I'm taking care of this mission with or without you. Unlike you, I still have a job to keep."

With that, Aiden slammed the door and started the vehicle. He backed all the way down the driveway and then tore off down the deserted street, leaving Jack standing in his driveway feeling like dog shit.

How did a guy choose between the only person in the world who had ever really been there for him and murdering someone. Sure, that someone was a Keeper whom he'd only just met, but it was still murder.

Not to mention that something had happened to him when Aiden had attacked her. That feeling was one he had never, ever experienced before. As if driven by unseen forces, he had felt the intense urge to safeguard her from harm.

"Son of a bitch!" Jack kicked the fender of his truck with his boot. Then, he stared at the dent for a few seconds and didn't feel like it was enough so he kicked it again, and again, until he decided it wasn't making him feel any better. He was just beating the shit out of his truck.

Well, why do with violence what beer and fucking could do. He got back inside his truck and sped out of his driveway following the direction that Aiden had gone.

When he got to Knight's, he saw Reese behind the bar and waved at her.

"You look like shit," she called out to him as she extracted an MGD and set it on the bar for him.

"I know," he told her. "It's been a shitty day."

"Looks like it," she responded.

"Do you ever let anyone else tend the bar?" he asked, looking around as if there might be a replacement waiting for her in the wings.

She shook her head. "Not usually, I don't trust a whole lot of people enough for that. This place is my baby."

"Yeah, I get that." He took a swig of his beer and cringed. "Ugh. Can I get a shot of Jameson with this too?"

"I thought you tried to stay away from the hard stuff." Her dark eyes penetrated him, looking for a reason that he would want to be drinking the hard A.

"Not tonight I don't."

"Fine. But, because I'm your friend I'm only allowing you one shot, then it's back to the hangover beer for you."

Friend. What a fucked up word. The F word for sure.

He gave her a twisted smile as she handed him the shot of amber colored liquid. "I don't have any friends. Not anymore."

She shot him a concerned look and put the Jameson bottle back on the shelf. "You do now. I think we hit it off as far as friends go. See, I'm going to help you out right now, just like a dude would. There's Janette."

"Who?"

"Are you fucking kidding me?"

Jack raised his eyebrows and shrugged his shoulders, then tilted his head back and slammed his shot.

Reese had her hands on her hips. "Janette. The girl you took home the other night," she explained.

"Oh! You mean Janice." He turned around to see

who she was talking about.

"No, I mean Janette. That is her name, asshole."

"Oh shit, really?"

Reese shook her head and laughed. "You may be good looking, but you are the poster child for guys women shouldn't date. I have no idea why I like you at all."

With a smile, Jack turned around and wiggled his eyebrows. "Maybe we should take that to the next level." He was totally joking and she knew it. The two of them seemed to have a mutual no touchy code.

"Not a chance in hell, Casanova."

Jack laughed and then once again looked over his shoulder at Janette. Now, *that* was exactly what he needed right now. Nothing calms the nerves after an attempted murder and a fight with your friend like a good night of fucking out the frustration. He grabbed his beer and got up off the stool.

"Really, Jack?"

He ignored Reese and set off for Janette, who stood leaning over the pool table, flirting with a guy who looked like the senior quarterback of the high school football team, fucking letter jacket and all. Most likely this was the idiot from every town who graduated and just couldn't give up the glory of the good ol' days.

"Hey Janette."

With a giggle, she turned around and he was rewarded with a look at those amazing tits all encased in a halter top that pushed them up, creating cleavage any guy would end up drooling over. Hell, chicks probably drooled over it too.

When she saw him her giggle disappeared. "Oh, it's you."

Yeah, she was still pissed. Oh well, she could take it out on him later. He may be an asshole, but one thing was for sure, they always came back for more. Always.

"You want to get out of here?" That's right, straight to the point.

She raised one eyebrow and looked at him like he

was crazy. "Now, why in the world would I want to go anywhere with you?" She took a long swig of her Budweiser.

"You know why."

"Listen, Jack. I don't like to be used." She tilted her head up defiantly.

With a smile, Jack set his beer on the table beside him and leaned forward, placing one hand on the pool table on either side of her so that she was trapped, her body almost, but not quite, touching his. "Oh, I think you do," he whispered against her ear.

"Dude, seriously?"

The sound of Mr. Letterman Jacket's voice forced him to look away from Janette and her perfectly pouty lips. The guy stood there with a pool stick clutched in his hand, obviously upset that Jack had moved in on what he'd been working on.

"Yeah, seriously," he told the guy without missing a beat and then directed his attention back to Janette. "So, what's it going to be?"

She tilted her head to the side as if contemplating whether or not she should go. "Well, I guess." She moved forward to stand, so Jack moved his hands and backed up. "Let's go then." He grabbed his beer bottle and chugged down every last drop, then grabbed Janette's hand and pulled her away from the kid who was clearly losing any hope he had of bagging her.

"See ya Lance," Janette giggled, grabbing her purse off the table as she let Jack pull her away.

Oh shit, seriously, his name was Lance. Perfect jock name to go along with the rest of his persona.

He passed by the bar and saw Reese shaking her head. She caught his eye and flipped him off. He shot the finger back at her and hurried out the door into the warm air of small town Summer Hollow.

For some reason, he felt like he was in a huge hurry. Usually when he picked up women, he didn't mind taking his time. Nothing was wrong with flirting and foreplay, it always led to the same place, so why not take your time getting there.

After they were in the truck he sped through town and took a side road that eventually turned to dirt and took them down by one of the little creeks that ran through Summer Hollow. "This looks like a nice spot to hang out," he told Janette as he pulled the truck into a spot alongside the water. Reaching behind the seat he fumbled around with all the crap back there until his fingers found the six pack of emergency beer he'd stashed back there a while ago.

Extracting the beer, he handed one to Janette and then opened one for himself. "Thanks." She accepted the beer and popped it open. "Look, about last time we were together …"

"We don't need to talk about that," Jack cut her off. More like *he* didn't want to talk about that. He opened the door. "Come on."

"Okay fine, we don't have to talk about it." She stepped down from the passenger side. Before he got out, he leaned over, opened the glove box and grabbed a condom. He was in a hurry, but not *that* much of a hurry. He met her at the back of the truck where he pulled down the tailgate. He set his beer down and then reached out and pulled her against him.

"Mmmm," she moaned, tilting her head up so that he had full access to her lips. One of his arms spanned around her torso and the other hand reached up and found her hair. He looked down at her face. She had opened her eyes, trying to meet his gaze and when their eyes locked, he saw utter emptiness. Suddenly, he didn't want to kiss her. Not even to take some of her soul.

For fucks sake. He barely wanted to touch her at all.

Normally, when a chick was with him, he gave them his undivided attention. He actually liked kissing, and touching, and all that other shit girls liked. Intimacy didn't bother him, relationships did.

"Turn around," he growled.

"Oh, hell yeah." She turned so that her ass was

pressed against his cock and gave a little wiggle, which was doing to his erection exactly what she wanted it to do. As quick as he could he unbuckled his belt and unbuttoned his jeans, letting them drop to the ground.

He slid the condom on in record time, then he reached down and yanked the skirt she was wearing up over her ass. Normally he would have fingered her until she was dripping wet and begging for it, but not this time. This time, he grabbed ahold of her hips and slammed the length of himself inside of her.

"Holy fucking shit!" she cried out, arching her back. "Oh, my ..."

She couldn't finish because suddenly Jack was trying to fuck out every single problem in his life. It was all about him this time. He thrust, harder and harder, pushing her midsection against the tailgate of the truck.

Janette was making all kinds of noise and it only made Jack drill her even harder. He needed release, not sexually, but to purge himself of all the shit that was going on inside of him. He felt the sweet, hot core of the woman he was inside clench against him and knew that she was going to climax.

Without warning, as Janette began her orgasm, Lucy's face swam before him. "Oh fuck!" he cried out in surprise.

"Fuck yeah, oh my God, *yes*!" Janette pretty much screamed in response, probably thinking that he had cried out because of the sex. He felt her finally release and then she collapsed onto the tailgate beneath him.

He didn't get his, and that was all right. After seeing that Keepers face while fucking someone else, his equipment was deflating rapidly. Janette assumed he'd gotten off and that was all right. Now, he could just take her home.

What the hell was wrong with him?

Sex usually worked as a temporary patch for his problems. This time, it just seemed to be making the problems worse. He'd hoped for a little taste of her soul before this all began, but now the thought of that almost repulsed him.

"Oh, Jack." Janette pushed her skirt back down and turned to face him. "*That* was awesome."

Jack quickly took care of the condom and then pulled up his jeans. Not wanting her to see his flaccid junk. "Hell yeah it was."

She licked her lips and then reached for the beer that sat on the bed of the truck that had, by some act of God, not tipped over. She took a long swig and then pulled herself up and sat on the tailgate. "I like the sound of the water."

"Huh?" What did she say? He had been staring up at the stars, his mind wandering to Aiden and what he was doing.

"I said, I like the sound of the water. You know, the calming sound of a babbling brook and all that. They even have this sound on CD's that help you sleep."

"Oh. I like it too, very soothing." Was that the right answer?

Something was nagging him and he couldn't place it. Like he needed to be somewhere and he'd forgotten about it. While he sat listening to the babbling brook, and the babbling Janette, he remembered Aiden's words. 'Well, I can. I still have a job to do.'

"Oh fuck!"

Janette jumped a little at his sudden outburst. "What?"

"I … I think I forgot to do something." He lifted her off the tailgate. "I'm sorry, I'm going to have to take you home."

She sighed. "And why am I not surprised?"

He slammed the tailgate shut. "That's not what this is about. I have a serious issue I need to take care of."

She offered him a fake smile. "I'm sure you do." With that, she adjusted her top and disappeared around the side of the truck, on her way to the passenger door.

Jack rolled his eyes and slipped behind the wheel. Dropping off Janette was uneventful, thank God, because he wasn't sure he could handle another clingy chick right now. Once he had her safely deposited at her house he didn't go back to his place like he should have.

He drove slowly back across town and turned off on cemetery road. His dashboard clock read that it was two thirty-five a.m. and the sun rose at about five a.m., so there was still a couple of hours until the sun rose.

He parked his truck discreetly down the road from the cemetery, but in a spot where he could see most of the expanse of headstones and also Lucy's house. He turned off all the lights on the truck and killed the engine. Leaving him in complete darkness.

LUCY

12

"Lucy!" Ethan had yanked the door open to find her bleeding and traumatized on his front porch. "What the hell happened?" He quickly put his arm around her and guided her inside. "Oh my God, you're neck!" He ran out of the room and was back in an instant with a wet towel, a dry towel and a bunch of stuff like peroxide and creams. "Now, tell me what happened."

"I ... the Reapers," she breathed out slowly, knowing that she couldn't speak clearly because of her rapid breaths. After a couple of long inhales and exhales she tried again. "I was talking to Dad while I was out on patrol and I was attacked by Reapers."

Ethan shook his head. "I don't get it Luce, you fight Reapers all the time."

"No, Ethan. They tried to kill me. Like ... slit my throat kill me."

"Well, I can see that," he retorted in a 'duh' type tone. "I mean why are they trying to kill you?"

"Isn't it obvious, ouch!" She recoiled when he touched the wet towel to her neck wound. "Fuck, be careful."

"I have to clean it, Lucy. Just lay down on the couch. It will be easier to get to it that way. Now what were you saying?"

"I was saying that the reason why they want to kill me is because of that Chosen One bullshit. They think I'm going to be the one to bring down the Reapers, so they want me dead."

Ethan held the compress to Lucy's neck and leaned back a little, his blue eyes iced over. "This isn't good. If they are going to attempt a murder in a small town like this than they probably won't stop until they get the job done."

Lucy closed her eyes, trying to block out the fact that her neck hurt like a bitch. "I'm not used to this sort of thing. We've been raised to kill if we have to, but mostly we just have fights and run the Reapers off. Neither side wants to worry about disposing of bodies and all the shit that goes along with committing crimes like that."

"Well, the Reapers know that you could be the end of their race. They don't want that, so apparently having to do a little clean up this time isn't going to bother them." He dabbed the cut on her neck with some peroxide on a cotton ball, dried it and then put some triple antibiotic cream on it. "We can't really put a bandage on this right now, so you're going to have to stay away from town until this heals. There is no way to cover it up."

Her lids fluttered up and she looked into Ethan's eyes. She was still stuck on the attack, not her wound. "You want to know the weirdest part of all of this? One of them saved me. Right when the one had his knife at my throat, the other jumped in out of nowhere and grabbed him off of me. That was when I ran away. If it wasn't for that guy, I'd be dead on the graveyard trail right now."

Ethan's eyes narrowed. "Why would he save you if they were here to kill you? That *is* really strange."

"I know. I can't figure it out either. Liv and I had an altercation with him earlier today in the bakery. He seemed surprised to see us in there, and I actually didn't get any bad vibes from him then."

"I've never heard of a Reaper actually saving a Keeper from another Reaper though."

Lucy shrugged. "I don't know. That's what happened."

Ethan rubbed his forehead and she noticed that he was wearing only plaid cotton pajama pants. This was another of those moments when she wished that she could be more than friends with him. His upper body was totally ripped. Like, panty-dropping ripped. He had several tattoos covering his arms and back, which only added to his hotness, in her opinion.

"I'm going to get you something to drink." Ethan stood up and left the room, obviously still tired from being woken up in the middle of the night.

A few minutes later he came back holding a steaming mug in one hand. "Here, I made you some hot chocolate."

"Thank you." She accepted the mug and took an experimental sip. The warm liquid tasted like someone was trying to shove bitter bakers chocolate down her throat.

She grimaced. "I wish you had coffee."

Ethan was currently pacing the floor in front of where she sat on the couch. "You know I don't drink that crap."

"It's not crap and you should keep some here for me."

He stopped and stared at her for a second. "You never come over here, why would I keep any special drinks around for you?"

She shrugged. "I don't know. Sorry." As much as she loved Ethan, maybe their friendship *was* sort of one sided. She didn't come over to his house, he always came to hers. He was always around, so she had never thought of it that way. But now that she had a moment to really consider the situation, she realized that he was the instigator for everything that they did together. She never just stopped by for coffee or asked him if he wanted to go do something.

I am the worst best friend ever.

"Lucy. Hey, Lucy." She came back from her thoughts to find Ethan waving his hands in front of her face.

"What?"

"Are you all right? You spaced off there for a minute."

She took another long drink of the nasty hot chocolate. "I'm fine. Just thinking."

Ethan nodded and turned toward his bedroom. "I need to get dressed. I'm going to go back to the house with you."

"You don't have to do that. You have classes tomorrow."

"I can take a day off. I am so far ahead in most of my classes it won't hurt anything if I miss a day."

"Ethan …"

"No." He turned back to face her, his expression hardening into that don't fuck with me look he got when his mind was made up. "I'm going back to the house with you, so stop trying to argue with me."

"Fine." She nodded. She didn't know why she was trying to argue about it in the first place. Those fucking Reapers had tried to kill her, so of course she didn't want to be there by herself.

Once Ethan had thrown on a pair of jeans and a tee shirt with a black hoodie, he came out of his room and grabbed the keys to his jeep off the table. "Let's go. We can't leave the souls unattended for too long while we know there are Reapers running around out there."

Yeah, especially with her dad out there. She had to talk to him soon and let him know she was okay after the attack. He was probably pretty worried. "All right. But I have to drive my car home. I can follow you there."

They both went out to their cars with Lucy feeling ten times calmer than she had been when she'd first pulled up into the driveway. She drove home with Ethan following close behind. When she finally pulled into her driveway, she didn't see the black truck hidden far down the road in the darkness. What she did see was five cars parked in the dirt lot right in front of her front lawn.

"Son of a bitch," she whispered as she turned the key, shutting down the engine. Then she pushed her car door open and stalked over to Ethan just as he was parking the jeep. "I can't believe you called them."

He slammed the door shut. "Seriously, you're surprised? What else was I supposed to do? Someone tried to cut your throat, Lucy! They tried to *murder* you!"

"Ethan, I want to prove I can do this on my own. Dad left the graveyard to me. He's only been gone for like a minute and now you've already called in the cavalry because I'm incompetent. It looks like I can't do my job."

Ethan's icy blue eyes bore into her. "It's not every day that this happens. As a matter of fact this has never happened in the Summer Hollow cemetery as far as I know. Not since I've been patrolling with your family."

"I don't care," she huffed and turned away, heading toward the house.

"Lucy. I just want you to be safe and I don't care if you are pissed at me about that."

"I'm not pissed," she called back. "I'll deal. Let's go in and get this over with."

The last thing she wanted to do at the moment was go in and fight with her brothers and sisters. They were going to be gunning for blood when they found out about this, and she was going to be lucky if she could go to the bathroom alone until the Reaper situation was taken care of.

She may be a Keeper, able to hold her own … well, usually able to hold her own, but she was still the baby of an entire family of Keepers and an Estmond to boot. If you messed with one then you got the entire clan up your ass.

Just about every light in the house was on and she could already hear the commotion of voices and arguing coming from within. This was really going to suck. A bath and a carton of mint chocolate chip sounded more the way she wanted the rest of the night to go. She looked up at the sky. Well … the rest of the morning anyway. It was still dark but the horizon was just starting to show the dim light of the approaching dawn. Normally, Lucy would just be heading in to hit the sack after a long night of patrol.

With a sigh, she mounted the stairs of the front porch and headed into what she could already hear was chaos.

She pushed open the door and found all of her brothers and sisters were there except for Greg, of course. But knowing her family, they had already told Greg what had happened and he was probably speeding toward Summer Hollow, giving his piece of shit car a reason to finally conk out on him.

Everyone was talking, no … yelling, over each other. She couldn't even gage what exactly the argument was about. Bits and pieces filtered through all the voices and she caught 'can't be alone,' 'fucking Reapers,' and 'no more patrolling.'

"Hey!" she yelled, slamming the door behind her after making sure Ethan had crossed the threshold and wasn't in the way. "What the hell is going on here?"

Every single one of her siblings silenced and swiveled their heads in her direction. She couldn't help but notice the look of utter relief that took over the expression of each and every one of them. God, how she loved them.

"Come here," Hannah ordered, but was first to stride across the living room to meet her. First, she grabbed Lucy and wrapped her arms around her, hugging her as if she hadn't seen her in years.

Returning the affection, she hung onto her sister just as hard.

When Hannah finally released her she stepped back

and then reached out, lifting Lucy's chin with her fingertips. "Let me see this."

"It's fine, Ethan took care of me."

"Good, just make sure that you keep it clean."

"I know how to take care of cuts and scrapes, Hannah."

Damn, sometimes being the baby of a family of seven kids was the worst shit in the world. No one had any confidence in her, even when it came to the smallest things.

"I know you can," Hannah apologized, "I'm sorry."

Even though she knew Hannah was just trying to help, the feeling of failure she'd had since the attack just got worse. Ethan stood silently at her side, ever her quiet bodyguard. Knowing he was there beside her was oddly comforting, even though he was the one who called in the Estmond clan.

Let's just get this over with so I can get some freaking sleep.

She looked past Hannah and ran her eyes over each of her siblings. "So, what are we arguing about?"

Yeah, let's just put it all on the table right now.

Everyone suddenly erupted into the chaotic yelling and hand waving that they had been in the middle of when she first opened the door. Again, she couldn't make out a damn thing.

"Wait, wait, wait. One at a time."

Surprisingly, they all shut up. Daniel waited for the last person to silence and then stepped forward, closer to Lucy. "We don't want you to be alone. Someone needs to stay here with you." He had on that fucking trench coat that he liked so much, but at least his eyes weren't bloodshot for once.

Oh hell no. "I don't need anyone to stay here with me."

Dan seemed to know this was coming. Of course he knew it was coming, anyone who knew Lucy would know that she wasn't one to ask or admit that she needed any help for anything. She was as stubborn as the rest of the Estmonds.

Hannah shook her head. "You either agree that someone will stay here with you, or we are going to have to send you somewhere where the Reapers can't find you."

What the fuck! "You would send me away? You can't do that!" Dang, could she sound any more childish than that, all she needed to do now was stomp her foot.

Hannah's dark brown eyes didn't show even one ounce of humor. "We can, and we will if you don't agree to this. This is for your safety, and since you are apparently the Chosen One for that crazy ass prophecy, then they won't stop with one failed attack, Lucy."

"You can't send me away. How the fuck would you do that? I'm an adult and I can make my own decisions."

James sat in the arm chair opposite of the couch with his feet on the coffee table. She couldn't help but think that if her dad were in the room that he would never attempt putting his nasty shoes up on their ancient coffee table. "You have to make a decision Luce, we won't let them get to you."

"You can't go patrolling anymore either," Steph added.

Lucy did stomp her foot this time. "You all are batshit crazy. I'm a Keeper! This is my graveyard. Mine! I will not abandon it because one Reaper tried to kill me."

"There were two, Lucy."

She swung her head around and gave Ethan the most furious glare that she could muster. "Shut up, Ethan."

"Wait, what?" Daniel raised his eyebrows. "Why would you tell us there was only one Reaper if there are two running around town trying to get to you?"

Fuck, fuck, fuck.

She knew that the last thing she should care about was outing a Reaper to her siblings. But, for some reason she felt the need to protect this one. He had saved her from having her throat slit open like an Easter ham. She kind of owed him.

But ... he was a Reaper, she didn't owe him anything. Not really.

"I ... he ... one of the Reapers had me on the ground with the knife at my throat when the other came out of nowhere and grabbed him off of me and gave me enough time to run. If he hadn't done that, I would be dead right now."

She said the last part with remorse, that fucking feeling of failure taking every opportunity to rear its ugly head.

"He *saved* you?" Daniel repeated incredulously.

Lucy nodded. Knowing how crazy it sounded.

Liv caught Lucy's eye. "Which one was the one we kicked out of the shop?"

"The one who helped me."

Liv nodded, giving Lucy a knowing look. "He didn't seem lethal when we saw him down at the shop today."

"Whoa, wait a minute," Steph finally spoke up. "You mean to tell us that you ran into one of those fucktards in your shop and didn't think it was something you should tell us?"

Liv shrugged. "It didn't seem important. We ran him off. They usually don't come back after they have a run in with any Keepers."

Lucy looked over at her brother and saw that James was fuming. "All right. There is no fucking way that we are going to let you stay here alone while there are two Reapers running around." He threw Steph one of their twin looks that clearly said 'agree with me now.' And, of course, she did.

"Yeah, Luce, I agree. We can't risk another attack like that."

Lucy sighed. "You guys. I am a Keeper ... not to mention the Chosen One, I can't just run off and hide. I have to do my job."

"Bullshit," Daniel grunted.

She turned to him. "Excuse me."

He pulled his flask out of the pocket of his coat and uncapped it. "I don't give a flying fuck about this Chosen One shit. What I *do* care about, is my sister and the fact that she has a cut on her neck caused by the knife of a Reaper."

"Dan …" Hannah tried to calm him down.

"No, fuck that. I am going to make sure that mother fucker doesn't ever have the chance to hurt any of my family again."

Hannah's eyes turned as cold as the warm brown color would allow. "We do this as a family, you hear me?"

Daniel took a long swig off his flask. "You don't get to make the decisions. Dad's not here anymore, but no one put you in charge of making the family decisions."

"Dan, you're hardly capable of making *any* decisions because you're always drunk off your ass."

"Leave him alone," Liv shot at Hannah. "We are all upset about this."

"Stay out of it, Liv!"

Lucy watched the conflict escalate, swinging her head back and forth between her brothers and sisters, and then finally turned around and headed toward the door. "I'm going to see Dad. He can make the final decisions just like he always did."

Dan tucked his flask back into his pocket. "Sounds like a grand plan. You know he's going to agree with us about you not being alone."

And she did know that, because it was one of the last things he said to her before the Reapers attacked her. But, at least if Dad laid down the law, they wouldn't have to worry about all the fighting. They may be a crazy stubborn bunch of kids, but when their dad told them what to do, they sure as hell did it.

"Fine!" She flung the door open and stomped out onto the porch. Ethan was right beside her in an instant, his large silver knife at his side. The rest of the

Estmonds followed close behind them, each prepared for conflict if the situation arose.

What's it gonna take for a girl to get some sleep. Lucy thought. She was covered in dirt and blood and just wanted to go to bed. The last thing she wanted to do was to be trekking across the cemetery to find their ghost dad to settle an argument between her siblings.

Once they had cleared the lawn and the fence, they took to the trails. "Dad," she called out. "Dad, we're all here and we need you."

It took about five minutes before Gregory Sr. appeared.

"Lucy Mae, thank goodness you're all right." Their father's voice came out of the darkness and the shimmering blue mist of his soul solidified into his human form before their eyes. "I didn't know what happened to you after you ran off."

"You shouldn't have seen that, Dad. I told you to hide."

"I wouldn't have left you there alone and you know it." He narrowed his eyes and set his ghostly lips in a firm line.

"I don't care, you shouldn't have given them the chance to get to you."

"They weren't after me, Lucy Mae, they were here for you this time."

Lucy was preparing a witty, Lucy style retort, when Liv stepped forward. The argument of what to do about the Reapers and Lucy appeared to be pushed to the back burner for now, because her eyes were glistening with tears. "Dad …" She choked back a sob. "Daddy, I miss you so much."

Their father's face softened once again. "Oh, honey, you shouldn't worry so much."

"And you shouldn't be here at all." The words came out hoarse and soft. Lucy knew she was trying hard not to break down.

"I have made my decisions about the fate of my own soul. That is a choice only I get to make. As much as I love you all, you don't get to choose for me."

"But Dad …"

He moved his gaze from Liv to the rest of his adult children, setting his eyes on them one by one. "I have never wished so much that a ghost could make contact with humans before. I want to hug you all so badly right now."

There was a chorus of 'me too's,' mingled with a few choked up 'yeah's,' and, of course, the tears that almost every one of them had brimming in the corners of their eyes.

"Now," he clasped his shimmering hands together, "I know for a fact if you are all out here right now, there is some family dispute that you need me to settle. So, what is it?"

Oh, he knew his children so well. How is it possible that a bastard illness like cancer could take their father from them? He just seemed like the kind of man that would kick cancer's ass and come back stronger than ever.

But, that was not the case. Now, here he was, another soul in the graveyard that they had to protect from the Reapers.

This argument seemed so petty compared to losing him, Lucy thought as Dan moved to the front of the pack. "Dad. Lucy doesn't want anyone to stay with her. She is insisting she can do this on her own."

Her father's eyes darted toward her. "Lucy. We talked about this. No more patrol on your own."

Frustrated, she threw her hands in the air. "Dad, they aren't just talking about patrol. They want someone to come and stay with me twenty-four seven. I don't need a bodyguard."

"It's for your safety, Lucy! Why do you have to be so stubborn?" James shot back at her. "It's not about making you look incompetent or whatever you think it's about. We just don't want you dead!"

"Ugh!" Lucy kicked at the gravel on the pathway.

"Real mature, Luce." Steph crossed her arms,

officially on the side of those who would lock her away if they could.

Their father held up his semitransparent hand for silence and waited until they had all calmed down enough that he could get a few words in. "Look, Lucy Mae, I agree that you shouldn't be alone. They are going to come back for you."

"I'll stay with her," Ethan volunteered before Lucy could get another defiant word in. None of her brothers or sisters appeared very surprised that Ethan was the first to volunteer.

"I will too," James offered.

Daniel spread his hands. "I should be the one to stay with her. Greg's not around so that makes me the oldest. Plus, I have a fucking score to settle."

Hannah set her hands on her hips. "You're also a Goddamn drunk. We can't trust you to take care of her."

Mother of God. This was getting worse and worse.

"For the last time, I don't need anyone to take care of me!"

"Enough," their father ordered. "James and Ethan will stay with you, and you won't go anywhere without at least one other Keeper. Understood?" It was the tone that told her there would be no more argument about it.

"Fine."

"And about this other Reaper, the one who allowed you to run off. Remember, he is still a Reaper and he was obviously with the one who held the knife to your neck. One valiant move from him does not make him any less dangerous."

"Yes Dad."

"Got it?"

"I got it!" she cried out in exasperation. "Can I go shower and get cleaned up now?"

"Go," he told her and she turned to leave him with the rest of her siblings. "But, Lucy, remember that I love you honey. We just want you to be safe."

"I know." She offered him a smile and then blew him a kiss. "I'll deal with it." With that, she left him with the family so that they could talk about all the things they wanted to say to him. Well, all except James and Ethan who hurried to flank her as she made her way back to the house.

Once she made it to the front porch, she turned to get a glimpse of the sunrise. James and Ethan went inside, but she knew they were hovering by the window, watching her. The glowing ball of fire had already risen into the sky. The few clouds around the small mountain ranges were various shades of pink and orange.

So pretty, she thought as she stared out at the perfection of nature. But then, something else caught her eye. On the street, beyond the cemetery, a black truck was pulled off to the side of the road. May have been her eyes playing tricks on her, but she could have sworn she saw a tiny bit of red flash inside of the cab.

"Dammit." She turned to go in so that she could let James and Ethan know, but as soon as her fingers touched the door knob, she heard the truck start up and pull out into the road. She watched closely as he drove by and saw that it was the dark haired one from the bakery, the one who saved her.

She couldn't help but notice that he was looking directly at her as he drove by. Their eyes met and he gave her a slight nod.

God he was sexy.

Then, he hit the gas and sped off. She watched until the truck was completely out of sight and then went inside with even more to contemplate than she had before.

AIDEN
13

Aiden leaned back in the steaming hot bath water of the jetted tub. He'd left Jack in his driveway and headed back toward Santa Rosa where he could get a better hotel room and keep a lower profile at the same time.

Fucking Jack. He'd known that his friend wouldn't have been able to do the deed, but he never once thought that he was going to interfere and stop him from killing that young Keeper.

Now he was going to have to report to the Empress about why the job wasn't finished already.

Dammit. This had been his chance to move up in the rankings of the Reaper army and prove himself to Jack's mom. He knew that Jack had a softer heart than most, covering it up with his slutty asshole ways, but Jack's allegiance to him had never wavered.

"Son of a bitch," he muttered to himself, then submerged his wounded leg into the scalding water. He hissed in pain as the water seeped into the hole where the silver arrow had been. That fucking Keeper had surprised him with that little stunt.

Because of the silver, it was going to take him at least overnight to get his strength back. Any time silver went into the body of a Reaper it slowed everything down. It wasn't just a leg injury. It affected his whole body, like getting high on downers. His system was compromised, making his reactions slow and his thinking might get fucked up. There was no way he could fight right now.

Having a weakness was a total bitch. It was common knowledge among the Keepers that silver was what you used on the Reapers, so he was constantly getting cut or stabbed, it was annoying as shit. The worst part about it was the headache. Yup, going along with the whole getting high metaphor meant you get the hangover too.

He lay there until the water grew cold and his skin looked like prunes, thinking about what the hell to do about Jack. Seems Jack had already made his decision though, he wanted out of the life of a Reaper, away from the critical eye of his mother.

Aiden couldn't help but feel betrayed. Even though Jack wanted out and could just up and leave, it wasn't that easy for him. All he knew was the life he was already living. Not to mention that if Aiden went off the radar it would be would be far worse than if Jack did. Camille Walker would have no problem punishing him, whereas Jack was her son and would probably just get bitched at for an hour and put on house arrest.

He wanted to be there for his friend, but his friend needed to be there for him. The door swings both ways mother fucker.

After the water was so cold he couldn't tolerate it anymore, he carefully stepped out of the tub and wrapped himself in one of the fluffy white hotel towels.

God he needed a drink. Without putting on any clothes he made his way into the sitting room of his suite and headed for the little bar in the corner. He found a bottle of bourbon and poured himself a short glass. Yeah, that should help him sleep off that fucking silver in his system.

He needed some time to get right in the head before he spoke with the Empress. This was one fucked up situation. One Keeper. Dammit Jack, one fucking Keeper and they would have been home free.

He groaned and took a swig of his bourbon and sat down on the sofa. Just as he was searching for the remote control, his cell phone chirped. He glanced over at the bedside table where he'd left the damn thing earlier. That was the ringtone that he had set specifically for the Empress.

He sure as hell didn't want to talk to her right now, but if he didn't he knew that she would just keep calling until he answered. At this point he didn't think the situation was going to get any better so he may as well answer the call.

"Your Highness," he turned on his voice of servitude.

"Aiden," the Empress's voice clipped through the receiver. "How goes your assignment?"

"Not well, I admit."

"What do you mean, not well? I would have thought that with your record you would have had this mission done and been on your way home by now."

"Under normal circumstances that would be the case. However, I've run into a snag."

To out Jack or to help Jack. What to do, what to do.

There was a silence that was obviously meant to intimidate him and then she spoke. "Explain."

"I had the Keeper, but someone intervened and she got away." The words were like acid rolling off his tongue.

"Intervened?"

"Unfortunately, yes."

Again, there was another thick silence. "What aren't you telling me, Aiden?"

Seriously.

"I have told you everything."

"Who saved the girl?"

"It was another Keeper, they grabbed me from behind. This place is crawling with Keepers. There are eight of them that I know of."

"Hmmm."

Aw fuck, she knew he was lying. "I'm sorry Empress, I am going to need a bit more time to proceed. Hopefully give them enough time to think I'm not coming back. Right now they are probably on full alert."

"What about my son. Where is he?"

"He is in the shower at the moment."

Lies, lies, and more fucking lies.

"All right, Aiden. I understand the need for more time. I will stop harassing you. However, I admit, I am actually pleased that you were not able to accomplish the task. I have changed my mind about killing the girl. I want you to get her and hold her."

What the fuck?

"With all due respect, highness, why do we want to abduct her?"

"Do not question my reason. Bring her to the Napa estate and I will meet you there. I am preparing for the trip as we speak."

"If we kidnap her, the entire family is going to come after us."

She sighed. "Are you questioning my orders?"

Aiden kept silent.

"I didn't think so. Now, I will give you more time, but get the girl and don't screw it up this time."

I didn't screw it up, it was your son, dammit.

"Yes Empress."

"Good. Call me when you have her." With that, she hung up on him.

He rolled his eyes and clicked off his phone. "Yes Empress. Goodbye Empress. Fuck off Empress."

He lifted his glass to take a sip of his bourbon and discovered that the glass was empty, so he made a beeline for the bar and refilled the glass. Only this time he filled it up to the top.

Dammit, this job was getting shittier and shittier. The last thing he wanted to do was hang out with a

Keeper. In fact, he'd almost rather kill her than have to abduct her and keep her around until he could deliver her to the Empress.

He lay back down on the bed and looked at his phone. Normally, he'd be calling Jack and telling him what was going on. Damn him.

Oh well, time to get his strength back so that he could do this job and get the fuck home.

JACK 14

J ack closed his eyes and let the steaming hot water of the shower beat down onto him. He couldn't get the image of Lucy's wide, fearful eyes out of his head. He never wanted to see a look like that on her face ever again.

She had seen him drive by as he was leaving the cemetery. They had made eye contact, so he was certain that she'd seen him.

For hours he had hidden in his truck, watching her house and waiting for Aiden to come back for her. The whole time he wondered what the fuck he was doing there in the first place. There was absolutely no reason that he should be protecting her. Saving her from Aiden had been wrong. No, it had been the right thing … but also the wrong thing.

Mother fucker.

Nothing like this had ever happened to him before. And why did it have to happen with a Keeper, out of all the chicks in the world. If he was going to get an overwhelming urge to protect someone, he would have preferred it *not* be an Estmond Keeper.

He had seen that love at first sight shit in the movies and never believed in it. Shit, he barely believed in love to begin with. This … this sure as hell wasn't love at first sight. Yeah, she was fucking awesome to look at, but this was more like an instinct to protect. Like a mother over her babies. Now that was a disturbing analogy if there ever was one.

He had no reasonable explanation for his actions, but one thing was for certain. Nothing ... fucking nothing, was going to hurt Lucy if he had anything to do with it.

And that was that.

But why?

Aiden hadn't come back. He was probably recuperating from the silver in his system. That would keep him off for a day or so, but it wouldn't be long before Aiden was back on the job.

He had seen the entire family of Estmond Keepers speeding down the farmhouse driveway and he'd known that all of them were now aware of the attack on Lucy. He had to be more careful now than ever. If he was smart, he would pack his shit and head out of town now. But, no ... he couldn't go yet. Not until he was sure Lucy was going to be safe.

Except, that probably wasn't going to happen anytime soon. She was the Chosen One, which meant she was always going to be in danger from his kind. The only way she was ever going to be safe was if he offed his parents and maybe even Aiden ... and that sure as hell wasn't going to happen.

He wanted to punch something, or fuck something. Only he was pretty sure that wasn't going to work because the last time he tried that he'd seen Lucy's face when she wasn't the one he was fucking.

He felt his cock responding to even the mere association of Lucy and sex together.

Well ... that was *just* great.

He shut the shower off, dried with a towel and threw on a pair of pajama pants, then headed for his bed. He needed to try and catch a few hours of sleep since he'd been up all night. The summer warmth was enough that he didn't need to get underneath the covers, so he flopped down on top of the fluffy comforter and threw his arm over his eyes, hoping it wouldn't take long to pass out.

Only about five minutes had gone by before he heard the dreaded sound of his mother's ringtone. "No fucking way." Without opening his eyes he flipped his middle finger in the direction of his phone. He let it ring until the voicemail picked it up and then let out a rather large sigh for someone who was supposed to be so rugged and manly.

Fifteen minutes later, just as he was in that place where you are just a little bit asleep, but still aware of what is going on around you, some asshole started pounding on his door.

He jolted up into a sitting position, wondering for a moment if he had dreamt it.

Bang, Bang, Bang!

The person behind the door went for another round of pounding on it.

Son of a bitch. He moved off the bed and reached into his duffel to grab his gun. Whoever was at the door was pretty intent on getting him to answer. They knew he was here, obviously, because his truck was outside. So, really, his choices were either to answer the damn door, or run out the back door like a bitch.

He wasn't a bitch.

With soft footing he crept toward the door, hoping that he could take the person out there by surprise. First, he took a peek out the window. He knew damn well that he couldn't see the doorstep from the window, but he could see if there were any vehicles out there.

Yup. A dark green minivan was parked right behind his truck. Who the fuck drove a minivan anymore, besides soccer moms.

His fingers wrapped gently around the door knob, trying not to jiggle it too much as he turned it. Then, when it was completely turned he flung the door wide and aimed his Glock at whoever was on the porch.

"Is that how you greet all your guests?"

What in the fresh hell? It was the older sister Keeper from the bakery.

"What do you want?" he demanded.

She shook her head, acting like she didn't even care that there was a gun pointed at her head. "You know exactly what I want. I know you were out at our place. I know you tore that Reaper off of Lucy and I want to know why."

"What, you want to know why I didn't want to witness a murder? I think that kinda explains itself."

"No. It doesn't."

Jack didn't say anything. What was he supposed to say? He sure as hell wasn't going to spill his guts to this Keeper at his doorstep, but on the other hand ... he had a Keeper on his doorstep and probably more outside in the fucking bushes or something. "How did you find out where I was?"

She actually laughed at him. "I have lived in this town my entire life and I know pretty much everyone else who lives here. I work in a shop that most of the townspeople frequent, and if *that* isn't enough, I can see your truck from the road. Now tell me what I want to know." She paused. "And put that damn gun away." She swatted the air as if the Glock were a pesky mosquito.

"I don't trust you. I'd rather keep it out."

She lifted an eyebrow. "Uh, do you actually think that I trust *you*? No, I don't. Not even a little bit, but you don't see me pointing a gun at you ... and you are the one who was with the guy who tried to murder my sister."

Jack was having a hard time believing that she was just here to talk, for the very reason that she just specified. "I don't understand what exactly it is that you want to know."

She tilted her head. "I don't understand why you still have your gun pointed at me."

God, if anything, he appreciated the quick wit and

sheer stubbornness of the women in their family. He lowered the gun but didn't put it away. "Tell me how she is."

Liv shook her head. "Nope. You don't get that kind of information."

"Oh, but you want answers from me."

She nodded. "Yes. So, to start with, you obviously know who we are and who my sister is, which is why one of your buddies tried to off her. Why didn't you just let him?"

"I don't approve of murder."

"Apparently. You Reapers have been a pain in our asses for generations, but in today's day and age the amount of murders is minimal."

Jack shook his head. "Not true, the big cities have a shit ton of murders caused by both sides."

"That's not the point, though," Liv continued. "If my sister is of the prophecy, the Chosen One, why didn't you let your friend kill her."

"I told you."

"Liar."

"I'm not lying," Jack insisted.

"Look man, I saw you and Lucy wrestling in the shop. I saw what happened … or didn't happen when you guys touched. Then, you save her from being murdered by one of your own kind. And she, for some reason, doesn't think you're a threat."

Jack wished for a beer so hard he wouldn't have been surprised if one popped out of the clouds and fell into his hand. "I'm offended. I'm one badass mother fucker."

She rolled her eyes. "Anyone who calls themselves a badass mother fucker really isn't one."

His free hand went to his heart. "You wound me, Keeper."

"And frankly, I don't feel like you're a threat either."

Shit, time to get serious again. "Look, I'm not the one you need to worry about. But, Lucy is still in danger. The guy coming after her is someone I know very well. He doesn't like to commit murder either, but he will if he has to. He is very dedicated to his job and will do whatever the Empress requests of him."

"And that request is the death of my sister?"

Jack nodded, feeling kind of sick to his stomach at the thought of Lucy dying. "Yes, it is."

Liv cracked her neck to the side. She had her dark red hair pulled up into a huge bun on top of her head, secured with a light blue ribbon, and she wore jeans that had the white residue of flour or something streaked across the material. "So, if you aren't here to kill her, what are you doing in Summer Hollow?" she pressed.

"I like it here, it's quaint. I'm thinking about settling down."

"Again, you're a liar."

He was done messing around. "Look, I told you that I wasn't the one you have to worry about. I don't have all the answers."

Her eyes narrowed with suspicion. "But, you do have some of them. Namely, about this friend of yours who is going to come back for Lucy."

He paused for a moment, contemplating how he should respond and then decided to go with honesty. "I'll be helping watch for him. I'm going to do my best to make sure he doesn't get to her."

"What's it going to take to get him to stay away?"

"You'll probably have to kill him. He's under orders from the Empress and will continue the attacks until he succeeds."

"Shit," she muttered under her breath.

"Make sure she is never alone," he told her.

Liv looked up at him, her face plastered with concern. "That is a lot harder than it sounds. Lucy isn't someone who deals well with being told what to do or being assigned bodyguards."

He nodded. "Yeah, I kinda figured."

Really, how did he know that? He shouldn't have a fucking clue about Lucy and her reactions. "Well, do your best and I will do what I can from my end, just don't let any of the other Keepers off me if they see me around."

"I can't make any promises," she told him. "I'm not telling them I came here, and I'm sure as hell not going to tell them that you aren't the enemy ... because you still are."

"Same goes for you. I don't even know why I'm sticking around to help as it is."

Her eyebrows lifted. "You seriously *don't* know do you?"

"Not a fucking clue."

"Can you explain it to me?"

He leaned against the door jamb. "I don't know. It's just ..." He trailed off, why the hell should he tell her anything. Oh yeah, cause telling a chick about your crazy is better than telling your friend who you're supposed to only be manly around. That's right.

She waited and when he didn't continue she looked him in the eye and said softly. "It's all right. You can tell me."

"I can't explain the feelings. It's not like romantic comedy bullshit or anything, but ever since we met in your bakery and my skin came into contact with Lucy's, my intentions have completely changed."

"What do you mean?" Liv looked like she might beat the shit out of him if he didn't tell her.

"I mean that ... when I came here I was supposed to find Lucy and kill her. Then we met, and when our skin touches there is no burning, no shocks, nothing that is painful. Ever since that moment, I have felt this *insane* urge to protect her, to keep her safe. When my friend had his knife to her throat I moved on instinct, like I had no choice.

"I would have killed him if he hadn't been someone I knew."

He had been staring off into the trees while he spoke and came back to reality as he finished the last sentence. "I don't know what the fuck it is. I wish I didn't have it at all, but I do and I am going to do what I can to make sure nothing happens to her. At least until this particular threat is taken care of."

"That could be a long time. Won't the Reapers just keep coming until she's gone?" Liv's voice was soft and barely audible.

He nodded. "Yes, yes they will ... as long as the Empress has ordered it."

"I don't understand this."

"She is the Chosen One, simple as that. Our Empress isn't going to take a chance that the Chosen One will fulfill the prophecy."

Turning slightly, with her hands on her hips she looked away from him. "That's not what I meant."

Ah, she meant him. "You mean how fucked up I am?"

"You're not fucked up."

"That means a lot coming from you, Keeper."

"You don't have to be rude."

"Why not, that's my specialty, and for the record I wasn't being rude or sarcastic, I actually mean that."

She rolled her eyes. "What I was talking about is the fact that I'm even here in the first place and that I don't want to kick your ass."

Jack smiled. "Yeah, it's pretty fuckin' weird."

Liv stepped back a couple of paces and then looked up at Jack. "All right, I don't believe a lot of what you say, but the one thing that I do believe is that you won't hurt Lucy. I still think you need to stay away because my family isn't going to be as thoughtful as I am about things, they will act first and think later."

"Don't worry, I have no plans for camp fires and Kumbaya quite yet."

"I have to go. But I will tell Lucy, and only Lucy, that I came here. The others don't need to know."

Why was she doing this? His whole life he had been taught that Keepers were the enemy. That concept had been burned into his brain. Liv was the first Keeper he had ever really spoken to and she seemed like an all right person, for being the enemy and all.

"I'd appreciate that." Yeah, the last thing he needed was the entire Estmond family up his ass. "And, I'm Jack, by the way."

She eyed him cautiously and then held out her hand. "Olivia, but everyone calls me Liv."

He reached out and clasped her hand tightly. The flash of heat was equivalent to sticking his hand into a fire. They shook, sealing their new partnership with pain, just as some would cut their palm and swear a blood oath.

He released her hand after a moment. The burn had grown worse and worse by the second, but he'd kept their hands connected, hopefully to send some message that he wasn't the enemy that she had been taught that he was.

Well, maybe he had been … maybe he could have been, but he wasn't now.

That's what counted right?

He rubbed his hand on his pajama pants after his hand had been freed. "That burning is a bitch."

She nodded. "Normally, it's a weapon."

"Yeah," he laughed, "but now it's just a bitch."

She joined him by letting out a small chuckle. "Yes, yes it is. Well, I have to make a couple of deliveries and get back to work. I'm sure we will meet again if you are sticking around."

Oh, yeah … that's why she drove a mini-van, for the bakery. "I don't plan on going anywhere any time soon."

"Goodbye then, Jack." She turned away, a sign of trust that she took her eyes off of him. She opened the door to her van, gave him a wave and then slid behind the wheel. He waved back at her and then waited until she had pulled completely out of the driveway before turning around to head back into the house.

"Holy shit," he breathed out the words.

Now that was something he would have never expected to happen.

LUCY
15

This was total crap.

Lucy sat on the couch in her living room pretending to watch television, but she couldn't concentrate on anything enough to actually watch it.

The door to the kitchen swung open and she looked up to find Greg Jr. juggling a beer, a bag of chips and a paper plate with a gigantic sandwich on it.

"Do you even eat at your place?" Lucy asked as he set all his goods on the coffee table.

"Of course I do. I'm just hungry."

She stretched out on the couch while Greg settled into a recliner. "You don't have to be here, you know."

He opened his mouth and took a bite of his sandwich. "I know," he said after he finished chewing. "But, to think I wouldn't be here is just stupid, you're my sister."

"What did you do about your patrols … and work?"

Another bite, more chewing, wash it down with beer. "I called in some of the other Keepers to take over for a few days and I called in sick to work. I'll call again in the morning." Another bite of the sandwich, followed by a swig of beer. "Did you let your instructors know you will be out for a few days?"

She nodded. "Yeah. I emailed."

That cut on her neck was not something she could hide so she had to miss her classes, which meant she was stuck in the house with her brothers and Ethan watching over her like some helpless damsel in distress.

Sitting around doing nothing all day just wasn't her thing, but everyone insisted that she not be alone. At this point she was lucky that she got to shower and go to the bathroom by herself.

"Good." Greg nodded and continued to demolish his sandwich. "Where did James and Ethan go?"

She waved dismissively, "They're out back putting extra locks on the doors and ground floor windows. How long are you going to stay?"

His eyes narrowed. "For as long as it takes to make sure you're out of danger."

"Great."

Yeah, freaking awesome.

She did like having her family around, but she didn't like feeling like she was incompetent or needed babysitting.

The sound of a car in the driveway had them both out of their seats, heading to the window to see who it was. Greg lifted the curtain away from the window and they saw the green minivan crunching slowly over the gravel and then come to a stop beside Greg's Escort. Awesome, now Liv was here to check on her too.

She watched Liv get out of the driver seat and open the sliding door on the side of the van. She reached in and withdrew a large flat box and balanced it in her hand while slamming the van door shut with the other.

"I hope that box is full of chocolate doughnuts," she told Greg as they both pulled away from the window.

"Me too." Greg let the curtain fall back down. "I'm starving."

"How can you possibly still be hungry?"

He shrugged. "I'm a guy. I like to eat."

"Weirdo." She hit him on the shoulder and flopped back down onto the couch where she continued to flip through the channels. "I don't know why I even have TV," she told Greg. "I never watch it, and when I do there is never anything on."

"So get rid of it."

She shrugged. "I might. It would save money."

"Can't go wrong there," he told her as he opened the door for Liv so she wouldn't have to struggle with the box again. "Hey Liv."

Lucy watched Liv look up at her big brother and smile. "Hey brother. I brought doughnuts." She lifted the box up a little bit.

"Yes!" Lucy fist pumped, jumping back up off the couch and setting Liv free from the burden of the heavy doughnut box. "You have chocolate in here right?"

Liv rolled her eyes. "Duh."

Lucy headed for the kitchen and the two followed her. "God, I need something sweet so bad." Lucy opened the box and skimmed over what her sister had brought them. It was a variety of different kinds. There were four chocolate glazed that she got to choose from. Lifting one out of the box she pointed at a plain glazed. "What kind of filling is in this one?"

Liv leaned over to see which one she was talking about. "Oh, that one is lemon."

A flash of memory hit her hard 'Do you have any with lemon filling?' The sexy, dark haired Reaper. The one who had saved her ... the one she couldn't get out of her head for some ridiculous reason.

"Oh." She quickly turned away from the box with her chocolate doughnut and ripped a paper towel off the dispenser that was mounted on the wall by the refrigerator. What the hell, it was just a fucking lemon doughnut. What was wrong with her?

Along with the lemon doughnut, she remembered his weight on top of her, how he held her down and looked into her eyes.

Fuck. This was sooo not a good thing.

Liv picked one out for herself. "Are you all right, Luce?"

Get it together, Lucy.

"Yeah, I'm fine. I think I'm going to head up to my room for a while though. I could use a nap."

Liv nodded, understanding that she probably needed rest. Greg, on the other hand knew damn well that she had slept until like ten in the morning, but kept his mouth shut anyway.

She polished off the last of her doughnut quickly, washed it down with a glass of water and then headed up the stairs, leaving Greg and Liv to talk about whatever they were going to talk about.

James and Ethan should be finishing up with the windows soon, then the whole house was going to be packed with people. Since Greg was down from the Bay Area, Liv was most likely going to call for a big family dinner and the others would inevitably show up.

She opened the door to her room and headed for the bed. Going up to her room was just an excuse to get away from everyone, but maybe it was a good idea to actually try and get some sleep.

After about twenty minutes of shifting uncomfortably, Lucy knew that it wasn't going to happen. That freaking Reaper would not get out of her head. She knew that she should be more concerned about the one that tried to kill her, but no … she was thinking about his skin on hers, the lack of any burning sensation, and the fierce look in his eyes when he pulled his friend away from her.

If he wasn't a Reaper she would be hitting that so fast, even if it meant breaking her rule of no dating anyone who wasn't Keeper. God, he was hot, but there was something else that made her adrenaline pump at just the mere thought of him.

Tap, Tap, Tap.

Lucy looked up at the soft knocking on her bedroom

door. "Come in," she called out.

Liv opened the door and peeked in. "Are you actually sleeping?"

She didn't move. "Nah, I'm laying here contemplating the meaning of life."

Liv stepped inside and closed the door behind her. Lucy saw the intent expression on her sister's face and knew there was something up, so she shifted into a sitting position and waited for Liv to come sit down next to her.

"Okay, what's going on?" she asked as her sister made herself comfortable.

"Something crazy happened."

Lucy raised her eye brows. "You think? I was attacked and almost murdered."

"That's not what I meant." Liv shook her head. "I mean, something else."

"Well spill it. Don't be all dramatic."

"I found that Reaper who saved you."

Lucy felt her eyes go wide and a flush passed over her body. "You *what*?"

"I found him and I questioned him."

Lucy didn't think she was ever going to see him again. She was fairly sure the one who tried to kill her was going to come back, but she'd thought the one who helped her get away would be long gone by now.

"You mean, you went and found him on purpose? By yourself?"

Liv nodded. "Yeah, I went to the house he is staying at."

"Oh my God, Liv, he could have killed you."

Her sister Olivia was one of the more sensible children of the Estmond clan, the fact that she had actively gone seeking a Reaper by herself after the attempted murder made Lucy fume. "How could you put yourself in that kind of danger?"

Liv didn't look away from Lucy's accusing eyes. "I took a chance."

"Are you fucking kidding me, Liv! They are all

concerned about protecting me and you're the one who went running off and putting yourself in a situation like that. Son of a bitch!" Lucy jumped up and started to pace her bedroom floor.

"It's all right. He isn't going to hurt me, and he sure as hell isn't going to hurt you."

"What does that mean?" Lucy snapped. "I'm so fucking pissed at you right now."

"Well, be pissed. I don't care." Liv stayed where she was on the bed. "This Reaper, something crazy is going on. He is like ... hell bent on making sure that you are safe."

"Huh?"

Yeah, that was pretty much the last thing that she had expected to hear about her sisters visit with the Reaper.

"His name is Jack and I don't think he is going to hurt you."

She couldn't help it, a giggle burst from between her lips. "Seriously! Jack the Reaper?"

Liv closed her eyes while Lucy continued to laugh. "My God, that's like a notch off from Jack the Ripper. Holy shit, what kind of Reaper parents would saddle their child with that kind of name. Oh my effing goodness!"

"Are you done?" Liv asked her calmly, with no note of laughter in her own voice.

"Almost." Lucy bent over and held her stomach and took long breaths in and out. "Oh my goodness that was funny."

"So anyway," Liv continued, "I need to know if you've been having any weird feelings about this guy."

Any laughter Lucy had left in her was quickly extinguished. "Why do you want to know that?"

"I think maybe you know why. So, have you?"

Any sarcasm that Lucy usually responded with faltered. "Maybe," she said with slow uncertainty.

"Tell me."

Lucy thought for a moment. She didn't know if she could explain the strange attraction she felt for the Reaper. "It's ... it's like I know that he's good. I think about him a lot, like way more than I should, that's for sure."

"Anything else."

"Not really."

Liv narrowed her eyes like she didn't believe her. "So that's it?"

She sure as hell wasn't going to tell her that she thought the Reaper was the hottest thing since ... well, since ever. "Yeah, why?"

"Did this start after you met him in the shop, or after he saved you?"

Why was she asking all these questions? What did this have to do with anything? "Both. After the shop, but way more after the attack. What is this all about, Liv?"

Liv lowered her voice. "I am going to tell you this, but you can't tell anyone else that I went over there or anything that I found out."

"All right," Lucy agreed. "Now tell me."

"Okay. Jack says that he doesn't understand this either. After you two fought in the shop, you both realized that when your skin comes into contact neither of you get the burning sensation. That is one strange thing, but he also told me that ever since then, he has felt this insane need to protect you. That is why he tore his friend off of you, his instincts kicked in."

"That is crazy." Lucy didn't know what she thought about that. "So, it's like ... like we are connected or something."

Liv tilted her head as she thought over her words before speaking. "Maybe. I don't know what it is, but Lucy, he was so adamant about not hurting you ... or any of us. And, he did tell me the guy who tried to kill you will be back."

Lucy stopped her pacing around and went to the window seat. The window had a beautiful view that looked out over the graveyard. Ever since she was a little girl, she would sit in the window seat at night and watch the shimmering blue mist of the souls glitter throughout the cemetery.

"Was he in on the attack?" she asked softly. She was fairly sure that she knew the answer already, but she needed to hear it.

Liv nodded gently. "Yes. He was. He had been sent by their Empress to kill you, to stop the prophecy from coming true."

"Mother fucker."

"But, after he came across us in the bakery everything changed. He couldn't do it. He told me that when his friend attacked you, his instincts took over and he felt like he would have killed the attacker if it hadn't been someone he knew."

Lucy turned away from the window to stare at her sister. "What do you think about this guy?"

"I don't fully trust him, but I feel it in my gut that he will do his best to protect you. I don't know why, but even he seems confused about why he needs to keep you safe."

"Well, if he's telling the truth, at least I only have the other Reaper to worry about for now. I can take on one a lot easier than two."

"I don't think he's lying," Liv told her.

Lucy rolled her eyes. "How would you know?"

Liv shrugged. "I've lived in a house full of trouble-makers all my life, I have a pretty decent sixth sense when it comes to that kind of stuff. Not to mention that he kept saying how he just wanted to make sure you were going to be all right."

The image of him driving by in his truck that morning flashed into Lucy's mind and she realized that he had probably been there for several hours while her whole family was out in the graveyard arguing.

"I want to talk to him."

"Luce, I don't think that's a good idea right now."

"Help me go see him. I have questions too."

"Lucy ..."

She jumped up from the window seat. "Please, please, please. Liv, will you do this for me?"

Liv shook her head. "I don't think we should take that chance right now."

"Oh, so you can go put yourself in danger, but it's not all right for you to take me there."

"Yes!" Liv threw her hands up. "That is exactly it, Lucy, I'm not the Chosen One, you are."

With a glare, Lucy pointed at her sister. "In this family ... we are all equally important. You fucking got that?"

Liv didn't answer.

"I mean it Liv."

"I know you do. But, my answer is still the same. I'm not going to help you. It's too risky."

Lucy thought about it for a minute and decided that she didn't want to get Liv involved in that kind of risky business anyway. She wished like hell that Liv hadn't gone over there by herself, but if she took Lucy over there and the family found out, it was going to turn into World War Three, Estmond style.

But, no one said she couldn't go by herself.

"Fine. Whatever. I get where you're coming from." Lucy waved her off and moved back to the window seat. "We have to come up with an offensive plan to take care of this other Reaper though."

Liv let out a long breath. She was probably relieved that Lucy let the subject of going to see Jack drop. "Yeah, it sucks just having to sit around a wait for it to happen again. I don't know what else we can do though."

Lucy agreed. "Hey Liv, did you ever think that we would be facing problems like this? I mean, fighting the Reapers yeah ... but, putting a hit out on one us is pretty crazy. We live in one of the smallest towns ever and I've always thought that made us safer as Keepers."

"I feel the same way. Summer Hollow has always

been a bit off the radar for the violence. The Reapers who come here are usually just passing through. But, it is what it is. We will deal with it and then everything will go back to normal."

"Normal isn't always awesome," Lucy told her.

"I know, believe me, I know. But, it's better than being chased by a murderer." Liv got up off the bed and headed for the door. "I just wanted to let you know about Jack, so if you see him around, that's why."

"I just don't understand why you don't want me to go see him and question him myself, especially if he's going to be like … following me around or something."

"It's one thing for me to allow someone to keep you safe, but it's another to enable socializing with the Reapers. If he wants to follow you around and take out anyone who tries to hurt you, that's totally fine because when you're here, you're with all of us. Taking you to him alone just isn't something I'm comfortable with yet."

Lucy nodded. "All right, I get it."

Like fuck she did.

"I'll be downstairs if you need me," Liv told her as she slipped out the bedroom door and closed it softly behind her.

Lucy moved back to the bed and lay on top of the covers. Now, how in the hell was she going to get out of this place without anyone knowing she was gone?

LUCY
16

The day passed so slowly, Lucy thought she might lose her mind. Sitting around doing nothing wasn't really her thing, so after pretending to rest in her bedroom for a while, she put on a tank and a pair of shorts, then grabbed a set of gardening gloves and headed out back to the severely neglected garden her father had left her with.

The garden consisted of a variety of different flowers planted at the corners of the fenced in area and raised boxes with vegetables. Mostly, there were snap peas, chard, lettuce, and zucchini. The cherry tomatoes added a lovely splash of color to all of the green, which dominated the garden.

She eyeballed the weeds and lifted her trowel, "Let's do this, you assholes." With that, she went to town, taking out the weeds with a vengeance that would have made her father proud. Garden duty was one of the rotating chores their father tasked his children out with. He tended to it too, but it was a rather large garden and needed more care than he alone could provide.

She was only out there for about two minutes before a shadow appeared at her side. She knew it was Ethan before she even looked up.

149

"Why didn't you tell anyone you were going outside?"

She glanced up at him, shading her eyes from the sun so she could see him better. "Because, I'm a big girl."

"The whole point of us being here is to protect you. If we don't know where you are then someone could just walk right up to you and kill you."

She bent down and went back to work on the weeds. "Good grief, Ethan, that's not going to happen in broad daylight right in front of my own house."

"Sure, and you didn't almost get murdered in the graveyard, which is basically your own yard."

Details ... "That was different."

"Not by much." He squatted down next to her and began helping her pull the weeds out.

She glanced at his hands. "You should get some gloves on."

"No way, gloves are for chicks. I can handle a little dirt."

"Fine, have it your way."

They worked on the garden in silence, neither needing to say much. They had an easy relationship which, often, did not need words. She knew Ethan was worried about her and he wanted to keep her safe, but she also knew that he cherished these small moments they spent together doing the most basic of things.

After a while, Lucy heard cars pulling up at the front of the house and knew that the rest of the family had arrived, and that dinner must be almost ready. "We better go in."

Ethan stood and held out his hand for her. She grasped it and he yanked her up. "Yeah, we better change too or Liv will have a fit."

Lucy smiled, loving that Ethan was as much a part of their family as any of the kids were.

They entered the house through the side door and found the kitchen bustling with people once again. Liv was lugging a gigantic bowl of spaghetti into the dining room, where there was already another bowl of the pasta on the table just as large as the one she was carrying in. James had just finished setting out the plates and silverware. Hannah swung through the door with a basket full of garlic bread and Steph followed right behind with a salad bowl. Greg was setting out wine glasses and water, while Daniel sat at the table pretty much just doing nothing and being in the way.

After the table was set and laden with food, they all sat down to eat. Lucy wasn't really that hungry, but she knew better than to try and opt out of a family dinner. Liv was a stickler about things like that.

Lucy always thought it was funny how Hannah was older, yet Liv was sort of the mother figure to the kids. They all helped take care of each other, but Hannah didn't like to cook, clean, or anything like that. She was more the nerdy type who preferred books and *Star Wars* to pretty much anything else. She did take her Keeper job very seriously though, so like the rest of the family, she could kick some major ass if she had to.

Hannah also worked a regular job in the morgue at the hospital. It worked out because she could Keep the souls there. The Reapers who roamed the bigger cities often liked to peruse the morgues, looking for a little soul snack.

No one wanted to talk about the attack, thank God. It had been argued to death already. Lucy didn't feel like talking at all and relief filled her when Steph started in on Daniel about his drinking. Not that it was a good thing, it was just nice to have the attention on someone else.

"Jesus, Dan! Its wine, not a fucking shot glass."

Daniel had just finished guzzling the red wine out of his glass and was reaching for the bottle so he could refill. "Shut up, Steph, I'm an adult. I can drink as much as I want."

"You are a drunk. We shouldn't have even had this

wine with dinner. You fucktard, now none of us can even drink around you because you can't control yourself. If you don't knock this shit off we're going to take you to a rehab center."

Daniel glared at her. "You can't just put me in a rehab center."

"Wanna fucking bet?"

"I have to check myself in or get sent there by someone like the cops."

Steph straightened in her chair. "Well I happen to know a few cops who might help me out, so don't push it, Dan. You need to stop drinking so much and get your shit together."

"Fuck. Off." Dan poured the remainder of the dark red liquid into his glass and took a large drink of it while looking very pointedly at Steph.

"Asshole," she muttered and then took a bite of spaghetti.

Greg, who was already almost done with his first serving, pointed his fork at Steph. "You guys need to watch your mouths, you know Dad never allows that kind of language at the table. At least *try* to be a tiny bit respectful."

Dan stood up and threw his fork onto his untouched plate of food. "I don't have to deal with this shit. I come here because you are all I have left and this happens every time. Every fucking time! I'm not going to sit here and listen to you all try to run my life." He spun around and headed for the door and then turned back. "Thanks for including me, Liv, but I can't do this right now.

Hannah pushed her chair out and stood up. "I'm driving you home."

Dan turned his back and stalked out the door. "No, you're not. I'm fine."

"Shut up and let me drive you." She picked up her pace and followed him out.

From the other room they could hear the argument ensue.

"Give me the keys."

"No, I can drive myself. Why is everyone treating me like a kid?"

"Because you're acting like one. Give me the keys."

Lucy sat with her family at the table and took small bites while listening to them go at it. The others were just as quiet, most probably hoping that Hannah would get the keys.

"Get the fuck away from me," Dan's voice escalated.

"If you're not going to give them to me, I'll take them from you."

"Ouch, get off!"

Lucy took a bite of garlic bread and then washed it down with a sip of wine.

"Give me the keys!"

A loud crash resounded from the living room, startling everyone. Lucy jumped to her feet dropping her fork on the table. She and most of the siblings rushed into the living room just in time to see Hannah's fist connect with Dan's cheek.

"You bitch!" Dan yelled, clutching his cheek with his hand.

Greg lunged forward, grabbing Hannah around the waist before she could go after Dan again. "I am going to drive his ass home. Stupid mother fuc…"

"Hannah! Knock it off," Greg hollered at her as she tried to squirm out of his grip.

"He can't be driving around like that." Her body relaxed a little bit.

James stalked forward and yanked on Dan's coat before he could react and stuck his hand down into the large outer pocket. He came up with the keys in an instant. "You're not driving, man. That settles it."

With his cheek a bit flushed from where Hannah had struck him, Dan retreated to the front door. "You all are a bunch of assholes," he told them flatly, with hurt evident in his deep brown eyes. "I'll fucking walk."

James jingled the keys. "I'll drive him in my car," he said as he tossed the keys at Steph. "You guys keep

153

these here for now."

Hannah shoved Greg away from her. "I'm so tired of worrying about him."

Steph put the keys in the drawer by the front door. "We all are. But, he has to want to do something about it and he just doesn't. Losing Theresa and then Dad ... I kinda get where he's coming from."

"Yeah," Hannah agreed as they headed back to the dining room. "But, this is getting bad. He is going to get himself arrested ... or killed in a freaking car accident or something. I don't want to lose him too, just because he can't get some self-control."

Lucy had watched the entire scene without involving herself. On any normal day she would have been right in the center of it trying to help, that's just how she was. But, this time she held back. The more they thought about Dan, the less they worried about her.

She sat down to finish her dinner and looked over to find Ethan staring at her. "What?"

"Why are you so quiet today?" he whispered.

The others didn't hear him because they were still holding their own conversation about what could be done about their drunkard brother.

She lifted her shoulders in a nonchalant shrug. "I just don't feel much like talking, I've got a lot on my mind."

This seemed to appease Ethan's curiosity. "About the prophecy and the Chosen One stuff."

She nodded. "And the attack. I think that took a lot more out of me than I thought. I'm still sore and tired."

"That's understandable."

"Yeah, I think I'm going to go up and take a bath and then try and get some more sleep. You and James are taking over patrol right?"

He swallowed a bite of spaghetti and cleared his throat. "Yeah, we got it. You just get some rest. Hopefully we don't have any problems tonight."

She hoped not. She didn't want to get attacked

again, but she would rather fight for herself than see anyone she loved hurt "Be careful out there, and if you see Dad, tell him to stay hidden until we can get rid of these Reapers. I hate having him out there all vulnerable."

Ethan shook his head and laughed a little bit. "He may be a ghost now, but he is still Gregory Estmond, and he would find a way to kick a Reapers ass all the way from the other side."

Lucy smiled. "You're probably right. He is one stubborn old man, isn't he?"

"He sure is, and he passed that trait onto each and every one of you kids."

"He says that we got it from our mom."

Ethan finished up the last bit of salad off his plate and stood up so he could take his dishes into the kitchen. "I didn't know your mom, but I'm assuming your dad was just trying to blame it on her," he laughed. "I'm sure you got just as much from him as you did from her. Which makes you all double the trouble."

She left the family at the table and followed him out with her own dishes. Once in the kitchen, they deposited the contents of their arms into the sink.

Lucy opened the dishwasher while Ethan started the water and rinsed off the dishes. They took a few minutes to clean up the piles of dishes left from cooking and chatted a bit more about her father.

"Well," Lucy dried her hands on a dish towel just as her brothers and sisters piled in from the dining room with more dishes, "I'm heading up to bed. You all can do your own dishes. We cleaned up the mess from cooking."

"Hey, I didn't make a mess." Liv actually appeared offended that Lucy would say she had made a mess."

Lucy directed an eye roll at her sister. "That is not what I meant. Geeze."

"Oh," Liv rinsed her own plate and stuck it in the dishwasher. "Well, go on up and rest. We got the rest of this."

Just then the door slammed and James strode into the house. "I delivered the package. He passed out in the car and I had to lug his ass into the apartment." He tossed his keys on the table and looked at Ethan. "You 'bout ready to head out there. I don't want to give these fuckers a chance to get close."

Ethan nodded. "Just about, let me go get my sweatshirt."

"Hurry up, dude."

"Good night." Lucy waved as she strode through the kitchen door and headed for the stairs. A chorus of 'goodnight' and 'get some rest' followed her.

Once she was in her room she closed the door behind her and leaned against it. Oh, the sweet, sweet silence. She loved her family, but being around them was exhausting.

She looked at the clock and figured most everyone would be going home soon except Greg, James and Ethan. James and Ethan were going out on patrol pretty soon and Greg would probably sit downstairs and read for most of the night.

A shower was severely needed after working in the garden, so she decided to do that first.

The steaming water filled the bathroom quickly. She let the water just roll over her for a while, soothing her sore muscles and opening her pores.

Lucy tried to tell herself that she was just going to question this Jack the Reaper, but at the same time she felt an excitement buzzing within her. She wanted to see him … more than she should ever want to see a Reaper.

Why in the hell was she so excited to see this guy? Seriously was there a reason that she was shaving her legs? Was there a logical reason as to why she sprayed her favorite perfume onto her skin? What about wearing her favorite jeans … the ones that she knew damn well made her ass look good? Or topping off her outfit with a tight fitting tank that showed off a little bit of cleavage? Did any of that sound like a girl who is just dropping by to thank a guy and ask him a few questions?

No ... it sounded like what a girl did when she was getting ready for a date.

Mother of God, she was going crazy. This Chosen One bullshit, and the attack, was getting to her head. Did they have special shrinks for Keepers? Maybe she should find out just in case she needed one.

It wasn't long before she heard cars starting up and pulling out of the driveway. She went to the window seat and watched, letting out a relieved breath when they were all gone.

Changing direction, she moved her gaze over to the graveyard. There, among the trees and gravestones, she saw two forms of shimmering silver mist milling about. James and Ethan were already out and about in the graveyard.

Time to get ready.

She hadn't done this since she was a teenager and felt terribly juvenile for doing it. Opening the closet door, she extracted a few extra blankets she stored there for when it got chilly. She peeled back the blankets on her bed and rolled the extra ones until they looked like a human form underneath the covers.

Then, she went back to the closet and dug way in the back until she found the awful doll that her grandmother had given her when she was three. This doll stood about two feet tall and looked just like the Estmond children. Meaning, it had the red hair she needed to pull off her little stunt.

She set the doll underneath the blankets, covering the face and then spread the hair out over the pillows.

There. That should do it. Most likely anyone checking on her would just crack the door open a little bit, see the body in the bed and then close the door again. Well, hopefully that's what would happen.

Back at the closet, she pulled out one last thing, a long, black, soft leather coat with a very large hood.

She had worn it a couple of times over the years, mostly during her dark stage when she was sixteen.

She donned the coat and pulled the hood up over her head then headed for the window.

Looking down, she cursed. Getting down there with this giant coat on was going to be extremely difficult. But, she needed the coat to hide her aura or James and Ethan might see her.

With careful precision, she threw her leg out the window and found the ledge. Then, she grabbed onto the top ledge with her fingertips and slowly pulled her other leg out.

The overhanging tree branches weren't very big, but should hold her weight. Reaching out, she grabbed the branch and then held her breath as she jumped, swinging herself out and grasping the branch with her other hand.

It was about four feet from window to tree. With her coat fanning out behind her and the hood blocking most of her vision, she used all her upper body strength to move across the branch. The process was excruciatingly slow.

Please, please, please don't let the branch break. Please, please, please, don't let me fall ... she chanted over and over again in her head until she made it to the trunk of the tree. Still hanging on to the branch for dear life, she tested around with her feet until she found another branch and let most of her weight settle onto it.

From there, it was easy peasy. She scoured down the branches quickly, just like she did when she was a teenager. The only issue was the fucking coat kept catching on the branches as she went down. The last branch was five feet up from the ground. Not a problem. She dropped down and landed on her feet without even losing the hood.

Quickly, she pulled the hood down farther, covering her face more. Not wanting to chance a look over at the graveyard, she took off toward the trees on the other side of the house, wanting to get out of sight before anyone saw her.

Once she got through the trees, which was a total bitch in the dark, she popped out on the road that led up to her house, but was far enough away that no one at the house could see her.

She jogged down the side of the road, and then took a shortcut onto another side road, which led over the little bridge and then straight into town.

Summer Hollow was a town where everyone knew everyone, but there was one place she knew she could get the information she needed. The place where everyone talks to everyone.

When she arrived at the door to the bar, she dropped the hood down before she stepped inside.

The place was pretty busy, as it always was. Not much to do in this little town for socialization, so drinking at the bar was one of the obvious solutions.

Reese was behind the bar, uncapping a beer for a customer. Not wasting any time, Lucy headed straight for her. "Reese."

"Hey, Lucy. How's it going?"

"I'm … Can I talk to you in private for a minute."

Reese lifted her eyebrows and shot her a curious look, then jerked her head to the side. "Down here, best I can do. I can't leave the bar."

Lucy nodded and followed Reese down to the end of the bar where there weren't any customers.

"What's up?" Reese folded her stained, white bar towel.

"I need help finding someone."

Again with the eyebrow lift. "I'll do what I can. Who is it?"

"His name is Jack, he's new around here …"

Before she could finish her description Reese had her hands up. "Whoa, Lucy, are you serious?"

"Yes. Why?"

"Jack is not a guy I would recommend any of my friends getting involved with."

Lucy's turn for an eyebrow lift. "Why, what did he do?"

Reese looked out over the patrons of the bar to make sure everyone was behaving themselves. "Don't get me wrong, I like Jack. He seems like an all right guy, but he's kinda slutty."

"Ummm ... oh." There wasn't one reason that this information should bother her, but suddenly she felt angry and ... hurt. The only other describable feeling Lucy could come up with was betrayal. "I ... um ... I still need to find him. It's important."

Reese shook her head. "All right, but don't say I didn't warn you when he breaks your heart."

Oh my God, what had this guy been up to when he wasn't reaping souls or saving Keepers.

"He's been staying out at Mr. Landry's old rental house."

"Thank you!" Lucy turned to go.

"Just be careful. Jack is a bad boy who needs a whole lotta fixin'."

Lucy smiled. "Gotcha. Thank you, Reese."

She pushed open the door and headed out into the night, lifting her hood as she strode quickly in the direction she needed to go. She had about a mile to walk before she got to the rental house that old man Landry owned. Luckily, she knew exactly where it was.

The walk wasn't too bad, sort of calming really, allowing her to gather her nerves and plan out what she wanted to say.

Finally, the mile was up and she turned off onto the side road. Even in the dark, she could see the little white house sitting among the little forest of trees. She stopped at the start of the gravel driveway and looked at the house.

A big black truck was parked outside and lights shone through several windows, so she knew he was in there.

The feeling of climbing the four stairs up to the front

door was extremely anticlimactic. She was here. Yay! Now what.

She raised her hand and knocked on the door. When no one answered, she knocked again, only harder.

It took over a minute, but she heard the knob turning and then the door was yanked open and suddenly the barrel of a gun was in her face.

"Oh my God, don't shoot me!" The words were out of her mouth before she could rethink something better to say.

Jack, who had answered the door and, to Lucy's delight, wasn't wearing a shirt, quickly dropped the gun to his side. "Lucy!" His gaze tried to get a better look at her face.

She lowered the hood down. "Yes, it's me."

For a moment, his dark eyes seemed to devour every inch of her. Then, his gaze moved beyond her, looking out into the trees and scouring his yard for any other Keepers.

"I'm alone," she told him. "You don't need to worry."

His eyes darkened and he suddenly looked angry. "Well, what the hell are you doing here at all?"

JACK
17

When he pulled open the door and saw the hooded figure on his porch, he'd figured that his mother had simply given up on giving them any more time and sent the Reaper Council after him. It wouldn't have surprised him at all.

What *did* fucking surprise him was that underneath that hood was the object of all his craziness lately. As she pulled the hood down, his red headed Keeper stood there, bathed in a shimmering silver mist.

What the fuck was she thinking, running around out in the dark by herself without any protection. Was she *trying* to get herself killed?

"Excuse me?" she responded to his rude ass question.

"I asked, what the hell you think you are doing here?"

He watched Lucy recoil a bit and felt like an ass. But, in his defense, she was the one putting herself in danger. Aiden could be out there looking for her right now and here she was making herself the perfect victim.

She looked away from him and seemed to consider turning around and leaving. "I, uh … I just … needed to see you. I'm sorry." She backed up and turned to descend the porch steps.

Oh hell no. He was pissed off enough that she was running around out in the dark by herself in the first place, he sure as hell wasn't going to let her walk all the way back home again. That is, assuming she walked, which he was pretty sure she did. Without thinking about it, he reached out and grabbed her arm.

"What the fuck, let go!" she screamed.

Oh great, now he was scaring her. "Shut up, I'm not going to hurt you." He pulled on her arm and yanked her inside the house, slamming the door behind him.

"Are you fucking crazy?" he demanded, letting go of her arm just as she pulled herself away from him and stumbled back a few feet.

"You're the crazy one! Do you always treat people like this, or is that just a Reaper trait? Liv told me you weren't that bad, but I'm wondering what the hell made her think that."

"Your sister doesn't know a damn thing about me."

He watched her gaze bounce around, inspecting the inside of his little house and then settle back onto him. "She knows enough to tell me she came here. She knows enough to think that you wouldn't hurt me."

Fuck, fuck, fuck.

Even as he was cursing Liv for talking to Lucy at all, he was fighting the urge to touch Lucy's skin, to feel that she was indeed here in his house.

He took a step closer to her. "Like I said, she doesn't know me. Neither do you. I could hurt you if I wanted to. Don't forget, I'm a Reaper and you have a soul."

She lifted her chin defiantly, and mimicking his actions, took a step toward him as well. "I'm not scared of you."

By now they were less than six inches apart. "You should be scared."

What was wrong with her? She just waltzes in here without thinking of her own safety. But, God fucking damn, her lips …

Their eyes were locked on each other, both of them

163

unwilling to turn away. "Why should I be scared of you?" she demanded. "Why would you save me from the other Reaper if you wanted to hurt me?"

With strength he didn't know he had, he tore his eyes away from hers and spun around, grabbing his truck keys off the table. "I'm taking you home. You should have never left."

"I need to talk to you. That's why I came here." With both hands she unbuttoned the long coat she was wearing and slid it down her arms.

Oh holy hell. So much skin.

She turned to set her coat on the back of one of the dining chairs and he was rewarded with an amazing view of her perfect ass. Again, oh holy hell. He let out a long breath and tried to send a brain signal to Mr. 'gets excited over everything,' down there, to tell him to behave himself.

"I don't know what I can do to help you that I haven't already told your sister."

"You didn't tell her everything." Lucy wandered around the room. He could see her taking in the details of his temporary home. Normally that kind of shit bothered him, but not this time. Nope.

"How would you know?" he demanded.

She peeked into the bedroom and then glanced back at him. "Because I didn't tell her everything either."

Well fuck, he leaned on the doorframe by the kitchen and watched her poke around the house. "So, are you ready to go now? We can talk in the truck."

"Why are you trying to get rid of me?"

"Because you're a Keeper. I don't associate with the likes of you."

"Well, under normal circumstances I'd feel the same way about you. But, I think you know as well as I do that we don't have normal circumstances."

"And you are putting yourself in danger by coming here, walking around in the fucking dark, what the hell is wrong with you, there is someone out there trying to kill you!" As soon as the words were out of his mouth his eyes went to her neck and he saw red.

Son of a bitch.

Mother fucker.

The faint scabbed line from where Aiden's knife had dragged across her throat stood out against her pale white skin. He wanted to choke the shit out of Aiden for marking her.

Her hands fluttered up and touched the wound. "I can take care of myself."

Without thinking, he closed the gap of space between them and dropped his keys on the floor. Reaching out and clutching her arms, he yanked her toward him. "You think you can take care of yourself, huh?" She let out a tiny gasp as he crushed their bodies together. "Those Reapers you fight on a regular basis do not want to kill you. They want souls. The Reaper after you now, he wants you *dead*." He shook her a bit. "Do you fucking hear me?"

"Yes! Now get away." She was demanding that he let her go, but she didn't fight or struggle against him. It almost felt like she was relaxing against him. "

"If I wanted to hurt you, I could, and there is nothing that you could do about it."

What the hell, was he *trying* to piss her off? She was here, she was safe.

She lifted her chin, looking up into his eyes. "That's not true. You have no idea what I am capable of."

His eyes zeroed in on her lips, slightly parted and shiny with some kind of gloss that smelled like strawberries. His gaze continued down her neck, beyond the knife wound, to her chest which was heaving gently, lifting her exposed cleavage up with every breath.

Fucking hell.

He raised his eyes and locked them with hers again. "Is that so?" he barked. "Fight me then, show me how fucking tough you are. Show me how you can protect yourself." With that, all control was lost. He pushed himself against her and crushed his mouth to hers.

As soon as their lips met, his body erupted with electric tingles that could be felt over every single nerve in his body. Her lips parted, making way for his tongue to graze hers. He moved forward, walking her back until she was pressed against the wall. Her hands were clutched in his, and he raised them up pinning her against the hard surface.

"Fucking fight me, Lucy." He pulled away only enough that he could mumble against her lips. "Show me."

With her lips against his and the connection made, he realized how hungry for souls he was. It had been a while since he had any soul other than the little bits he'd taken from those girls he'd been with.

She moaned and then abruptly turned her head to the side, forcing their lips apart. "I just came here to talk. I don't need to prove anything to you."

With a push, Jack forced himself to move away from her. "Well, like I said, let's talk in the truck."

Lucy shook her head, smoothing down her top and getting her nerves back in order. "Why … um …" She paused and shook her head, as if trying to clear the sexual thoughts out of her head and make way for the actual questions she'd come to him with. "There isn't any burn when we touch, why is that?"

"I don't have a clue."

"Has this ever happened to you before, with another Keeper?" She began moving around the house again.

"Nope, never." He went into his bedroom and found his jeans. "I'm going to get dressed now." Without even bothering to shut the door, he slid out of his pajama bottoms. Before he reached for the jeans, he glanced up, wondering if she had been curious enough to look in at him while he was changing. But, no, she wasn't anywhere near the doorway.

"Do you know what would cause the contact between you and me to be different than it is with every other Keeper and Reaper?"

He pulled on his jeans and a black tee shirt and

headed back into the living area. "No, I don't know what the hell it is. Supposedly, the burning sensation is caused by something that's in our DNA that goes against the nature of each species. It's some kind of a reaction. Maybe we just don't have whatever that is. It's some kinda super scientific shit that I wouldn't know anything about."

Lucy looked him over, eyes scanning from his feet, up his legs and torso, finally meeting his eyes once again. "So, Liv told me some stuff ... stuff about how you've been feeling since we first met."

He gave her a nod and sat on the couch with his boots. "Yeah, I don't know what the hell it is. I don't know what started it. I don't know if it will last, but I wish it would go away because, frankly, it's a real pain in the ass."

"I know."

His head snapped up. "What do you mean?"

"I mean, that I know ... because I've been experiencing a weird attraction to you."

What the fuck? He could only stare at her with his mouth hanging open.

"Maybe not as severely as you are, but it's there, nonetheless."

This whole situation just got a hell of a lot more dangerous than Aiden being after her. If she had even half the attraction for him that he had for her, then they were both staring trouble right in the face. On the other hand, he had spent the last few days thinking he was just going crazy, and now it turned out that he wasn't alone in his craziness. The fact that she was going through the same shit he was could be an upside or a serious downside.

He finished lacing up his boots and pulled the strings tight. "Yeah, let's get you home."

She stepped away from him a couple of feet. "But, we need to talk about this. It's important."

"Well, I'm going. You can either come with me and talk in the truck or walk home and not talk to me."

He pulled open the front door, hoping to God that she would follow him.

She did.

He stalked out the door and she hurried after him, grabbing up her coat on the way. Once they were out at the truck, he watched her hesitate by the door and then reach out and yank the handle.

Why couldn't she have just stayed home? This whole situation was going to shit as it was, and he didn't need even more Keepers up his ass because she couldn't sit at home where she was safe.

He slid behind the wheel, fired up the engine and backed out of the driveway. Once they were on the main road she started up again. "Do you think that when you leave here the attraction will fade?"

He shrugged "I don't know." He paused. "I hope so." Well, he kind of hoped it did.

Out of the corner of his eye, he saw her turn toward him in the darkness of the truck. "Look, I know that this situation isn't exactly normal and we aren't supposed to get along, but I don't understand why the hell you're treating me like this if you are supposedly feeling so protective of me."

Good God, why didn't she get it? He was careful not to look at her and kept his eyes on the road. "Because, it's exactly the reason that you said. We aren't supposed to get along. We are enemies, Lucy."

He heard her flop back in her seat in a huff. "I don't feel like we're enemies. Maybe that's what this Chosen One bullshit is all about. Maybe you're a part of it too."

Yeah right.

"I highly doubt that is the case. The Chosen One is supposed to bring forth and end to the Reapers, remember. I don't think that a Reaper can be part of bringing himself to an end."

He glanced at her again and she shrugged. "Maybe … maybe not."

A few minutes later he turned into a pullout a ways down from Lucy's house and killed the engine. Then, he reached behind the seat and pulled out his hoodie. Slipping it on, he made sure that it was zipped and the hood was up.

"Put your coat on. I don't want anyone to see us."

She did as he asked, but kicked up her chin in defiance. "I don't need you to walk me, I'll be fine."

"I'm walking you at least until I can see that you've gone into the house."

"I don't need you."

"Shut up, Lucy. This is happening."

He didn't really expect her to shut her mouth. He barely knew her, but from the small amount of time he had spent with her, he did know that she was stubborn and used to fighting to get her way. Surprisingly, she kept silent as she slipped down from his truck.

She had covered her hair and face with that giant hood, which, ironically, reminded him of the Grim Reaper. He followed behind her as she cut through the woods. His eyes were everywhere, searching for any movement or flashes of color. At this point the color didn't matter, both red and silver were just as dangerous.

As the farmhouse came into view, she stopped at the edge of the trees and turned to face him. He could barely see her with her hood pulled up, but he could see the tiniest bit of silver floating on the warm summer air.

"We're here."

Fucking right they were. And the shittiest part about it was that now that they were at her house and he had to send her back inside, he didn't fucking want to. Whatever the hell was happening to him seemed to multiply every time he saw her, but when he was with her it was even worse than that.

When he didn't say anything, she turned back toward the house. "I'd better go now. Sorry you had to do this." With that, she stepped out beyond the trees.

Aw, fuck it. "Wait!" He reached out and grabbed her arm, dragging her back toward him.

"What?" Her head was tilted up and he could see her eyes underneath the hood, they were wide with surprise, but he didn't sense or see any fear from her.

He pulled her back a little bit further so that they were completely out of view of the house. What was he going to say to her? Shit. He didn't have a clue, the only thing he knew was that he didn't want her to leave him. Not yet.

So fucking strange when, not a half an hour ago, he had basically kicked her out of his house.

"Jack?"

"I … I just needed another minute."

She glanced back at the house and then back at him. "I'm glad. I don't know why. But, I am."

God, her voice was just as sexy as the rest of her. "I want you to do what your family tells you to do." His voice was uncharacteristically soft.

"But …"

He held his hand up to stop her protests. "But nothing. They are only doing what is best for you. I will be helping find the Reaper who is after you. Hopefully soon, this can all be over."

"And then you will leave Summer Hollow?"

He nodded. "I think that is probably what's best."

Then she smiled. "This is like some fucked up movie about two very different people falling for each other for no reason, isn't it?"

He let out a low chuckle and tapped the top of her hood. "Hey, we even sparkle, it must be fate."

"Don't even go there!"

He paused and then reached down and found her hand, which was buried within the confines of her sleeve. It was so odd, not having the burn when he touched her. "I am an asshole, this isn't just my reaction to you. It's just how I am."

She gripped his hand tightly and then found his other hand and took hold of that one too. She held fast to both of his hands. "Crazy thing is, I really don't care if you're an asshole. We are supposed to be enemies, but right now, maybe we should just concentrate on our common goal."

He loosened his grip and flattened his hands against hers. "What exactly is our common goal?" God, how he loved the feel of her skin against his. Not exactly the thought of an asshole, now was it.

She moved their hands up a little, so that they stood face to face with their hands pressed against each other. "To find out what is going on with us."

He shook his head. "No. The fact that someone is trying to kill you is more important."

He wanted to send her away, to shove her back and force her into the house, but at the same time, he wanted exactly the opposite of that. "I'm fucking confused about all this, so just do what your family tells you to do, all right."

He could barely see it, but she offered him a small smile. "I can't make any guarantees. That's just how I am, but I'll try. Okay?"

"Okay." He pretty much had to summon the willpower to pull his hands away from hers and take a step back. "You should get in there before they realize you're gone."

"Yeah," she agreed. "I don't know when I'll see you again, but I'm sure I will."

Suddenly grim, he found that he couldn't fucking wait until the next time he saw her. "Go." He waved her off. "I don't need your family out for my blood."

She turned toward the house and then paused, appearing to contemplate leaving, but after a few seconds she hurried off across the expanse of lawn to the safety of the yellow farmhouse.

He moved to a spot where he could see the side of the house that her bedroom was on. Vaguely, he could see the dark shape climbing up the low branches of the tree, up to the second floor window where he finally saw her crawl inside. Once she was safely in her room, he released a breath that he hadn't even realized he was holding.

Wow. Shit certainly wasn't going the way he expected.

LUCY 18

The next morning, Lucy woke to her alarm, even though she had no reason to get up. Still no classes for her since she was on Estmond family lock down. Not quite ready to get out of bed yet, she lay there, staring at the ceiling and thinking about Jack.

This was so wrong ... sooooo wrong, and she totally knew it. But, on the other hand, she had never felt so attracted and connected to one person in her entire life.

Sure, she and Ethan had a connection, but what she felt with Jack blew Ethan right out of the water, and that was saying a lot.

Of all the men in the world, *this* was the one that she had to go and feel something for.

Like he said, he was an asshole. She could tell that from the very beginning when she met him in the bakery. Or maybe not quite an asshole ... most likely just a smart-ass. But, damn, he was hot. When she was around him, there was something else there ... something that was missing when she was with anyone else.

And ... he had kissed her. Sure, it was meant to prove something to her or some shit, but she didn't care. It was phenomenal. If he had kissed her much longer, she may have taken things into her own hands and tried to get him to sleep with her. Yeah, it was that fucking good.

This was almost like *Romeo and Juliet*, two houses at war and two people forbidden to be together. Damn, could she possibly get anymore chick flick over this? Where's the chocolate and wine when you need it.

"No more," she said out loud as she sat up and flung the comforter away from her. Ugh, time to think about something else.

After a long shower, she went down to the kitchen for coffee and found Greg underneath the sink with only his legs sticking out.

She headed straight for the coffee pot. "Hey bro, what are you doing under there?" she asked as she poured her coffee into a large mug.

There was a grunt and a shift and then, "I'm relaxing. Seriously Luce, what the hell does it look like I'm doing?"

She shrugged, even though he couldn't see her, and then pulled out a chair at the kitchen table.

"I'm fixing the leak that you never told anyone was leaking for God knows how long. Now there's damage under the cabinet."

Fuck. "I'm sorry, Greg. I didn't even know that it was leaking."

"We can all fix this stuff for you, you just need to keep an eye out and let us know when shit goes wrong."

Shit was going very wrong lately.

"I said I was sorry. I'll keep a better watch on things from now on."

Greg pulled himself out from under the sink and sat up. His hair was sticking up in some places and his eyes were wide with mock surprise. "What, no arguments?"

She took a sip of her coffee. "Nope."

"I don't understand." He kept up the rouse, feigning

confusion. "You," his hand went to his heart, "you agree with me?"

"Knock it off before I change my mind and give you a run for your money."

Greg laughed and disappeared back underneath the sink.

"Where are James and Ethan?"

"Sleeping. They were up all night on patrol."

"Oh." Of course they would be sleeping off their all-nighter. Thankfully, whatever they were doing, neither of them caught her sneaking in or out of the house, or realized that she was gone. Thank goodness. She hadn't wanted to leave Jack, but she was sure relieved when she was safely back in the house.

She sipped on her coffee some more and stared at the kitchen table. "I'm going to go check out that trunk some more. See if there are any clues."

Greg's muffled voice floated out from under the sink. "Ok Velma. Make sure you keep an eye on Fred and Daphne when you split up."

"Ha ha, very funny."

"Have fun. I'll be here."

They had stashed the trunk up in her room, having decided it was hers since she was the Chosen One and all.

She stood in the doorway of her room staring at the ancient trunk. Her crossbow was sitting on top, the pouch of arrows resting beside it. She hadn't needed it for anything since the night she had been attacked, since no one would let her out of the house.

Moving the crossbow and its arrows aside, she lifted the lid and then pulled the white silk completely out of the trunk. The book lay exactly where they had left it, as well as the parchment, which had been carefully re-rolled and the ribbon tied back around it.

Lifting the book out, she set it on the floor in front of her and ran her hand over the emblem on the cover. Apparently, this was their family symbol. It was weird that neither she, nor her siblings, had known about the family symbol. It wasn't important really, but drove home the fact that her father had kept this from her.

Opening the book, she carefully turned the old pages one by one, looking for any entries that she would be able to read. As the pages flipped by, she noted the handwriting changes and the types of ink were different. She couldn't read any of it, until about three-quarters of the way through.

The first English entry that was legible was dated 1892.

My name is Amelia Estmond, daughter of Thomas Estmond, and this entry is the first of my language in the Estmond family records. It had been passed into my hands several years ago. However, no ink has stained this parchment until now. I give no excuse to my neglect, and shall get to the matter of recording my endeavors as a Keeper.

This day was not a day I wish to repeat. I was forced to kill my first Reaper. I shall never forget, for the bloodshed is written in my memory forever. Now, it will be written here as well.

We, the Keepers, do not wish to kill. We only wish to save the souls. The souls, if taken by a Reaper will never cross over to wherever it is they are destined to go. If a Reaper takes them, from what we know, they are then consumed into the body of the Reaper forevermore. Therefore, we must protect them at all costs.

My life as a Keeper thus far has been simple. Battle the Reapers and they shall eventually run. The Reapers are not afraid of us, and they would simply rather not have to make acquaintance with a Keeper at all.

Each day that passes, there is yet another death. People are being murdered, and are frequently falling ill with disease so terrible that death finally takes them. I have no husband, no children, so my life is committed to protecting the souls in the crude and ever growing graveyards.

This night, the Reaper came looking, and came upon me before he found a soul. I carried twin daggers, the blades of which were silver. I fully admit to having stolen the items from which they were forged. In any case, I drew my blades

176

and ordered him to leave the graveyard.

He charged me, wielding his own large knife. We fought, both giving and receiving wounds, which weakened us. In the end, it was my dagger which struck the final blow.

I cannot put into words exactly how it feels to have taken a life, even the life of a Reaper. However, I shall honor my commitment just as my ancestors have.

We are born Keepers, it is a calling which lies in our blood. Some of our line thus far have chosen to ignore the calling and attempt to live what they think is a normal life. Sadly, they eventually discover that it is not something which can simply be discarded.

The souls are everywhere and they cannot be avoided, even if you try to pretend they are not there. Yet, where there are souls, there are Reapers, and no matter how hard one may try to deny the urge, a Keeper will act on instinct to protect those souls.

I do not like the things I have to do, especially when I must act as I have this eve, but I will never turn my back on my commitment to the souls. I do not deny my calling.

So, in closing to this first entry I must say that I do not regret having to take a life. Not one ounce of regret lies within me, because I know that I saved a soul in doing so.

No, I do not wish to kill again ... but I will if my hand is forced to do so.

Lucy looked up from the pages of Amelia's first entry. It was pretty cool to read about how her ancestors had fought, and how they perceived the life of a Keeper. Her father had never really told them much about any of their relatives, except for their grandmother.

She was beginning to think that her father had intentionally tried to keep them secluded from a lot of the Keeper heritage, but why? That was something she was definitely going to have to ask her dad about next time she saw him.

Sitting on the floor was beginning to get uncomfortable. She picked up the book and took it over to the window seat so she could sit on a cushion and lean back. After she had settled in, she found another entry from Amelia and had just begun to read when soft knock sounded on her bedroom door.

"Come in," she called, looking up expectantly.

The door cracked open and Ethan poked his head in. "Hey, just checking on you."

"I'm all right, just checking this out." She gestured to the book before her. "It's a record from the Estmond Keepers."

He entered the room and bent down beside her. "Really? That's pretty awesome."

Ethan knew just as much, or as little, as she did about the Keepers of the past, so it probably was pretty exciting for him too. "I found some of it in English, not much, but there are some that we can read. Check it out." She patted the cushion next to her, motioning for him to sit.

She turned back to Amelia's first entry and let him read it for himself. "Wow," he said when he was done. "She is certainly committed to the life."

Lucy nodded. "Yeah, we all are, but, I sort of feel like living in a small town has secluded us from a lot of what happens in the real world, with Keepers and Reapers. Not that I'm complaining or anything, I just feel like there is a lot we may not know."

Ethan shrugged. "I don't mind this. If we don't know what we are missing, who really cares."

"Yeah ... you're probably right," she agreed.

"That stuff she wrote, about Keepers denying their calling. Have you ever felt like you wanted to be normal, you know, not see the souls?"

Like when she is going through a relationship crisis, and there is no one to date because the only available Keeper in the area is her best friend, and even though she loved him, she didn't love him like that. Yeah, that would be one of those moments. "Yes, I have, but it's never lasted long. I love my life."

"Back when Mom and Dad were around, I used to wish that I wasn't able to see them. But, now ... I never do."

Man, Ethan had had a tough life, she often wondered what would have happened if the Estmonds hadn't taken him in. They didn't usually bring up his parents or how she and Ethan felt about each other, but Lucy suddenly felt like apologizing to him and it was out before she could stop herself. "I'm sorry."

He furrowed his eyebrows and managed to look sincerely confused. "What on Earth are you sorry about?"

"I don't know … about your parents, about us … about everything."

"I don't know why you would bring all that up, but as far as my parents go, you and I both know I'm better off without them. If they hadn't been such shitty parents than I wouldn't have become as close to you and your family as I am. You are my family, they aren't." He paused, as if contemplating on continuing. "And as far as you and I go, we've had this discussion. You know my stance."

"I wish it was different." Lucy turned away and stared out at the graveyard. The sun was peeking through the fluffy clouds that filled the brilliant blue sky.

Ethan reached over and gently touched her chin with his fingertips, turning her head toward him so that he could look into her eyes.

God, his eyes were such an intense shade of blue.

"I wish it was different too," he whispered. "You feel how you feel, *I* know how you feel, and that is just the way it is."

Lucy looked into his eyes as he spoke and knew that this was a man who loved her. Maybe, just maybe, she could force the feelings for Jack away by trying to feel something for someone else.

She leaned in just a little bit closer and let her hand drift over and settle on Ethan's leg.

"Lucy, what are you doing?" He didn't move.

"I don't know." She shrugged. "I want to kiss you right now."

He shook his head. "We can't do this anymore. That ended a long ti…"

She cut him off by closing the gap between them. Their lips met and he immediately responded to her, opening slightly. Suddenly he took hold of Lucy's arms, holding her firmly in his grasp and hauled her into his lap.

Lucy ran her fingertips over his bicep, feeling the hard muscles built from construction work and fight training.

His arms slid around her back, holding her tightly against him, as if he were trying to savor each second of the moment he knew wouldn't last.

Even as his hands wound their way up into her hair, the pangs of guilt began. She was using him. She was positive that he knew she was using him for something, but his feelings for her were so much that he didn't care and would take what he could get.

This man loved her.

Why couldn't she love him the way he loved her.

As the urgent kisses continued, Lucy fought to send Jack out of her mind. Kissing Ethan didn't feel wrong, but it didn't feel right either. When Jack had kissed her before, back at his house, there had been a sense of perfection that just wasn't there with Ethan.

Finally, it was Ethan who broke away and gently pulled back. "Lucy." His breathing was heavy and his voice huskier than usual.

She tilted her head down so her forehead pressed into his shoulder. "I'm sorry. I just … I'm sorry."

She felt his hand smooth down her hair. "It's all right, I understand."

With her head still against him she shook it back and forth. "No, no, it's not all right."

"Is something going on that you need to talk about. What brought this on?"

Pulling up her head, she looked into his eyes and said nothing. Right then, she knew that he could tell she was hiding something. "It's nothing," she told him and then scooted off his lap, back over to her spot on the window seat. "I guess I'm just messed up from all the commotion lately."

He reached over and took her hand. "I am here for you *always*. Do you understand that? There is nothing you can't tell me."

Yeah, she highly doubted that.

"I won't push you, but I'm not stupid. We stopped this kind of thing a long time ago, and something had to have happened for you to kiss me."

Damn, when he said it like that it made her look like a big asshole. She was the worst friend in the world.

"I'm sorry," she whispered again. "I don't know what happened."

Finally he smiled. "Well, I'm not going to complain too much. It's certainly nothing to be sorry about. I'm not."

Yup, she was right, he would take what he could get, which only made the whole thing even more fucked up. Maybe she should just tell him and get all this shit off her chest. Maybe he would be all right with the whole thing. On the other hand, it could make things worse and he would take his bodyguard job even more seriously than he already was.

Probably best just to keep it to herself ... even though she sort of owed him an explanation.

She flashed him a small smile in return and patted him on the shoulder. "I'm so glad that you can always find positivity. That's one of your best qualities."

"If there is one thing I've learned in my lifetime, it's that you have to make the best out of bad situations, and that you don't always get what you want. If you don't keep a good attitude during those times then all the bad things will eat you alive."

Lucy nodded. "Yeah, I get that."

Ethan stood and stretched. "Well, as awesome as this little visit has been, I have to go find some food. I haven't eaten yet today."

"Go on, I'm going to stay here and read some more

of this."

He gave her a wave and a smile then opened the door and stepped out.

After he was gone, she let out a huge sigh and leaned back on the wall behind her. Well that didn't work for shit and only made her feel worse than she had before.

Fucking wonderful.

She turned her head and gazed out at the graveyard. She could barely see the faint blue glimmering from some of the souls. A sudden movement at the edge of the woods caught her eye. Directing her gaze to where she had seen the rustle within the trees, she searched until she saw it again.

When she focused, she realized that she was looking directly at a face hidden among the trees and bushes.

With a gasp, she pulled back away from the window and yanked the curtain in front of her enough so that she could still peek around it.

Oh God, what if that Reaper had come back?

She could, indeed, see the misty red aura floating around the face. He wore a hood and a pair of sunglasses to try and conceal his presence, but if you looked close enough you could still see it.

He was watching her, she realized, because after he saw her pull back from the window, he lowered his sunglasses and nodded to her. She saw the dark brown eyes focused on her and let out a long breath filled with relief. It was Jack.

Yeah, it was Jack, and he was watching in the window where she had just been kissing Ethan.

Son of a bitch.

She nodded back and then motioned for him to get back farther into the woods. Without waiting to see if he complied, she quickly got up from the window seat and hurried out the door.

JACK
19

Even though he was protected by the shade of the trees and brush, he was still roasting his ass off. In order to stay concealed, he had worn a thin hoodie and gloves, as well as sunglasses. This shit was crazy. It had to be at least a hundred degrees out and here he was, standing in the woods baking like an idiot.

To make matters worse, he was waiting here to make sure that Lucy was safe and what did he get? Front fucking row to her make-out session with another Keeper, that's fucking what.

In a way, he actually hoped that Aiden would just try and attack so that he could get the hell out of Summer Hollow and away from Lucy. Hopefully, like she suggested, the feelings would fade the farther away from each other that they get.

But for now, it was just getting worse with each passing moment.

He had watched her in the window, reading or something and then that mother fucker had come in and sat down with her. It had been agonizing watching the whole thing take place. The kind of agony where you don't want to watch, but, at the same time, you can't look away.

Watching her kiss another man had brought up the kind of feelings that were on the same level as when Aiden had attacked her. Yeah, he wanted to rip the guy limb from fucking limb. No one touched her ... except for him.

Well, that's how he felt, and he couldn't help how he felt, so he'd forced back the urge to smash that Keepers face in and just watched. Luckily for him though, it didn't last long. If it had, he wasn't sure he could have controlled himself at all, and that was the last thing that any of them needed. He could see it so clearly, him busting into the house and running up the stairs to beat the shit out of that guy.

He shook his head, trying to get the vision out of his head. Yeah, that would have only gotten his ass killed since none of the other Keepers, aside from Liv, knew what was going on.

Then, he'd been staring up there when she fucking saw him.

Awesome. Just awesome. Busted, staring into her window like a peeping tom or some shit.

"Hey."

He turned and spun, reaching for his gun at the same time. Of course he was prepared to fight. Sitting outside of a place that housed a hell of a lot of Keepers was not a place that he was going to go unarmed.

Before he could even draw his weapon his eyes met with Lucy's.

"What the fuck are you doing out here? Go inside!"

She lifted her chin. "What the fuck are *you* doing out here? This is my property and you are the trespasser."

He turned and backed off into the trees a bit more. "God dammit, Lucy! You're lucky it's only me out here."

His red haired Keeper was not about to back down. "Every time I see you, you tell me that I need to be careful and stay safe and all that other bullshit, but did it ever occur to you that maybe I'm worried about your safety as well."

Uh, no. "This isn't about me."

She waved him off. "Yeah, yeah, I'm the Chosen One … blah, blah, blah. Well it isn't about just me. Now it's about us. I don't want my family to kill you just as much as you don't want your buddy to kill me. So fucking deal with it. If you're going to be running around out in my yard I am going to come out and talk to you."

"Not a good idea."

"Says you."

Their eyes were locked in challenge. "And I know what I'm talking about. Go home, Lucy."

"And, you know," she continued "it's kind of stalkerish that you're out here lurking about in the woods outside my house too."

"You know why I'm here."

She nodded. "Yes, I do, but that doesn't mean it's not creepy."

Shit. It was creepy. "Sorry," was all that he could think to say.

"No need to be sorry, just stop trying to feed me this bullshit about keeping me safe when you're putting yourself at risk too."

He hadn't really thought about it that way. All he knew was that he had to make sure that she was all right. He didn't care about himself. The fact that someone else might was not factored in.

"So who's the guy?"

She didn't pretend to be surprised. "That's my best friend."

"Ah, well, that's a pretty good benefit for being friends." He broke a small branch off one of the trees and fiddled with it.

"Shut up, he's like a brother."

Jack smiled, unable to keep his expression serious. "Yeah, that doesn't make it better."

"Dammit, you know what I mean." She threw her hands up in frustration. "It's nothing."

He picked some of the little leaves off of the branch

and dropped them absent-mindedly to the floor of the woods. "I'm so happy to see how you view that sort of thing."

Jack could not believe what was coming out of his mouth. What was he, sixteen? And to top it off, he'd slept with several women in town already and he was giving her a lecture on kissing her best friend.

"You sound jealous?" she countered, her eyes wide and questioning.

He tossed the whole branch down to the ground. "Of course I'm jealous. I told you what was going on with me. I told you how these feelings were fucking me up! I don't want to see another man touch you ever again, regardless of if it's to hurt you or to fuck you, it's all the same to me."

He expected her to realize just how fucking nuts he was and get the hell away from him. To his surprise, her reaction was completely the opposite. Her eyes softened and she came toward him so that there was only about a foot of space between them. "I was trying to see if kissing him would get you out of my head," she admitted.

He had been ready to tell her that he didn't want to hear any more about it, but her last words stopped him. "You wh … did it work?"

She shook her head, her red hair swaying with the movement. "No, it made it worse."

"Worse?"

"It only made me feel bad for using him. I realize that, even though the only time you and I kissed, you were trying to prove a point … but, it was still a kiss that felt like it was meant to be … it was perfect in every way."

Stonewalled. He couldn't find the words to respond, mostly because he felt the same way.

She continued since he stayed silent. "So, there are a few things I want to know. One, do you believe that people are meant to be together? Like … um … soul mates or fated partners? Second, if this," she gestured to herself and to him, "doesn't go away and space doesn't get rid of it, what will we do?"

He closed his eyes, trying to picture a life without Lucy in it. Not that she was in it to begin with. He barely knew her, and had only spent moments with her, yet it wrenched his heart to even think of never seeing her again.

When he opened his eyes, his gaze locked with hers. "No, I have never believed that every person had someone who was meant for them. And for the second question, we will cross that bridge when we come to it."

"Jack, that bridge is right in front of us."

She was right. He leaned against a tree and wiped his hand across his forehead. God, it was fucking hot outside. He couldn't wait to get out of the heat and into some air conditioning. "I know."

Lucy pushed twigs and rocks around in the dirt with her toe. "This is weird, and I feel like a dumbass even saying this, but maybe you should think about leaving now."

He totally should. Yup, pack his shit and go. "I can't. It wouldn't feel right until we take care of the guy who's after you."

"We talked about this before. If the one who attacked me is taken out, the Empress of the Reapers will only send another and another after that. She won't quit until I am gone. It's not going to stop, Jack."

"I am not just going to leave you here to die. I won't do that."

"But, *you* came here to kill me."

He felt his heart speed up a few beats. "Things have changed. If anyone else even comes close to you now, it will be them who dies."

"It's time to try and end this, Jack. I can't concentrate on anything but you, and that's not good."

She wanted him to leave and he knew that he should, but damn if it wasn't harder than he expected to actually do it. "Is this what you really want?"

187

For a moment she only stood there staring into his eyes and then she offered him a slight nod. "Yes. It is."

"Well, if that is the way you want it, then I'll be gone in the morning." Even as he said the words it felt so wrong. For one, he never gave in when there was something he wanted and for two, he had never felt so much emotion for a woman and now he was just going to leave her to die. But, it was what she wanted and she needed to focus on keeping herself safe.

"It has to be this way. Both of us keep putting ourselves at risk in the name of the other, and that is what is going to get us killed."

He turned away from her and looked off into the woods. "I said I would be gone by morning." He knew that he sounded angry and didn't care.

"We both know this is the right thing to do."

"Yeah, I know, but it doesn't *feel* right."

An awkward silence filled the space between them. "I'm sorry," Lucy blurted, like she had to say something … anything to rid them of the silence.

Jack tilted his head wondering why the hell she was apologizing. "Why?"

"I don't know."

"You don't need to be sorry," he told her in a low voice. "You should probably go back inside though."

She was still pushing the debris around with the tip of her shoe. "Yeah, probably."

There it was again, the awkward silence. "It …" she began and then paused, "I want to tell you it was nice to meet you, but it hasn't been exactly the most awesome of meetings. But, I feel like you deserve more than a 'cool, I'll see ya later.' You know?"

"Yeah, I know exactly what you mean," he told her. He did, indeed, understand what she was talking about because he felt the same way. Knowing that she was going to walk away, and he was going to go pack his things and leave town, seemed impossible.

She gave him a little smile and turned toward the opening in the trees. "I'd better get back before someone notices that I'm gone. Jack, it has not been a pleasure meeting you, but I am glad that I know not every Reaper is the heartless being that we have always thought they were."

But he was, before he met Lucy, he was heartless. She didn't know what she was talking about. "I'm happy to hear that," he told her coldly. "I can't say I've been exactly thrilled with our unexpected situation either, but it sure has been a learning experience, if anything."

Lucy nodded, her eyes never straying from his. "Well ... goodbye ... Jack." Then, she turned and stepped toward the opening of the trees.

No, no, no. There was no way it was ending like this. "Fuck it." He lunged forward and grabbed her arm, turning her quickly so that she was facing him. Then, his arm snaked around her, crushing her body to his. Without giving her anytime to resist, he lowered his head until his lips found hers.

She responded immediately, her lips parting to let his tongue urgently meet with hers. She let out a soft moan and her arms went around his neck.

He didn't know how long they kissed, but he could have stayed like that forever. Even with the heat and the danger all around them, he didn't care, she was fucking perfect.

She was first to come up for air, pulling away and taking a deep breath.

"Was that the type of goodbye you were looking for?" he teased as he stared down into her dark brown eyes.

She smiled. "Something like that."

They still had their arms around each other, both unwilling to release the other.

"I'm sorry," he told her. "I couldn't let you go without doing that."

She shook her head so vigorously that her hair swayed around her shoulders. "Don't be sorry. *Never* be sorry for that. That was the most epic kiss I have ever had in my life."

A perfect goodbye, he thought.

"All right, then I'm not sorry." He leaned down and nipped at her lip. "But you really need to go inside now."

"I know," she whispered. But, instead of pulling away, she stood on her tiptoes and touched her lips to his again. The kiss was slow, less urgent than before. The kind of kiss that built up until they were both panting with desire for each other when they parted.

"Lucy," he gasped and then pulled away quicker than he would have liked.

"What's wrong?"

"Nothing … nothing is wrong at all." Yeah, nothing except that he was getting a fucking hard on. "It's pretty much exactly the opposite of wrong."

"God dammit!" She cursed and spun around. She looked out in the direction of her house while Jack stared at her back and tried to get his lower half to calm the fuck down. When she turned back to him, his heart sunk. Her eyes had welled with tears which were escaping from the corners and sliding down her cheeks. "I have to go, Jack. I … I have to go."

"Lucy!" He stepped forward to stop her. She had anticipated this and moved backward, out of his reach.

"Thank you … thank you … for this." She wiped her cheek, then spun on her toes and ran.

"Lucy, wait!" he followed her to the edge of the trees and then stopped abruptly before he stepped out into the open, he couldn't go chasing her across the yard to her house. So, instead, he watched her run aimlessly across the yard until she disappeared from his sight.

That was probably the last time he would see her, and he was stuck with the image of her running from him in tears.

"Mother fucker!" He charged forward and kicked an innocent tree. "Dammit!" He took a deep breath and tried to calm down. Hitting and kicking shit, like a two year old throwing a fit because he didn't get what he wanted, wasn't going to help matters any.

Breathe in … breathe out.

Lather, rinse, repeat.

All right. Now, he needed to get the hell out of the heat before he passed the fuck out. His truck was parked down near the bridge, so he jogged most of the way back to it, even though he felt like he was on the brink of heat stroke.

Once he got to the truck, he fired it up and headed back to the house.

He could not wait to pack up and get out of this hell hole of a town that had managed to ruin his life in a matter of days.

AIDEN
20

M
other fucker, Aiden thought as he crouched down in his own little section of the woods around the farmhouse. It was no wonder that Jack had saved that Keeper.

He had been scouting the area, hoping to see how many Keepers were in and out of the house, and whether the Chosen One was confined to house.

Yeah, there he was, minding his own business when he saw the young Keeper step out of the house, close the door softly behind her, and jog across the yard where she suddenly disappeared into the woods.

He was curious about what she was doing, but also thinking that maybe the whole kidnapping idea was going to be easier than he had originally thought it was going to be. As quietly as he could, he moved over the rough terrain until he could once again see the Keeper.

He spotted her red hair and the silver shimmering around her instantly. There was someone with her, though. Someone she had sneaked out of the house to meet in secret. It felt like it took forever until she finally moved to the side and he saw who it was.

"You son of a bitch," Aiden mumbled under his breath.

There was Jack, talking to that Keeper. He couldn't believe his eyes, and it wasn't because he was talking to the Keeper, probably warning her about the impending attack. It was the look in Jack's eyes.

He had known Jack a long time, and not once had he ever seen him look like he was in love. Not fucking once. He knew every expression the bastard had, and never had this particular one ever appeared.

He watched carefully, wondering what they could possibly be talking about, and then his mind managed to be blown for the second time in the same day when she turned to leave and Jack grabbed her, pulling her back and laying a romance novel kiss on her.

What. The. Fuck.

How in the hell were they kissing in the first place? That should hurt like a bastard. Neither of them appeared to feel the burn which should have been forcing them apart. No, the two of them looked like they were three seconds away from ripping off their clothes and going at it.

God, he really hoped they didn't do that.

Annnnnd they were still kissing. Shit, he was starting to feel uncomfortable watching them, like watching porn alone, hoping like hell that no one catches you. Yeah, it was that feeling.

Finally, they tore themselves away from each other. Well, for like two seconds, and then they were making out again.

What the hell was he going to do about Jack? Shit, it was one thing for him to be insubordinate to his mother, but this … this brought pissing off your mom to a whole new level.

The next thing he knew they were talking again, she turned away from him, looking in the direction of her house and then, before he knew it, she bolted. She ran over the expanse leading up to her house and then disappeared.

He should have followed her, to see where she went, but he couldn't take his eyes off his best friend. Jack stood there with his arm out, fingers reaching for the woman who was running from him.

He turned and kicked a tree, taking out his feelings on the forest. When he finally turned to give the farmhouse one last look, the only thing Aiden saw was what looked like the pieces of a broken heart reflecting in Jack's eyes.

"You have got to be kidding me." Aiden shook his head and scurried off further into the woods where he wouldn't be seen. Jack was taking a huge risk, standing around in the woods like that where people could see him. If Aiden could see him then the Keepers would be able to as well.

After he backed off into the woods a bit, he circled around until he could get a view on the farmhouse again. There she was. The little Keeper was standing up against the house by the side door. Sunlight glinted off the tears that stained her face and her hands were gripping her hair, like she wanted to rip it out.

Shit, whatever had just happened between her and Jack had to have been pretty serious, because they both looked pretty tore up about it.

Well, as much as it pained him to see Jack suffer, he had a job to do.

His eyes stayed with her as her sobbing ebbed and she took a few long, deep breaths. After she had finally calmed herself a bit, she gazed toward the graveyard. Slowly, she pushed herself off the wall and then headed that way.

He followed along with the cover of the trees which edged their entire property.

She stayed on the trails walking slowly and moving her gaze back and forth. "Dad, where are you?" he heard her call out. "Come on, I know you're here somewhere." She kept walking, trudging up the hill. "Please … Daddy, I need you."

"Lucy!" someone called out and her head swung toward the voice. Her expectant expression fell when she realized it wasn't her father. A red headed Keeper came running up the path. "Lucy, what the hell are you doing out here? No one knew where you were."

"I'm fine," she told him when he was close enough that she didn't have to yell. "I just want to talk to Dad … alone."

"Luce, you can't be out here by yourself."

She nodded. "I know, it's not safe." Her voice was mocking and she used air quotes to emphasize her irritation. "Dammit, Greg, I just want some fucking privacy. All right?"

He tilted his head and scrutinized her more closely. "You've been crying."

"Just go away."

"Why were you crying?"

"Greg! Go away … please."

"Lucy, what the hell is going on?"

She set her hands on her hips and looked up at him defiantly. "I am having some personal issues and I need some space."

For a moment, he said nothing. He merely looked her over as he appeared to be thinking about what the right decision was. "All right," he said finally. "I'll leave you alone but I'll be watching from the house."

A shimmering blue mist appeared beside them. The molecules gathered, solidifying into the form of an old man in a Hawaiian button up shirt and Khaki shorts. "I'll take care of her," the old man soul said.

Both Lucy and Greg quickly turned their heads toward the soul, who must have been their father.

"Dad!" Lucy's solemn expression perked up.

Her brother on the other hand wasn't quite so happy. "Dad, no offense but I don't think that you are quite equipped to take care of her if something were to happen."

Aiden watched with interest. Maybe this Keeper was the only one in the house besides the Chosen One. This would be the perfect time to take action. He could probably take both the brother and the sister, but no more. He might not have another opportunity if what he had heard was correct and they were keeping her pretty much prisoner in the house.

"I can take care of my own daughter, Jr.," the old man scolded his son sternly.

Greg shook his head. "Dad …"

"I know she needs to be watched, but give the girl some space. Just go over by the house or something."

Time to rock and roll. Aiden reached into his pocket and found his gloves. He slipped them on so that the burn wouldn't hinder him when he touched the Keepers, he would have that over them at least. Then, he pulled out his gun.

Normally, he preferred to be a bit more old-fashioned when fighting Keepers, but that was on his average soul hunts. This was an assignment that needed to be taken care of ASAP, and he couldn't risk losing in hand-to-hand combat.

For a moment he considered just shooting the brother, but then decided that would give Lucy time to run. He wasn't worried about the father. Souls didn't have enough ability to fight back. Plus, a gunshot would alert anyone around that something was up.

He raised his weapon and stepped out of his hiding place. "Don't move," he ordered, keeping his voice completely calm, while continuing to move toward them.

All three looked up in surprise and took their fighting stances, even the old man. He flashed the three Keepers his best lethal smile. "I don't know if you noticed, but I have a gun and I will fucking shoot you. So, don't even think about trying anything."

The older brother, idiot that he was, moved in front of the sister. "Greg!" she cried out.

By this time, Aiden was right in front of them and kicked out his weapon, then swung it hard. It connected with Greg's skull and the brother fell to the ground with a thud. Unconscious for now, he turned on the sister.

"If you're going to kill me, fucking do it already. Just

leave my family alone," she cried out and fell to the ground beside her brother.

"Lucy!" her father chastised her.

Aiden wanted this whole situation to be over, he was getting tired of chasing Keepers. "Shut up, both of you," he ordered then reached down with his free hand and grabbed Lucy by the hair. "You scream and I will shoot him, understand?"

Lucy choked back a sob and nodded that she understood.

"You too, old man," he warned as he dragged Lucy up into a standing position. He reached down into her jeans pocket and pulled out her phone, then threw it to the ground beside her brother.

"Don't hurt her," the father pleaded, "please."

"Yeah, not making any promises," Aiden told him.

"Let her go! There has to be something we can offer in exchange."

"I told you to shut your mouth." Aiden dropped Lucy and turned to the old man. Only an inch away from the shimmering soul, he opened his mouth and felt the surge of energy take him as the soul of the old man began to float toward him.

"Lucy," the old man moaned, unable to stop what was happening to him.

"Stop!" she cried out. "You can't have him." The next thing he knew, his feet were coming out from under him. She had grabbed one of his legs and pulled. The transfer of the soul halted and the old man's semi-solid form stumbled backward a few steps.

Aiden managed not to drop his gun, but Lucy was on top of him instantly. She pulled back her arm and then slammed her fist into his face. "You fucking bastard!

His cheekbone erupted in a spike of pain and metaphorical fire. She reared back and hit him again, but he blocked the third one and then remembered that his gun was in the other hand. He lifted it and rested the barrel against her midsection. "Get the fuck off me," he managed to say in a low voice.

"You are a cheat," she muttered, slowly sliding off of him.

"Careful now," he told her. "I don't like this gun any more than you do, if it makes you feel any better. But, I can't risk losing. Not this time." He once again grabbed her by the hair, wrapping it in his fist. Once they were in a standing position, he gave her a little yank. "It's time to go."

He glanced at the old man, whose expression was a cross between sadness and anger. Aiden actually felt bad for the guy for like five seconds. Poor guy was watching his daughter be kidnapped, and probably thought she was going to be killed, which she eventually would be if the Empress had anything to do with it.

"Lucy." The old man stretched his transparent hand out to his daughter.

"Dad. I'll be fine. Just tell the others what happened." She had begun to cry and wiped some of her tears away.

"Yeah," Aiden agreed sarcastically. "Tell the others, it won't do you any good though. It's over now."

With that, Aiden slammed the grip of his gun into the back of Lucy's head. Her weight slumped down in his hand, leaving her hanging from her hair where he had hold of it.

"You will be sorry," the old man hissed. "You are going to be so sorry that you have done this," he repeated.

Aiden turned and looked him straight in the eye. "It might surprise you, but I already am."

"Then why?"

"Orders, my man. Not that I owe you an explanation." He lifted the unconscious Lucy and threw her over his shoulder. "I hope to hell we never see each other again," Aiden told the old man, and then strode off into the woods with Lucy hanging over him.

"God dammit!" he heard the old man curse after he

was out of sight. "Greg! Wake up!"

Knowing that the son would be gaining consciousness pretty soon, he took off at a run. He needed to get out of there before they could give chase. The idea was to be on the road before the guy even woke up.

His SUV was parked on some deserted side road he'd found on the other side of the woods from the Keepers property. Well, he hoped it was deserted. He opened the back door and pulled out a set of handcuffs and some duct tape. He'd had to get the cuffs at a fucking sex store because he couldn't bring his own shit with him. Thank God the store had some hardcore stuff there, he didn't know what he'd have done if he had to restrain his kidnapping victim with handcuffs that had pink fur padding on them.

She moaned as he plopped her down into the back seat where he handcuffed her wrists together and then wrapped her ankles with the tape. She was in a sitting position and kept flopping forward and he kept pushing her back.

As soon as he finished taping her ankles together, her eyes popped wide open and she screamed so loud he wanted to cover his ears.

"Shut the fuck up!" He grabbed his gun from the floor of the SUV and pressed the barrel against her forehead. With one hand, he held the roll of tape to his mouth, and with a loud tearing noise he ripped off a good sized piece. "Guess I'm going to have to use this on your mouth too." He pressed the piece of tape onto her lips, and then removed the gun from its resting place on her forehead.

"Now, be a good girl and sit still." He slammed the door shut and rounded the vehicle to the driver seat.

In no time, they were flying over the mountain to where the Empress had told him to meet her with the Chosen One.

LUCY 21

She could only breathe through her nose, which was causing claustrophobia to set in. It took a lot of focus but she managed to take long slow breaths in and out to avoid panic.

She was sitting up in the back seat and could clearly see that they were going over the Saint Helena Mountain. What worried her most about this whole situation was that the Reaper who took her wasn't worried about her being able to see where she was going, which meant that he didn't expect her to be around to tell anyone about it.

Oh shit, she was totally fucked.

She eyeballed the Reaper who was driving. He had blond hair, she couldn't see his eyes, but she remembered from the attack that they were green. While he was driving, he dug around in his pocket until he came up with a phone. He hit a number on what must have been his speed dial and lifted the phone to his ear.

"Empress. Yes, I have her. Yes, she is alive. All right, okay. I look forward to the presence of your company." A long pause. "No, I haven't seen him. Yes, Empress. I look forward to your appearance."

Good God, he was taking her to the Empress of the

Reapers. Yeah, 'totally fucked' pretty much covered it.

She couldn't say anything with the tape over her mouth, and he didn't offer any conversation, so they drove in silence to wherever it was he was taking her. It was an odd feeling that came over her, as much as she hoped to get away from this alive, she really hoped that none of her family tried to rescue her.

It's not like they would be able to find her anyway and she would probably be dead by the time they did.

They had made it over the mountain and were entering the Napa Valley. She looked out across the expanse of vineyards. Wineries were set far back against the land and most had large homes built beside them.

Suddenly, she thought of how ironic it was that she had lived in the area her entire life and had not once gone wine tasting. There and then, she made a pact with herself. *If I get out of this alive, I am going wine tasting, dammit.*

After driving a little while longer, she felt the car slow to almost a stop and then take a turn. A look out the window told her that they were heading down a long, paved driveway that was lined with oaks on both sides.

They slowed again as the vehicle approached an iron gate. The Reaper stopped at the gate and rolled down the window so that he could enter a code into the little box with a keypad on it. Lucy watched everything as carefully as she could, just in case.

Once the code was properly entered, the gate rolled aside, opening the way to what appeared to be more paved driveway. It wasn't long, though, before they rolled into a circular driveway and were faced with a massive Victorian home. The lower half of the home was mostly gray stone from what she could see. Castle was the only word that Lucy felt could describe the second and third stories of the home.

The Reaper circled the gargantuan fountain, which was placed in the center of the drive, and came to a stop near the front entrance.

As he slid from the driver seat and came around the vehicle to get her out, the panic set in again. Shit, shit, shit! How in the hell was she going to get out of this?

The back door opened and he stared at her for a second before reaching down to heft her out of the car. "Come on, Chosen One, let's get this over with," he muttered.

Lucy couldn't help it, she wanted to tell him to fuck off, but the only thing that came through the heavy tape was a pathetic moan that made her sound like she was whining.

He threw her over his shoulder again and headed up the large set of stone stairs leading to the front doors. His shoulder dug into her stomach and both halves of her bounced off of his body.

She heard the door open before he could knock on it or ring a bell. "Good evening, Sir Aiden," a smooth voice greeted him.

"Evening," Aiden grunted under her weight.

"You will find the Empress in the sitting room. She is expecting you."

Aiden trudged forward. "Thanks man, which way is it."

"Oh, of course, I will take you there."

And then they were walking down a hall with hardwood flooring, then through a set of glass doors into a large room with the same kind of floors. She couldn't see much of the furniture from her view, but what she could see looked all antique.

"Here you are Sir. Would you be requiring anything else?"

Dang, guess it was no surprise to that guy to have someone show up at the door with a tied up girl draped over their shoulder.

"Nope, I'm good." Then he turned and managed to execute a small leaning bow. "Empress."

"Aiden. I'm so glad you're finally here."

Then she was going over. Aiden flipped her and

dumped her on a dark red velvet couch. Immediately, her eyes scanned the room until she found the woman who had been speaking.

She knew her eyes had to be wide with fear, because she was scared shitless, but she sure as hell wasn't going to show these fuckers just *how* scared.

The Empress had short dark hair and wicked cold, dark brown eyes. Something about her was familiar, but she couldn't quite place it. The woman was old, but she carried it well, and was most likely far older than she looked. She stood on the far end of the room by a set of glass doors that led out to a balcony.

Standing beside her was a young black girl who looked to be about the same age as Lucy. She wore a flowing burgundy skirt and a tight black tank top. The girl's hair fell down her back in loose ringlets. Those were the kind of curls that never stayed for more than five minutes when Lucy curled her straight-as-a-board hair.

"May I ask who your friend is?" Aiden questioned, caution thick in his voice. Why wouldn't it be, he just kidnapped someone. It's not like he wanted that shit on the front page of the paper anytime soon.

The Empress ripped her gaze away from Lucy and concentrated on Aiden. "This, is Emily, I will explain her presence shortly. You need not worry about her at the moment."

"With all due respect, Empress, I am worried when someone is involved in … matters which are to be kept under wraps."

The Empress waved her hand at Aiden in a dismissive manner. "Aiden, take the tape off the Keeper's mouth."

Realizing that the Empress had no intention of continuing that part of the conversation, Aiden reached down and took the corner of the tape then yanked it off so fast Lucy knew she wouldn't need to get her lip waxed for at least a year. "Mother fucker!" she cursed as soon as the tape was off. "Fuck!"

"Mind your manners," Aiden ordered.

"You kidnapped me you asshole, I don't have to mind shit!"

She looked at the Empress. "If you're going to kill me, just do it. Why the hell would you kidnap me instead of just offing me like he tried to do the first time." At least if they just killed her then her family would be safe. She knew better than to think that they would do nothing about her being taken.

The Empress sighed and strode across the room, her heels clicking prominently on the hard wood. "No one said we aren't going to kill you. Be patient."

The whole time Lucy and the Empress were bantering, Emily's face had gone from resting bitch face to really fucking worried. "Excuse me, but I didn't realize that all this was part of your intentions. I cannot be involved in such things."

The Reaper Empress turned her head, her eyes boring down into Emily's beautiful brown ones. "You have no choice, you *are* involved now and will not be allowed to leave the premises."

Emily didn't seem to care. Lucy watched her carefully take a step to the side. She wasn't the only one watching carefully, though, because Aiden side stepped as well. "Don't even think about it," he told her in one of the coldest voices she'd ever heard.

"This is not what my gift is for."

Camille cracked a smug smile. "It is now, darling."

Emily's face fell and she stepped back to where she had been, probably realizing that she would not be able to escape the grounds alive.

Lucy struggled against her bindings. "What do you want?"

The older woman sat down in a straight-back chair across from Lucy and crossed her legs. "You are the Chosen One, correct?"

"Apparently," Lucy spat.

"You see, the prophecy says that the Chosen One is descended from one of the seven original lines of

Keepers. What exactly is so special about you that you would be the one deemed worthy enough to 'bring forth an end to the Reapers?'

"There is nothing special about me, and frankly I don't give a fuck about this prophecy. All it has done is screw up my life."

The Empress closed her eyes and shook her head slightly. "First things first though." She stood up. "We are going to need a few samples from you."

"Samples?" What the hell kind of 'samples' could they possibly want from her.

The Empress went to a heavy wooden desk which was taking up space in one corner of the room. Lucy couldn't see what was on the desk, but she saw what she held up and began to squirm again.

"No fucking way!"

The Empress came back her way, holding up a syringe complete with a huge needle. "I am afraid that you don't have a choice, young Keeper."

"My name is Lucy, you bitch!"

The Empress merely smiled a thin, cold smile. "Well, since we are on a first name basis now, my name is Camille, Camille Walker."

Walker. Now why did that name set off alarms in her head?

"Now, we just need a little bit of blood. Aiden, hold her down."

No fucking way! Lucy tried to move off the couch. Maybe somehow she could roll to safety or something. What she ended up doing, though, was flopping around like a fish out of water.

"Leave her alone," Emily cried from the other side of the room.

The Empress glanced her way. "If you move an inch I will have you killed this very night. Understand?"

There was no answer, so Lucy assumed that Emily had nodded her response.

Aiden reached down, grasped her by both arms and hauled her up. He sat on the couch and pulled her into his lap, where he wrapped his legs around hers and held down her arms at the same time.

Lucy felt the tears on her cheeks and wished that she could wipe them away. She had failed so miserably with this whole Chosen One thing. "Why are you doing this?" She tilted her head up toward Aiden.

He didn't answer. He kept his face as emotionless as stone, just the way a henchman for his Empress should.

"Hold still, Lucy," Camille ordered as she approached, and then before Lucy could react, she felt the tightening of a tourniquet on her upper arm. "Please don't," Lucy pathetically tried again, but the Empress ignored her and a moment later, Lucy felt the slight prick of the needle sliding into one of her veins.

She closed her eyes and turned her head away. God dammit, what a violation. Not that she would compare it to rape or anything, but it pretty much was. They were taking something from her body without her permission and it made her feel dirty and disgusting.

"I hate you both," Lucy murmured with her eyes closed.

"You are mistaken if you think that I need or want you to like me." Camille's voice was icy cold. "There," she released the tourniquet on Lucy's arm, "that should do for now."

"Fuck off."

The Empress's hand struck out so fast that Lucy's head was forced far to the left. Lucy didn't scream, but she let out a long breath and tried to keep calm. She was sure she came pretty close to pulling an Exorcist move there for a minute.

"None of this is going to help you," Lucy hissed.

Aiden lifted her off of his lap set her aside and resumed his standing position like a good guard dog.

Camille rolled her eyes slightly, as if Lucy was the most ignorant person on earth. "Don't be so sure, Keeper. You have your prophecy, who is to say that we don't have our own?"

The Empress took the blood drawing equipment and the tube of blood over to the desk and set it on a silver tray. "This prophecy was given to me specifically, not passed down through the generations like yours has been." She returned to her chair and sat once again.

Lucy wished that they would take the tape off her legs. They were starting to feel a little numb from lack of movement.

"When I was a child," the Empress began, "I was already betrothed to the future Emperor. There are only three surviving royal families in Reaper society, and I was born into one of those families. I was the only female child my parents bore at the time, so I was the obvious choice to marry the Emperor.

"When I was twelve years old, still a young girl full of hopes and dreams, I begged my parents to take me to one of those county fairs that came around once every year. They denied my request, as that was not something that a future Empress of our people should be doing."

"Aw, so that's why you're such a bitch, you had shitty parents."

Aiden drew his knife from a sheath at his side. "Watch your mouth, Keeper."

Lucy rolled her eyes. "What? You gonna kill me? Please, get on with it or put your fucking knife away."

Aiden glared at her, but sheathed his knife anyway. "Shut up and let the Empress finish."

"By all means, continue," she slurred sarcastically.

"Of course, I thought they were awful parents for not allowing me to go run about and do anything remotely related to fun, so I went by myself. My mother and father didn't even notice I was gone, since I was mostly taken care of by one of our housemaids.

"The fair was more than I could have imagined. I had never been to a place where so many people were gathered together. I explored the little booths where people sold their crafts and goods, I watched boys play games to try and win a prize for their lady, and finally

I found myself in front of a fortune teller's tent."

She paused to take a sip of water from the small crystal glass on the table beside her. While she was telling the story, falling into her past, Lucy could almost feel for her. She knew it wouldn't last long. It was easier to think that this evil bitch didn't have any emotions.

"I don't know why I did it," the Empress continued, "but, I pushed the silk fabrics aside and stepped into the tent. There sat a beautiful woman. Just the kind you would imagine would be sitting there. She had long dark hair, large golden hoops in her ears, and wore the bright colored clothing of the stereotypical gypsy.

"She greeted me and offered me to sit down. I remember shaking my head, telling her no thank you. She asked me to please, sit down, and she would read my palms to find what my future held.

"Why not? I was at the fair for a reason. I'd wanted to see and experience what others my age did, so I sat down at the small table in front of her and held out my hands. Admittedly, I was excited to hear what she might say about my future, even though my future was basically written in stone since the day I was born.

"She reached out and took my young hands into hers. The moment our fingertips touched, she gasped and her eyes widened. 'What's this? You are a Reaper of Souls,' she had whispered urgently.

"I nodded and tried to pull my hands from hers. I needed to get out of there and fast. Even at my age, I knew that my identity was kept secret from normal humans. She held onto my hands even tighter though. 'Do not break the bond. I can see what is in store for you,' she warned me, but I did not care. I was frightened and knew I had to get home quickly.

"With one final yank, my hands were released from her grasp. I fell back onto the floor and she stood, towering over me. 'I see far into your life and must tell you this ... your blood will join with the enemy to stop

208

the warring with the guardians.'

"I could barely hear her last words calling after me as I scrambled up from the floor and hurried through the silk fabrics, almost twisting myself up in them in my haste. I ran all the way home and found our housemaid looking for me.

"I flew into her arms, so distraught and upset that I told her everything. She pulled me into her lap and rocked me until I had calmed. The whole time she was chanting a song, or what I thought was a song, and trailing her fingertips across my temple.

"After that, I remembered nothing of what happened. The memory had evaporated from my mind completely, as if it had never happened at all.

"This is where Emily comes in." She looked over her shoulder to the cowering woman against the wall. "While Aiden was sent on his mission to do away with you, I happened to come across Emily as I was coming out of the building my salon is located in. She stumbled in front of me and when she reached out to catch her fall, she grabbed my shoulder.

"Poor Emily was suddenly inundated with my lost memories. 'Your blood will join with the enemy to stop the warring with the guardians,' she'd cried out, right in the middle of the crowded sidewalk.

"I called her crazy. Obviously I realized that she knew of the Reapers and the Keepers through her reference to warring and guardians, but I was not about to have a discussion like that on the street.

"I ordered her to come with me, hoping that she would come willingly. My car was brought and we were allowed the privacy we needed. As soon as we were in the vehicle she looked to me with wonder and said. 'You do not remember do you?'

"I had no idea what she was talking about and told her so. 'Ma'am, someone has repressed some of your memories. They are hidden deep within your mind. When I touched you, I saw those lost moments.'

"Of course, I wanted to know how she could know

such a thing, and that is when she told me that she is a seer. A seer is not a witch of sorts, but they are more like an oracle who can catch glimpses of the future and the past. They can also, depending on the seer, manipulate the mind to an extent." The Empress raised her eyebrows. "Manipulation, meaning perform certain abilities, like memory repression ... and also bringing those memories back.

"Long story short, Emily is of the seer ancestry, as was the fortune teller, and also my housemaid. Emily has been able to detect the missing memory that my housemaid must have taken away."

The Empress rolled her eyes. "That woman must have decided to get rid of my experience to save herself from punishment, which she definitely would have endured for letting me go off by myself."

She chuckled softly. "Who knew that so many seers had been in my life and I didn't even know it." She sipped her water and then continued. "Emily here agreed to come with me and bring back my memories. I remembered it all. It came flooding back with every single emotion I had experienced at the age of twelve.

"Our young seer even agreed to stay and help convince you that what the fortune teller said was true, and hope you would offer your blood as a token for the cause, which is why she is here now."

Emily marched forward. "I didn't know that you were going to kidnap and probably kill someone." She waved her arm in Lucy's direction. "This is illegal ... and wrong, so very wrong."

The Empress ignored Emily's outburst and lifted her water glass to her lips again. "So, you see little Keeper, I've thought about this and realized that it will be something in my blood that ends this. However, there must be truth to your prophecy as well or it wouldn't have been passed down for so many generations.

"At first I was going to kill you, just get it over with, then Emily came along and now I am certain that perhaps our prophecies are one in the same. My blood will join with the enemies to end the warring. But, you" she pointed at Lucy "you are the Chosen One. I can't see the blood of any other Keeper being so special. Together, we will end this."

Oh God, she truly was a psycho. Lucy looked up at Aiden and found that he too had a very surprised look spread across his face.

"So let me get this straight. You want to mix our blood together?"

Camille nodded. "I have thought about this a lot over the last couple of days. The fortune teller was not a fake. She knew what I was, so I fully believe that she had foreseen the future."

Lucy squirmed against her bindings. "What will mixing our blood do?"

"I have no idea. That remains to be seen now, doesn't it?"

Lucy shook her head. "It ... it just seems like there should be more to it than a simple 'oh, let's mix this blood with that one.'

Once again, the Empress stood. "I agree. Which is why we are going to keep experimenting until we find out how exactly the blood needs to be joined."

Oh fuck. "So, I'm here for your own personal blood bank to experiment with?"

With a nod, the Empress stood. "Yes. Well ... until we figure it out and then we will dispose of you."

Lucy's heart began to pound again. She had felt a small inking of hope welling inside her when she heard the Empress say that the joined blood would stop the warring. She had hoped she could just dump off a bunch of blood and get the hell away from these people. "But ..."

Camille raised a thin eyebrow. "What, did you actually think that we would let you go after we attempted to murder you and then kidnapped you? No, this will be your last contribution to your people."

Holy shit.

"Aiden, take her to her room and watch her. I will

have another guard deliver Emily … since apparently she isn't so apt to help us now."

Lucy shot a scared look at Emily, who also looked terrified. She stood near the opposite wall, arms wrapped around herself, knowing that she had suddenly gotten into a very dangerous situation.

Looking back at the Empress she spoke in the best sarcastic voice she could muster. "Seriously, you mean you're not going to lock me up in a dungeon down in the cellar?"

Camille glared at her. "We don't have a dungeon, but if we did then that is where you would be. Watch your tone young lady. I have to deal with enough of that from my own son." She glanced at Aiden. "And *where* might my son be? Have you found him yet?"

Aiden took Lucy by the arm and looked her in the eye with his piercing green ones. "No, Empress, I have not been able to locate Jack yet."

Holy Mother of God.

Jack.

Jack Walker. That was why the last name rang a bell, the only time she had heard it was when she had asked Reese about Jack. She felt like her heart was going to explode.

Jack was the fucking Reaper prince.

JACK
22

He liked his little house. Too bad he was going to have to leave this place. He would find another one though, he was sure. There was no way that he was going to go back home to the mansion with his parents, that was for damn sure.

The really shitty part was that he was going to have to find a job. He'd never had to work before, so he didn't have any skills for a job that would pay him much. Hopefully he didn't end up working at Micky D's or some shit.

He was pretty much packed, since he had gathered up most of his things the day they attacked Lucy. Besides, he didn't have that much stuff to begin with. After throwing his bags in the truck, he went back into the house to close things up and give the place another once over.

All he had left to do was stop by Landry's house and drop off the rent money, and he wanted to swing by the bar to tell Reese that he was heading out of town for good. He probably had enough time to do that before it was totally dark. The sun had just fallen behind the hills, but it would still be light out for quite a while.

He was just opening the fridge door and bending

down to make sure he got everything when he heard the sound of a car. No, wait, more than one vehicle.

Oh shit.

He spun around and hurried to the kitchen window, which was on the same side of the house as the front door. He moved the curtain aside and peered through the glass.

Double shit. He saw Liv's green van, a white Escort and a truck coming to a stop in front of the house. Liv threw the van into park and bolted from the vehicle, nearly tripping as she headed for the porch.

He hurried to the front door and threw it wide. "What's wrong?" he asked her, not paying any attention to the Keepers who were assembling in a half circle around the porch. "Is it Lucy?"

"Is she here?" Liv demanded. "Please tell me your friend brought her here."

Jack shook his head. "No, she's not here. I haven't seen Aiden since the night of the attack." He was already pulling his keys from his pocket.

"He took her, Jack. Knocked Greg out, tried to reap my dad, and then kidnapped her ... Oh God."

Jack ran his gaze over the family of red headed Keepers and the blond guy, the one who Lucy claimed was her best friend, and then nodded his head their way. "Are they going to attack me?"

"Only if they feel like you're a threat. Shit, Jack ... I had to tell them everything so that they would let me come here and find you. Please, please tell me that you can do something to help us."

Every single one of the Keepers were glaring at him. He knew that not one of them trusted him and that was going to make it hard, but he was going to find Lucy and that was all there was to it.

He stepped forward and Liv moved aside as he continued down the stairs to face off with Lucy's family. "You guys going to let me help?"

The oldest brother, who had a bruise on his forehead, gave a slight nod, "We have no other choice." He kicked his chin out. "Besides, from what I hear, you would be out there looking for her anyway, so we may as well work together."

"Fucking right I will be," Jack agreed.

The Keepers all appeared willing to tolerate Jack helping as long as they found Lucy. That was the ultimate goal. The only two of them who looked like they wanted to rip his head off was the brother he had come across in the bar, and the best friend. Jack could only guess his reason for the death glares. Since Liv had told them all about Jack and Lucy, it made sense that this guy would be pissed.

"All right, quick intros so I don't have to keep thinking of you guys as 'the older red headed brother' and 'the blond one.'"

Liv appeared next to him again. "In line, that is Greg, Hannah, Daniel, James and Steph, and the 'blond one' is Ethan."

He memorized the names to the faces and then offered a lame wave. "Jackson Walker."

Hannah looked him over from head to toe, and then asked, "Do you know where they might have gone?"

Jack nodded. "Actually, I am pretty sure I know *exactly* where they went." He strode over to his truck and opened the door. "I'll meet you guys in the parking lot of the school. I have something I have to do before we go."

"What's more important than my sister? I thought you actually gave a fuck about her." Daniel sneered.

Jack turned, slowly, trying to keep his temper under control. "I do care about her. The *only* fuck I give at this point is about her. But, we are probably going to end up fighting tonight and I'm weak. I know you don't want to hear this, but I have to keep up a certain diet if I want to stay strong, and I haven't done that for quite a while."

Daniel strode up to Jack until they were practically nose to nose. "You stay the hell away from our graveyard."

James and Greg stepped forward, prepared to pull Daniel away from Jack if they had to. "I am too weak to fight other Reapers right now." Jack didn't back down, but he hated ever having to admit weakness. Fucking hated it.

"Those are our souls to guard. We can't just let you go in there and take them."

Jack stepped back away from the angry Keeper. "This is your sister, Daniel. I will do whatever it takes to find her and right now, that means souls."

Hannah stepped up and put a hand on Daniel's shoulder. "Dan, let him go. We need him to find Lucy."

Jack took another step away and then slid into the driver seat. "I'll meet you guys at the school, all right?"

None of them answered because they were all standing there staring at him, still conflicted between their life commitment of protecting souls and the life of their sister. Jack knew there was no contest there, but they were born, bred and trained to do whatever it took to protect the souls, so it was only natural for them to have inner turmoil about it.

"I have to do this," he told them in a soft voice. Believe me, I wouldn't if I didn't have to. But, I won't risk Lucy because I let myself get weak."

Liv waved him off. "Go, do what you have to do, but stay away from my dad. Clear?"

"Crystal."

Greg rubbed his face with his hands and his eyes met Jack's. Clearly, the brother was struggling with this decision. "You remember that this … this is a one-time thing. Our job is to protect those souls. But, this is our sister we are talking about and that changes the game."

"I assure you, I won't take more than I need. I don't want to have to do this at all."

Ethan turned away, looking like he wanted punch something. "Just hurry up," he snapped. "We need to move. Every minute lost is a minute she could die."

"I'll be fast." He gave the others a nod, and then

backed up and spun the truck around so that he could drive around the other vehicles in the driveway.

He drove through town at an excruciatingly slow speed. The last thing he wanted to do was get pulled over and waste any time. He had to get to the graveyard and then get to Lucy. The slow drive gave him time to crave the feeling of taking in a soul. As much as he hated being what he was, there was nothing better than Reaping a soul.

He made the turn into Lucy's driveway instead of parking on the road to the graveyard. His truck skidded to a stop, he threw it into park, and then opened the door in such a hurry he didn't even close the door before he was running across the expanse to the graveyard.

The only problem with this was that souls didn't just come out and say, 'Hey Reaper, here I am.' He had to sneak up on them or they would simply disappear before you had a chance to take hold.

Of course, this time was no different than any other. He didn't see a soul in sight as he ran up the path into the heart of the graveyard. Trying to calm himself, he found one of the benches and sat down. This was seriously the last thing he should be doing while Lucy was with Aiden. Time was not on his side here.

He thought about calling Aiden, but that might only tip him off that Jack was coming. They really needed the element of surprise on their side.

"Reaper."

He heard the voice behind him and swung around, ready to draw in the soul. But, as soon as he laid eyes on the soul, he stopped. It was an old man, the man he'd seen in the obituary. "Gregory Estmond?" he asked.

The old man nodded acknowledgment. "What are you doing here, Reaper?"

Jack offered him a weak smile. "Still guarding the souls, even though you are one, eh?"

"Always," Greg Sr. agreed with another brief nod,

217

after which he looked Jack over. "You're the one who saved my daughter from the other Reaper."

Jack's breeding to respect his elders came back quick. "Yes sir. And now she needs me to save her again."

"You know where to find her?"

"I think so, but I need to … um … refuel, if you know what I mean."

The old man wore a solemn expression and it did not waiver from his facial features. "I was there when Olivia explained what is happening and why you may be able to help. I won't claim to be completely on board with any of this, but my daughter's life is hanging in the balance. I can feel your energy and somehow I know you won't hurt her."

"No sir, I will do everything … anything, to bring her back to you."

Lucy's dad gave his nod of approval. "Then do what you have to do … just find her and bring her home safely."

"I will," Jack vowed as the old man's molecules separated and then disappeared into thin air.

Even with the final blessing from Gregory Estmond, he still hated that he had to do this in Lucy's graveyard. But, there was absolutely no time to go somewhere else.

Luckily, he didn't have to wait long.

He walked the path quietly, keeping his footsteps soft and light. Out of the corner of his eye he spotted the glittering blue of a soul. Heading in that direction he sped up until he was almost close enough to begin the transfer.

The soul was not solid yet. Its molecules were spread into thousands … or millions, of shimmering specks of blue. It had not detected him yet, so Jack approached quietly once again and lifted his arms so that his palms were up and directed at the soul.

He focused on the soul and pulled with his mind. When he was young and learning to take souls on his own, he had always thought of this part of the hunt as locking them into his tractor beams. Once they were locked in, they couldn't get away unless the Reaper broke the beam. Breaking the beam was usually when a Keeper would get to them because they were busy drawing the soul to them, but had not yet begun to reap.

All the particles of the soul floated toward him, swirling more rapidly with each passing second as the soul tried to fight back. It was useless for the soul to fight though. Once in the beam, they were pretty much a goner unless a Keeper was able to save them.

The shimmering mist of the soul gathered into the space between his hands, and then he opened his mouth and brought the soul close to his lips. Then, he breathed in deeply with both his mouth and his nose, letting the soul enter his body.

Oh God, why had he been putting this off? The immediate high ravaged through his body. He felt strong and alert and … and fucking immortal.

The transfer of the soul into himself didn't take very long. When it was over, he closed his eyes and pictured Lucy behind his lids. Then, he turned and took off at a dead run back to his truck. Time to get the fuck on the road so he could rescue his woman.

Well … she wasn't his woman. But, it felt like she was.

Once again, he forced himself to go the speed limit as he drove through town. He could see all the Keepers waiting for him as he pulled into the parking lot, just like they had arranged.

They were all out of their cars, leaning against them and talking. He came to a stop and jumped down from the vehicle.

Daniel was on his case before he could even get one word out. He sat on the hood of the Escort with his legs propped up on the bumper. "So, Reaper, are you ready now that you've had your fill of innocent souls."

"Shut up, Dan!" Steph moved over and punched him in the shoulder. "He's helping us, don't piss him off."

"Yeah, don't piss me off," Jack agreed. "Now, I only have one question before we take off." He paused dramatically. All the while the Keepers were waiting with expectant expressions on their faces. Finally he looked to Liv and Greg, "What kind of weapons do you have?"

It was James that answered though.

"What kind of weapons do we have?" With a smirk, the brother opened the driver door of the Escort and popped the hatch. Then he came around the back and lifted the hatchback. There, he reached in and removed a blanket that was strewn across the cargo area.

"You think this will do?"

Underneath the blanket there was a variety of knives, the crossbow Lucy had had the night of the attack, a few guns, two machetes and a crowbar.

He picked up the crowbar, tested its weight and looked over at James. "What's this for, you guys prepping for the zombie apocalypse?"

James reached over and grabbed the tool from him. "Greg just keeps that in the car in case he needs it. It's part of his tool kit. Geez man, we didn't pack a crowbar for a weapon." He threw the crowbar back into the pile and set the blanket back in place.

"Plus we have weapons on us," Hannah told him. "Can we go now?"

Jack nodded. He was just as anxious to find Lucy as the rest of them were. "Hell yeah, let's go get her."

JACK
23

They flew through the night at a speed which was probably way too fast for anyone to be traveling at. Jack had convinced Liv, Hannah and James to ride with him, while Ethan, Daniel and Steph followed in the Escort with Greg. They didn't bring Liv's van because it didn't do well on the turns going over the mountain. Taking them while speeding in a van was just asking for an accident.

"So, how do you know where they are?" Liv asked him. She was sitting in the back seat with Hannah but leaned between the seats to talk to them.

"My mother owns a small winery in Napa. It seems like that would be the most obvious place they would take her. The Reaper royals live in Florida now. I just can't see them traveling all that way with Lucy in a car … and they would have to take a car, since they wouldn't be able to get her on a plane."

"Um, why would your mother be involved in all of this?"

Damn, best just to tell them and get it out of the way. It was going to come out sooner or later anyway.

"My mother is the Reaper Empress," he announced, his voice void of any emotion.

Silence. Dead fucking silence.

Jack didn't let his eyes stray from the road, but felt all of their eyes boring into him. Talk about an uncomfortable situation.

James was the first to finally respond. "So … um … yeah, I've got nothing."

"Tell us more about what's going on with Lucy. We got most of it from Liv, but I want to know why you are risking so much to help her," Hannah asked.

God he wished he knew the answer to that.

"I don't really know what this is. It started when I first saw her and now it only gets worse each time I see her. I really wish I could explain it more, but I can't because I don't know. Lucy just told me that I should go, leave town and see if it fades as we get farther apart. That is just what I was doing when you guys came to find me."

"And you guys don't have the burn when you touch?"

Jack shook his head. "Nope."

"Incredible," Hannah muttered.

"What?"

James rolled his eyes and then explained. "Hannah went to med school. She is a medical examiner at the morgue, so she is fascinated with anything that has to do with the body or how it works."

"Oh, I see."

"Tell us more," Hannah urged.

"Look, all I really know is that I feel more for your sister than I ever have for anyone in my entire life. I wouldn't call it love or any shit like that, but when I'm not with her, I want to be. That guy who attacked her is my friend and I didn't even know Lucy, but when he went for her … I wanted to tear him apart."

"And Lucy feels the same?"

He nodded. "From what she has told me, yes. There are slight differences, like my instinct to protect her is not nearly as strong with her toward me. From what I can tell, she has more of a … sense of rightness when we are together."

"What will you guys do when this is over?"

Yup, just stare at the road and pretend that none of this was happening.

"Well, she asked me to leave, so if that is still what she wants, then that is what I will do."

He still refused to take his eyes off the road, but he could sense Hannah's gaze inspecting his expression. "What if she doesn't want you to leave after this?" she asked him in a soft voice.

He thought for a minute and then answered. "I have never been one to give a shit what anyone else thinks. If she wants me to stay I probably will, but unless you guys are all on board, it would only make our lives miserable. So, whatever she wants … that's what I do." He didn't want to hear what any of them had to say after that last part and, luckily, he didn't have to. They were rolling into Napa.

"We're almost there," he announced when they were close.

"Greg's car is still right behind us," Liv told him.

"Good."

It wasn't long before Jack found the turnoff onto a staff road beside the vineyard. The Escort turned and followed him until he came to a stop at a large metal building that served as a shop for the vineyard's heavy equipment. He cut the lights and the engine then jumped down from the driver seat. The others had just gotten out of the truck when the Escort came to a stop beside Jack's rig.

Once they were all there, Jack assembled them in a small circle and spoke in a low voice. "I guess I better get the full disclosure out of the way." He gave Liv, Hannah and James a knowing look.

Hannah nodded in agreement. "You need to tell them or they won't understand why you know so much."

Jack took a deep breath. This shit felt like a bad dream that just kept repeating itself. You know, the kind where you're naked in front of the whole school giving a speech. He took a deep breath and let it roll. "My mother is the Empress. I am next in line to lead when my father dies."

Again, the air was filled with a thick silence.

"You're serious?" Ethan asked, a 'what the fuck' look having completely taken over his face.

"Yes," Jack nodded, "I wouldn't make jokes about that. For one, I fucking hate my family and for two, I wasn't going back to them when I left Summer Hollow."

Greg stepped in. "Okay, there is nothing we can do about this right now. We just need to get Lucy and then we can hash all this out. Every minute that passes is another minute she is in danger."

"I agree." Jack ran his fingers through his hair. "All right, I can get onto the grounds and into the house from here. This isn't going to be as easy as it might sound because the place has cameras everywhere."

Greg nodded. "Just tell us what to do and we'll do it."

The others muttered their agreement, all anxious to go get their sister out of there.

"Okay, we are going to have to go on foot, cut through these grapes over here. See the house?" Collectively, they looked in the direction he was pointing. The lights from the main house were burning bright. There were also large light poles that were illuminating the grounds in front of the house.

"The grounds to the main house are surrounded by a brick wall. We are going to have to go over the wall from the backyard where the lights aren't as bright. If you stick with me, I will take you the path with the least cameras."

Dan rolled his eyes and leaned against the Escort. "How do you know how to get in and out of here without being seen?"

Annoyed, Jack glared at him and shrugged his shoulders. "My family has come here every summer for most of my life. I snuck out all the time and was never caught."

"Maybe they just didn't care." Dan returned the glare and then reached into his coat for his flask. Once he had it out, he took a long swig and then tucked it back into his pocket.

Well, that was a reasonable explanation, if you didn't know his mother. "That's possible, but unlikely that my mother wouldn't have punished me if she knew I'd done it.

"Now, once we are in the backyard, we are going to go into the side entrance that is mostly used by the staff. It will take us through a few bedrooms and then we will go into the main part of the house. Got it?"

A bunch of the Keepers nodded and a few muttered 'got it' in response.

"After we are in the main house, we will have to see what is happening in there before we can figure out where to go from there. Just watch for my signals."

Ethan stepped back and rubbed his fingers to his temple.

"Something wrong, Keeper?" Jack demanded.

"This just feels strange. I mean, we are following you right into the home of the Empress of the Reapers. What if we are walking right into a trap?"

Jack opened his mouth to make some smartass remark, but Greg beat him to it. "Then we still have no choice. Trap or not, Lucy is in there and we are going in to get her." He gave Jack a pointed look. "We will just have to trust that he is telling the truth."

Ethan only looked more pissed off. "We were taught never to trust a Reaper."

"Well get over it," Greg snapped. "We have also never had one of our lives hanging in the balance."

With a nod, Jack clapped his hands together. "You guys ready to do this."

Everyone agreed and then headed to the cars to get ready. Each of them donned a hoodie and some gloves to conceal their auras.

Then, they all strapped down with weapons. Jack

had a gun, but he also chose one of the knives that the Keepers had in the Escort. He needed something silver that could damage, but not kill, a Reaper.

The Keepers, on the other hand, already had a crap ton of knives on their bodies. Greg, Liv and Ethan selected guns, checking the clips to make sure they had bullets in them. As Jack watched the Keepers getting prepared, he desperately hoped that no one had to fire a weapon.

The least amount of death possible would be the best turnout for this infiltration. He also mentally prepared himself because he knew that he would see his mother in there, and probably Aiden too.

He was going to have to fight them … for Lucy, who was a Keeper.

Now that was definitely a situation he never thought would happen in his lifetime.

Once the Keepers were ready he led them into the vineyard. They ran, crouched over so that the long rows of grapes concealed their presence, following Jack until they reached the brick wall that Jack had assured them would be there.

He beckoned the group to follow him and they hurried along the wall until they reached the spot where they needed to go over. "I'll go first," Jack whispered. "Then, send the girls over, you guys follow after them."

Jack didn't need any help getting over the wall. He had done it a hundred times before, so for him, it was like riding a bike. He backed up and charged the wall, grabbed the top, and then swung his entire body over.

Landing softly on the other side, he quickly scanned the area and found it clear. He also checked the area where he knew there to be cameras. Good, that point of the fence line was still the gap in the cameras view. He just hoped they hadn't added any since he'd last been here.

The girls came over the top, one by one, and then the guys followed, each landing on the soft grass with ease. Thank goodness these Keepers were all in shape or he would have had a hell of a time trying to get them all over the top of that wall, even if it was only six feet high.

He put a finger to his lips, warning them to keep silent, and then signaled for them to follow him again.

They sprinted across the lawn at exactly the right moment between the movements of the cameras and gathered by the back door.

Before he opened the door, Jack closed his eyes and took a deep breath. This was fucking hard for him. It seemed so wrong. He was a traitor ... but, on the other hand he was saving Lucy, the woman who had somehow become his everything.

Beside the door, there was a keypad that required a code to be entered. Jack reached over and entered the numbers of his birthday and then gently turned the knob until he heard it click. Sweet, his code still worked.

He turned and waved his hand in a 'come on' manner. The group of Keepers followed, each of them moving silently over the hardwood hallways of the massive home. So far, the house was quiet and they hadn't come across anyone yet, but Jack knew that wouldn't last long. His mother always traveled with an entire entourage, and there were several staff members who lived at the home year round.

The hallway ended and opened up into a wide crossroad. The options would take them right, left or up. Jack had just begun to lead them up the staircase when they heard footsteps thundering toward them.

"Oh fuck." Jack turned, preparing to fight. He wasn't ready to draw his knife yet because he was hoping he wouldn't have to use it at all.

All the Keepers were staring in the direction the Reapers were coming from, but James looked to Jack. "You think she's up there?"

"I don't know, but we should search there."

James nodded. "Then you go, we will handle it

down here."

Just as he finished the sentence, four Reapers appeared in the hallway. He didn't recognize them, but he knew they were part of his mother's guard because they were all dressed alike in black jeans and matching tee shirts. "Stop right there!" one of the Reapers called out.

The Keepers weren't about to heed the warning, they were ready to fight. Greg drew his knife and took his fighting stance. "Jack, go! We got this."

Ethan had unsheathed his dagger, but he looked to the Reapers, and then to Jack. "I'm going with him," he told the others.

With a nod, Greg surged into the fray. "Go!" he called out, as he blocked a punch and swiped one of the Reaper's arms with his knife. The injured Reaper grunted and spun, throwing his weight at Greg.

"We got it!" Hannah shouted. "Just get going!"

He felt strange just leaving the Keepers down there to fight, but he also didn't want to waste a second while they were keeping the guards occupied.

They hit the landing and Jack bolted down the hallway until they reached some doorways. He began opening each door to check the interior. "Check that side," he ordered, pointing to the doors on the other side of the hallway. Ethan did as asked without giving him any flack. Thank God. The last thing he needed was to be trading snarky remarks back and forth with a jealous, wannabe lover.

Nothing. Nothing. Nothing.

They rounded the corner leading into another wing of the house and found a tall Reaper just closing one of the doors behind him. "What the fu…"

He didn't have time to finish his sentence because Jack careened forward, cocking back his arm and then slammed his fist into the guy's cheekbone. Before the guard could react, Jack hit him again with his left, a hard uppercut to the stomach which caused him to stumble backward and trip over his own feet.

Moving fast, he peeked inside the door the guy had just come out of and found nothing but a tousled bed and some clothes on the floor. "Let's go," he muttered. "She has to be around here somewhere."

"Hold on." Ethan stooped beside the injured guard, who was picking himself up off the ground, and clocked him in the face, nailing the exact same area where Jack had hit him. The guy went down without any more fight. "Pansy," Ethan spat at the guard. Then, bending down, he plunged his dagger into the Reapers muscular shoulder.

With a shout, the injured Reaper cursed and kicked his foot out. "Fucking silver." The guy swung at Ethan with his uninjured arm.

Ethan pulled the dagger out and casually wiped the blood on the guard's jeans, then looked up at Jack. "Your mom needs to get some better guards. These guys suck."

Jack nodded, completely in agreement. But, they hadn't come across Aiden yet, whom he knew could be lethal if he wanted to be. "Let's move."

They took off down the hallway, continuing their room checks. Again, they found each of the rooms empty, with perfectly made beds and meticulously dusted furniture inside to greet them.

The last door before they came to another turn in the hallway surprised them. Ethan opened the door quickly, expecting to find nothing, just like in all the other rooms. But, when he swung the door wide, he found a Reaper with dark hair and dark eyes standing there in his boxer briefs. He was bent slightly, reaching to put his black uniform jeans on. "Hey! Get the hell out of ... oh shit." The Reaper tossed his jeans aside and headed toward them.

"I got this one," Ethan told Jack as he moved into the room. "You keep checking. We're running out of time."

"No man, I'll stay and help," Jack told him. The last thing he needed was for him to get his ass kicked, or worse, and the family to blame him for it. That wouldn't get him very far with the whole trust issue.

"You made a big mistake," the Reaper growled at Ethan, and then swung at him. Ethan leaned back, dodging the Reaper's extra-large fist. Then he returned fire on him, nailing his cheekbone with his left, and then scaling his knife down the guy's bare arm. "Dude, I've got it," Ethan shouted at Jack. "Just go find her. You know this place better than any of us."

Jack threw his arms up. "Fine!" And turned to go, yelling "be careful" to the Keeper that he knew Lucy would be devastated to lose.

He bolted out the door, back into the hall, and began his room checks again. Finally, he rounded another corner and the hall opened up into a sitting room at the end of the wing. There, standing before one last door, was the one person he had been hoping he wouldn't have to fight.

Jack slowed to a walk. "Aiden."

"Jack, there you are," Aiden greeted him nonchalantly, as if nothing was amiss at all. "You're mother has been driving me crazy asking about you."

"Where is she?" Jack demanded.

Aiden somehow managed to look confused. "Your mom? She's downstairs thinking up ways to make your life miserable."

Jack stopped, leaving the sofa between him and Aiden. "You know exactly who I'm talking about."

"I assure you, I do not," Aiden insisted.

Jack gestured toward the door his friend guarded. "Then you won't mind if I go in there and check it out."

"Sorry man, but no."

"Aiden, I am going in that room. You can try to stop me, but it would be a lot easier if you just let me pass."

Aiden lifted an eyebrow and stepped forward. "I have orders not to let anyone in … or out. I'm sorry, Jack."

Son of a bitch. Aiden was actually going to choose

his mother, and her damn Reaper duties, over him. Jack flexed his fists and pushed up the sleeves of his hoodie.

"Jack, don't do this. You know that I'm gonna whip your ass if you fight me."

It was true that Aiden and Jack were never equally matched as fighters. Aiden always won ... always. But, this time was different. This time he was fighting *for* something. Jack shook his head. "No, not this time."

He saw sadness filter into his friend's green eyes. "All right, if that's the way you want it."

"I don't want it to be this way, but it has to be if you aren't going to let me go in there and get her."

"Dammit, Jack."

Jack took the moment of sympathy and surged forward. He went low, knowing that Aiden would expect him to go for the face.

Aiden, taken by surprise, grunted when Jack's fist slammed into his lower stomach, followed by an uppercut which cracked his chin. "Fuck!" Aiden staggered back a step. The element of surprise didn't last long. Aiden lunged, grabbing Jack by the front of his hoodie and turning him so that he could slam him up against the door.

Jack was pinned, getting ready to retaliate when something slammed into the other side of the door, near his head. Then, someone's fist was pounding against the hard wood that separated them. "Jack!" he heard Lucy's voice through the door.

That was all it took to spur him into action. With one fist he hit Aiden in the side while pushing him away from him with the other. He felt Aiden's fist land on his temple. Things got a little fuzzy for a few seconds, but he came back quickly.

The next few moments were a blur of fists and muscle, grunts and shouts, all while Lucy continued to pound on the door.

Finally, Jack bent low and swept his leg out, tumbling Aiden to the floor. Instantly he had his knife drawn and poised above Aiden's heart.

Aiden stared up at him, the feeling of betrayal clear in his expression. "You wouldn't."

He hated this, he hated every fucking moment of it. "I have to," Jack told him and then plunged the knife down. At the last second he changed his trajectory and shifted to the side, causing the large, silver blade to sink down into Aiden's shoulder.

Aiden's eyes went wide. "You son of a bitch. I am going to make you pay for this. God, Jack … fucking asshole."

Jack ignored him and bolted for the door. It was locked of course, so he turned around and kicked Aiden. "Where's the key."

"Fuck you!" Aiden groaned and tried to get up. Jack kicked him again and then bent down, searching his pockets. It didn't take long. He found the key in the front pocket of Aiden's jeans and had it in the lock of the door only seconds later.

"Jack," Lucy pounded on the door again, "hurry!"

Ethan ran into the room just as the door swung wide and Lucy came careening out … straight into his arms.

LUCY 24

S he heard the lock click, the thick wooden door opened and there he was. He was panting and sweaty, his dark hair strewn every which way and his eyes hardened by the fight with his fellow Reaper.

As she ran to him, calling his name, she watched those very same eyes fill with relief to see her. "Jack!" She flung herself against him. Her arms went around his neck and he grabbed her legs, hauling her up so that she could wrap them around his waist.

The tears she had been trying to hold back finally spilled over, sliding down her cheeks in celebration of the rescue that she hadn't known would happen. "I'm so sorry," she whispered, bending down to kiss him.

"What are you sorry for?" he asked when their lips separated, his voice low and husky.

She planted another short kiss on him. "I lied." And yet another kiss, God, she couldn't get enough. Never in her life had she been so happy to see someone. As soon as she'd told him that he should leave and ran away from him, the regret had hit her like a brick in the face.

He tilted his head and pressed his lips to hers. "What? You lied about what?"

"I don't want you to leave. I never wanted you to

leave."

He pulled her closer against him, as if that were even possible. "Then I'm staying."

Instead of the tears getting better, they got worse. "I'm sorry," she sobbed, wiping the tears away.

"Never be sorry for this," he told her, repeating what she had told him in the woods earlier in the day. Damn, had it really been only a day? It seemed like days ago that she had told him to go and they had been saying goodbye.

Even in the post kidnapping fog she was in, she knew they needed to get the hell out of there. But, still, she took a moment to rest her forehead against his. "Thank you for coming for me."

"There was no fucking way I wouldn't have come for you."

Just then she heard a familiar ... and irritated voice. "Excuse me, I hate to break this up, but, we have to get moving."

Lucy swung her head toward the intrusion. "Ethan! Oh, my God. What the hell are you doing here?" Guilt sliced through her as her eyes met with his and she saw the hurt lingering behind the piercing blue irises.

Ethan's gaze ran over the two of them. She could only imagine what was going through his head. Here she was, clinging to a Reaper, of all people, and sobbing like a baby.

Beside them, a groan and a muffled, "fuck you, mother fuckers," came from Aiden. Lucy ripped her gaze away from Ethan to see what kind of condition her captor was in. She had completely forgotten about him, or anything else around them. When that door had opened and she saw Jack on the other side, her world had suddenly become all about him once again.

"Let's go," Ethan growled. "We need to check on the others. Don't worry about him," he gestured to Aiden, "he won't be getting up for a little while."

"Yeah, we have to go help the others." Jack loosened his grip on her, letting her slide down his body until

234

her feet touched the ground. She knew it was not the place or time, but she could have stayed like that forever. "Can you walk?" he asked her.

"Yes." She nodded. "Nobody hurt me."

His eyes narrowed, as if the mere thought of someone harming her would trigger his wrath.

Oh shit. Suddenly she realized what Ethan and Jack had just said. "The others ... you mean my family is down there fighting Reapers?"

Both men nodded.

"Well let's go. Dammit, why didn't you guys say so?" She bolted for the door and then slowed. "Jack, I don't know where the hell I'm going."

She let him move into the lead and the three of them took off.

Oh, dammit ... Emily. She'd forgotten about her. "Hey, they have another prisoner here somewhere. We have to get her out too."

"Are you kidding me?" Ethan asked incredulously. "Who else would the Reaper Empress want to lock up?"

Lucy had stopped and was trying to decide if they should go back the way they came or continue forward.. "It's a long story and we don't have time. I'll explain later. Let's just find her."

"Well we already checked all the rooms that way, so let's continue on and check as we go." Jack gestured for them to keep going.

"Sounds like a plan," Lucy agreed and off they went. She hadn't realized before because she was so pissed, but the house was gargantuan. After a shit ton of turning corners, room checks, and fighting two Reapers, they finally came across another Reaper guarding a room. He saw them coming and took his fighting stance.

Jack broke away from the group and strode forward, drawing out his gun at the same moment. "I really, really don't have time for bullshit. Do you have a woman in there?"

The Reaper guard shook his head. "Like I would tell you. This is not your business, and why would a Reaper be hangin' around with Keepers anyway?"

Jack didn't fuck around. He fired his gun and shot the dude in the foot. The Reaper screamed and toppled to the side. Jack sighed a little. "I really didn't want to have to shoot anyone today, but I told you I didn't have time to fuck around." Then, Jack's hotness factor went up about ninety percent when he kicked the door, efficiently busting it open just like the heroes in the movies. "Cheap ass doors," he muttered.

Putting aside her admiration for Jack's hero skills, Lucy bolted into the room spun in a circle, calling out. "Emily! Emily, are you in here?"

At first she heard nothing and then she saw movement out of the corner of her eye. She turned her head and found Emily had opened the bathroom door just enough to peek out.

"Lucy?"

"Yes!" Lucy let out a relieved breath. "Come on, we're getting out of here."

"But …"

Lucy cut her off. "No buts, let go!" She waved her arms to emphasize the need to hurry.

The Seer caught sight of Jack and shrunk back into the bathroom again. Lucy realized why she was shying away … she could see the auras. She could see that Jack was a Reaper and didn't want to go with them.

"No, Emily, it's all right. He's on our side."

No luck. Emily stayed put on the other side of the door. Not wanting to waste any more time, Lucy took matters into her own hands and marched forward, shoving open the bathroom door. "Emily!"

The girl's eyes widened with fear and she held her hands up in front of her. "No! I can't go with one of them," she cried out.

Lucy swung her hand and gestured to Jack who, surprisingly, was letting Lucy handle everything. She didn't think his patience was going to last long though. Ethan's either. "Do you really think I would be hanging around 'one of them' if I didn't know he could be trusted?"

The Seer's face shifted from fear to confusion. "I assure you, he's on our side, but we need to get out of here. Now!"

Emily stepped forward and then appeared to hesitate. "Trust me," Lucy told her, holding her hand out as invitation.

Then, the Seer seemed to snap out of her fog of fear and realized that this was probably her only chance to escape. She nodded, a quick movement of the head, and hurried toward Lucy. "Okay, I'm okay. Let's go."

Lucy felt so bad for her, being pulled into all this by the Empress. The Seer seemed to be going through some form of shock. With good reason though. Being tricked into doing something you didn't know anything about, and then suddenly finding yourself a captive, was enough to traumatize anyone.

"Jack, lead the way," Lucy ordered and soon they were back out in the hallway. The guy Jack had shot in the foot was gone, who knows where. It was only a minute later and the small group pounded down a flight of fancy stairs which led into an entryway.

The amount of time it took to run from upstairs to downstairs seemed like freaking forever. The urge to get down there and help was so strong that she nearly tripped several times. It was because of her that they were all here, and she would never forgive herself if something were to happen to any of them.

Immediately, they heard the shouts of battle and headed that way.

The entryway led into a great room which was where the battle was taking place. Each of her brothers and sisters were engaged in combat with a Reaper. Everyone in the room, both Keeper and Reaper, were too busy to notice that the small group had entered. "Either of you have an extra knife?" she asked, holding her hand out.

Even though he only had the one, Jack unsheathed his knife and set it in her open palm.

"You good," she asked.

He nodded and withdrew his gun from its hiding place in the waistband of his jeans.

She looked to Emily and whispered, "I need you to go hide over there until this is over."

The Seer nodded. She was staring at the room full of Keepers and Reapers battling for the win with her eyes wide and her mouth hanging open.

"Emily, go!" Lucy told her with more urgency in her voice. This finally spurred Emily into action and she hurried over to the corner of the room where there was far less action.

Whew. She thought she was going to have to drag her over there and shove her under a desk or something.

Switching her gaze to Ethan she questioned him with her eyes. He nodded in response, signaling that he was ready. "Take 'em out," she whispered and then careened forward into the midst of the fighting.

Lucy headed straight for a female Reaper that had Steph pinned to a wall. Steph was holding her own, for being pinned against a wall, but the sight of someone hurting her siblings made her furious. She was already pissed beyond belief because … well, because she had been kidnapped.

Time to suck it up and get on with it. Mentally, she prepared herself to kill if she had to, but also gave herself silent instructions only to incapacitate them, if possible. That was how they were trained as Keepers, not to kill unless you were forced to do it.

Suppressing a battle cry, Lucy skidded to a stop behind the Reaper and Steph's eyes went wide with shock and relief. Lucy swung the knife sideways and stuck the Reaper in the side.

A piercing scream erupted from the wounded lady Reaper. Lucy pulled the knife easily from her flesh and stepped back, letting her stagger backward away from Steph. Not missing a beat, Steph picked up her foot and planted it in the now bleeding midsection of the Reaper and pushed her even further away.

"Thanks!" Steph lunged toward Lucy and threw her arms around her.

Lucy returned the hug but then shoved her away. "No time. Let's help!"

With a nod, Steph hurried away to help someone else. Lucy looked for Ethan and Jack while she made her way over to Daniel, who had a Reaper on the ground and was beating the ever living pulp out of him.

She found Jack behind another one, holding him in a headlock while Hannah plunged her knife into his thigh. She yanked the knife out and then repeated the procedure with the other thigh.

Ethan went for the back of a Reaper with his daggers. This one had Liv's arm twisted behind her back and her knife had fallen to the floor beneath them. Ethan used his dagger just as Lucy had, straight into the side.

Confident that they were all right, she went for Dan. "Hey bro." Dan paused his pummeling and glanced up at the sound of her voice. "Thank God!" He picked himself up off the bleeding and unconscious Reaper and pulled Lucy to him. "Now we can get the hell out of here."

"Damn straight," Lucy agreed.

Dan looked around. By then, there was only one Reaper left up and fighting. Greg had just dropped one, and Jack jogged over to take out the one James was fist fighting with. The two danced around each other like they were in a boxing ring, until Jack arrived behind him and slammed the grip of his Glock into the back of the Reapers head. The guy dropped to the ground mid-swing, landing with an anticlimactic thud on the beautiful hardwood floor. Too bad that pretty floor was now stained with blood that would probably take forever to clean.

The Keepers, and Jack, stood among the fallen Reapers. All of them were breathing heavily and holding onto their weapons.

Lucy clutched her knife tightly in her hand, hoping to God she wouldn't have to use the thing again. "Let's get the hell out of here," she said, rather calmly, as she stepped over one of the bodies.

Everyone muttered their agreement, but before they could move another inch, the French doors on the opposite side of the room swung open and the Empress strode into the room.

Flanked by two Reaper guards, she entered with the confidence ... and bitchiness ... of a royal. She wore a scarlet business suit and sensible black heels that clicked over the hardwood floor. The dark haired Empress examined the room, with all the bleeding bodies of her guards and the toppled furniture, then looked up and caught the eye of her son. "No one is going anywhere."

With a quick glance to the side, Lucy checked to make sure that Emily was still in her hiding spot. She couldn't see her, so that was reassuring.

Jack stepped forward before Lucy or any of her family could respond. "You can't stop us." He paused and then added, "We won this time and now we are leaving."

Somehow that bitch managed to crank her thin lips up into half a smile. "Why, Jackson, you speak as though you are one of them."

He thrust his shoulders back and stared his mother down. "Tonight, I *am* one of them. You kidnapped her," he gestured to Lucy. "You tried to have her *murdered*. I don't want any of that in my life."

Aiden stumbled in behind the Empress, holding his bloody shoulder and squinting through his newly blackened eyes. He didn't say anything, but leaned on the door jamb beside one of the other guards.

Lucy saw the confusion in Aiden's green eyes and knew that he and Jack had been close. Even though Aiden had been her kidnapper and the one who tried to kill her, she felt the tiniest bit sorry for him. Tiny ...

like, really, really, really small.

The Empress thrust her chin out. "You have no choice but for this to be part of your life," she retorted.

"No, mother, I do have a choice." He pointed to Lucy again. "And I choose *her*."

Lucy could have fainted at that moment had she not been in a room full of Reapers and danger. He chose her. What did that really even mean? Her mind tried to spin the logic on it, but her heart felt like it was going to explode from happiness.

The Empress glared at Lucy, but spoke to Jack. "You appear to be forgetting one little thing here, you are a *Reaper*, you must have souls to live ... and Keepers won't let you have them."

Jack stepped forward and spoke very calmly. "I don't care." Then, his voice rose as if he wanted the entire world to hear him. "I renounce my title as the next Emperor. I renounce my heritage and I renounce *you*!"

"You wouldn't dare ... over a Keeper, our enemy?"

"You are no longer my mother," he declared coldly. Then he turned to Lucy and her family. "Let's get out of here." He slid his arm around Lucy to guide her out. Thank goodness too, because she wasn't sure she could move very far without help. She was so shocked she felt like a statue.

"Now," the Empress ordered. That is when everything went into slow motion. The Reaper guards who flanked her both reached behind them, and when their hands reappeared they had guns.

"Nooo!" Jack yelled and stepped in front of Lucy. In a feeble attempt to protect him, she pushed him out of the way and tried to move into a position in front of him. She had no idea what her brothers and sisters were doing because her eyes were on the Reapers with the guns.

Just as the guard on the left was pulling back the trigger, Aiden jumped from his spot against the wall and kicked the guy's hand. The gun fired above all

241

their heads and went flying into the air.

Everyone ducked to avoid being shot by the stray bullet. The other guard had probably had aim on one of them, but he missed because of Aiden's surprise attack. The bullet from his gun lodged into the wall to the right, behind the group of Keepers.

The Empress turned her head and glared at Aiden. "What is the matter with you? How dare you intervene?"

He clutched his shoulder again and bent over, growing weak from the silver. "I don't give a flying fuck about these Keepers, and you may not care if one of these idiots shoots your son, but I fucking do."

"You are going to be severely punished for this." The Empress scolded him in an icy voice.

"Do what you want with me. I know how valued I am to you. So go right ahead and punish me however you see fit."

Lucy almost wanted to crack up. Aiden standing up to her made her seem so much less of a threat than she actually was.

Again, Jack slid his arm around her waist to urge her out of the room. "Let's go. We're done here."

The Empress tried one last time. "Jackson ..."

"Shut it. We are leaving so don't follow us."

Taking his verbal cue, the entire group backed slowly out of the room toward the entryway where the front door was located.

Frustrated and angry for having lost the battle and her claim on the Chosen One, The Empress called out to them. "I want you all to know that this is not over. In fact, it just got much, much worse. Enjoy the little time you have left, because it's not going to last long. And Jackson, you've actually done me a favor. My days have been spent wondering what we are going to do when your father dies since you aren't competent enough to lead. Now that you've renounced the throne as well as your family, I don't have to worry about that. I can appoint it to whomever I feel is deserving of the job." With that, she spun around and retreated back into the room from which she had come, the guards shutting the doors behind her.

"Holy shit," Greg breathed. "Let's go, let's just fucking go."

"Hold on," Lucy whispered to her brother and then strode over to the corner of the room as quick as she could. "Emily, are you still down there?"

Instantly, Emily's head appeared from underneath the desk she had crammed herself into. "Yes," she answered in a whisper. "I'm here."

Lucy held out her hand for Emily to grip and helped pull her out. "Come on, we have to go right now."

Everyone in the group, except Ethan and Jack had confused expressions on their faces since they didn't know who Emily was. Lucy shook her head as she approached with Emily. "It's a long story. I'll explain later, but she needs out of here too."

Emily's big brown eyes were wide as she inspected each of the Keepers who were grouped together in the room. "Thank you, thank you so much," she whispered.

"Pleasure," James winked and held his hand out. "I'm James."

Good grief, was her brother really flirting with the Seer right here in the Empress's house? Greg, on the other hand, was just staring at her the whole time, even as she took James's hand and gripped it. Then he shook his head as if coming out of a dream. "I'm getting the hell out of here."

The group made for the front door, practically clogging it up as they all tried to get out at the same time.

Once they were out in the fresh air, Lucy breathed in a long breath through her nose and blew it out through her mouth. God it felt good to be out of that place.

"Come on," Jack urged her across the large lawn. "We have to go over that wall."

She followed Jack and let him help her over the wall.

Everyone else did the same and then they were off and running through the grapes. The leaves from the vines slapped at them as they ran as fast as they could manage to wherever it was that Jack was leading them. Lowering her head, she plowed forward, not wanting to slow down until she was as far away from that awful place as she could possibly get.

After running for a bit, they emerged at an opening in the vineyard where a metal building sat. It was illuminated with fluorescent lights which were mounted to the outer walls. She bent over for a moment to catch her breath, then stood and found everyone else doing the same. A quick survey of how many bodies were with them told her they'd lost someone. "Where is Emily?"

The others glanced around them, looking back and forth as if she might pop out of the vineyard at any time. "Dammit." Lucy kicked the gravel.

Greg, looking a little wistful, pulled his hood down off his head. "She must have broken off from us in the grapes."

Liv shrugged. "Well, there's nothing we can do about it now. We need to get our own asses home."

Lucy agreed. They got her out of the Reapers compound, so there was nothing more they could do anyway. "Still sucks, I would have liked to know more about what she knows. I'll fill you guys in on that later."

That was when her eyes fell upon Greg's car and Jack's truck waiting for them near the building, and she realized she was actually going to make it home.

LUCY
25

It wasn't until they were on the highway, racing back toward Summer Hollow, that Lucy was able to relax. She sat in the middle of the front seat in Jack's truck, wedged somewhat uncomfortably between Jack and Ethan.

Apparently no one felt like talking and Lucy was all right with that. Liv and Hannah sat in the back seat, resting after the impromptu rescue mission. Ethan stared out the passenger window into the darkness, ignoring everyone else in the vehicle.

Jack had one hand on the wheel and the other resting on Lucy's thigh. She wanted to scoot over until she was practically sitting in his lap but didn't because, with Ethan there, it would definitely be weird. The disapproval radiated from Ethan so thickly that she was sure Liv and Hannah felt it too.

She couldn't worry about him and his feelings right now though. The last thing she ever wanted to do was hurt him, but she had an inkling his behavior was more about Jack being a Reaper than his relationship with Lucy. Most likely, if Jack had been some ordinary guy, he wouldn't be reacting the way he was.

When they rolled into Summer Hollow, Jack drove straight to Lucy's house and parked his truck beside all the other vehicles in the driveway. He helped her down from the truck and let the girls out of the back.

Greg's Escort pulled up behind him with the rest of her family cramped inside the tiny vehicle. Once they were all out and standing in the brisk night air, Greg eyeballed Jack and then held out his hand for a shake. "Thanks for the help man."

Jack gripped her brother's hand and they both grimaced. "Anytime," Jack responded and then released Greg's hand. "Well … I should probably…"

"Why don't you come in for a while and unwind. We should probably discuss a few things as far as further planning and …" he glanced at Lucy, "other stuff," her brother's voice trailed off.

Oh good lord. What were they going to talk about? She wished that this relationship, or whatever it was, was just between her and Jack. But, as much as she hated her business being a public matter, her family had to be a part of it. "Geez Greg, subtlety never was your strong suit."

She felt Jack take her hand. "Sure. I'd love to come in."

Everyone went into the house and piled into the kitchen where they proceeded to inspect all their wounds and start cleaning up. Hannah opened a cabinet and extracted two gigantic bottles of peroxide, a tube of triple antibiotic cream and a box full of bandages. The box had every size and shape of bandage you could imagine. They kept the supplies handy since they used the stuff all the time.

"Get over here," Hannah mumbled as she rifled through the box.

Lucy examined her arms, looking for an injury that she may not have noticed. Sure enough, there was a large cut on her shoulder. "Oh." She strode over to join Hannah by the sink. "I don't even know where or when I got that."

Hannah wet a cotton ball with some peroxide and touched it to Lucy's cut. "It doesn't matter. It was

chaos in there so it could have happened at any point."
She continued to treat Lucy's wound while the others
tended to their own.

Greg opened the fridge and rummaged around until
he found some bottles of beer in the back. He grabbed
two and offered one to Jack. "You want one?"

"That, is exactly what I need right now." Jack
accepted the beer and twisted off the cap. He closed
his eyes and took a long pull, then leaned back on the
counter beside Lucy. "Look, I know how awkward
and strange this is," he began.

Greg held up his hand. "Stop. I think we can be done
with that part. You helped us rescue Lucy and you …
um, you renounced your … mother. I think that pretty
much takes care of most of our trust issues."

Dan let out a noise that sounded a lot like a snort. "I
still don't trust him. I don't give a fuck how much he
helped us." He opened the fridge and got a beer out
for himself.

Having Jack inside of her house, hanging out and
having a beer with her family, was something she
never thought would happen. Her expectations
had never gone beyond trying to stop the attraction
between them. The fact that a Reaper was in their
home at all was mind blowing.

"What is this?" Hannah asked, pointing at the small
round bandage that Aiden had given her after the
blood draw.

Lucy shrugged. "They took some blood. They didn't
hurt me or anything."

Jack swung his head around, as did her brothers and
sisters. "What the fuck do you mean they took some
blood? What for?"

"Oh…" Lucy caught Jack's eye. "Um, you know
that girl … Emily?"

"Yeah."

James finished cleaning his cuts and scrapes and sat
down at the table. "Yeah, what was she doing there
anyway?" he asked.

247

Looking to each of the siblings, Lucy saw that they were all waiting for an answer. "Okay, hold on." She waited for Hannah to finish up with the antibiotic cream and slap a bandage on her arm. She moved to the table and sat down so that she could relax. Immediately, as if he were her shadow, Jack pulled out a chair and sat next to her.

"I'm not sure if this lady is just crazy, or if there is any truth to it, but they claim Emily is a Seer who has given the Empress a prophecy of her own concerning the Reapers and the Keepers." Jack's eyes met with hers. "No offence about your mom," she added.

He held up his hand. "No worries."

"So, anyway ..." She began, and then told them everything she knew about the Empress and Emily.

After hearing the whole story, Jack leaned back in his chair. "So that's why she changed her mind about killing you."

She nodded. "Yes. She thinks that, together, our blood will be able to put an end to the warring of the Keepers and the Reapers. But, like our prophecy, there aren't any specifics. The seer said that it doesn't work like that.

Daniel threw his empty beer bottle in the trash. "Well, that is all behind us for right now. What we have ahead is a bigger problem. We really, really pissed her off and I have a feeling that this place is going to be crawling with Reapers soon."

Greg nodded. "He's right. We need to figure out both our offensive and defensive moves here. This is obviously going to get worse before it gets better."

Lucy leaned forward on the table and yawned. "Can we do it tomorrow though? I'm exhausted."

There was a loud murmur throughout the room as the others agreed that they needed to get some rest.

She turned to Jack, wanting to say something but not sure how it was going to go over with her family ... or Ethan. "You're welcome to stay the night if you want. We have space on the couch."

248

Jack narrowed his eyes, the protective instinct appearing once again. "Sorry, but if I'm going to stay here, I'm staying with you. I don't want you out of my sight for one fucking minute."

And she was worried about what *she* was going to say. Looked like Jack took care of the shock factor for her.

Ethan shifted against the counter he was leaning on. "I don't think that's a good idea."

Lucy felt the panic fluttering into her stomach again. She started to speak, cleared her throat and then tried again. "I'm an adult Ethan. I can have sleepovers if I want to."

He rolled his eyes and turned away. "Whatever. Lucy, he is still a Reaper. We probably have a better chance of avoiding this whole mess if he weren't around."

Greg shook his head. "No. Lucy probably would have been killed that first night if Jack hadn't saved her. And even if she had avoided that, we wouldn't have been able to rescue her tonight if he wasn't around." He looked at Jack, "No offense here, but I don't really think the Empress cares that much about what you do. She is pissed at all of us and most of this would be still be happening without you involved. Right now she's probably more worried that you will tell us Reaper super secrets or some shit."

Jack closed his eyes for a second and then opened them. Lucy found herself reaching over to hold his hand. She gripped it in her own, letting him know that she was there for him. He focused his gaze back onto Greg. "No, you're right. She doesn't care. And she is going to come for all of you full force regardless of if I'm around or not. Now, it's not just about Lucy being the Chosen One, it's about the fact that she didn't get what she wanted. More Reapers will definitely be coming."

Greg considered this. "I won't make decisions as far as you and Lucy, although I admit this is fuckin' weird, but you are welcome to stay."

Jack nodded, but Lucy could see the look in his eye that said he wouldn't have left anyway.

"I think Dad's waiting for us?" Liv changed the subject. She stood near the window facing the graveyard. "I'm pretty sure that's him on the edge of the yard."

James scooted his chair out and stood. "We'd better go fill him in and let him see that Lucy is all right." He looked at Jack. "Maybe you should hang out here."

Jack also stood. "If you're worried about me and your dad and the soul eating thing, I already met him when I was here before we left."

"You met my dad?" Lucy asked.

He ran his hand through his dark hair, which was all messed up from the fighting and running. She thought it made him look even sexier. Then he shrugged as if it were no big deal. "Yeah, he gave me the go ahead to … well, he told me to do what I had to do as long as I brought you back."

Whoa … that was a shocker, but pretty much everything that had happened within the last twenty-four hours had a pretty high shock value.

"Well …" Lucy didn't want to make him stay in the house, so she nodded. "I guess you can come with."

"Don't worry," he reassured them, "I'm not going to go on a soul binge or anything. I'm good for a while."

Daniel rolled his eyes and headed for the door. "I feel so much better now," he muttered sarcastically.

Lucy watched Jack and realized he was, and had been, internally battling with himself. He looked like he wanted to get in Dan's face and tell him off. Instead, he just moved closer to Lucy and said, "Look man, I understand that you have a problem with me. Believe me, I get that, but unless Lucy asks me to leave I'm staying and you're going to have to get used to me."

Uh oh.

Dan turned around slowly until he was facing Jack. "Reaper, you know *nothing* about my problems.

The love of my life was killed by one of you mother fuckers. So excuse the hell out of me for not wanting you around at all, especially not around my sister."

Still battling, Jack kept his cool. Thank God. "I am not that Reaper. I am not like most Reapers, and I never have been. I helped you save your sister, but dude, you are her blood … If it came down to it, I would go through everything that we went through tonight all over again, even if *you* were the one who needed saving."

Suddenly, the tears wanted to make another appearance. He was telling her brother that her family meant just as much to him as she did. That was pretty much swoon-worthy.

"I don't need you to save me," Dan shot back, then spun, shoving open the door and headed out into the night.

Lucy squeezed Jacks hand. "Thank you."

Jack only let out a long breath and nodded. "Let's go."

So, out into the night they went, the entire clan of Estmond Keepers and one Reaper. They would have made quite a sight to anyone who could see the auras, with the misty red of a Reaper enveloped by the shimmering silver of the Keepers.

Lucy strode across the yard with Jack and her family. Indeed, she could see her father's soul waiting at the line between where the yard ended and the graveyard began. The moment he caught sight of all his children, her included, marching toward him, his transparent face lit up with a smile.

"Oh, thank the Lord, you're all right," he cried out as they approached, "all of you, thank God!"

"We're okay, Dad. Tired, but okay." Lucy stepped forward, wishing that she could give him a hug. She missed that so much.

"And you have brought your friend back with you?"

She reached out once again for Jack's hand and he entwined his fingers with hers. "I guess Liv explained

251

things."

Her father nodded. "She did. I got the quick version, but enough to comprehend what is going on between you two."

"I need him to stick around for a while until we can figure it all out. It's too hard for me to not have him near me."

Even as a soul, her father managed a sarcastic grin. "I would love to know what's happening here as well." He turned and gazed off into the cemetery for a moment and then continued. "I can't make these decisions for my children. I also can't tell you that I'm completely all right with a Reaper among us, but I don't really see any other option at the moment. He helped our family tonight and that is a debt we must pay back."

Jack held his free hand up. "No, there is no debt. I helped with the rescue, but I would have gone by myself if I had to. Lucy will never be any part of a debt that is being repaid, ever."

Wow, this was just getting better and better with each passing moment.

Her father nodded and looked to his other children. "All right then, no repayment. But, I have to agree that if this pull is as strong as Lucy and the Reaper both say it is, it's probably more dangerous for them to be apart."

Lucy breathed a sigh of relief. "Thanks Dad and his name is Jack."

"Well Jack, I would shake your hand, but …" He held up his wavering and transparent hand in explanation of his lack of manners.

Jack interrupted him with a wave of his own. "No worries. I understand."

"Just mind yourself, Reaper. We are far from alone and if you make one wrong move with my daughter or my family, I'm calling in more Keepers."

"Yes sir," Jack acknowledged him with a nod.

"Now, tell me everything about what happened

during the rescue."

The siblings took turns explaining to their father what had happened when they broke into the Empress's mansion. She did notice that the other's put in good words for Jack, all except Dan and Ethan, who took every opportunity to make a case for Jack not to be around.

After the story was told once again, Greg Sr. furrowed his brows with worry. "This is not good."

His eldest son nodded in agreement. "We know Dad, we all need to get showers and rest, and then tomorrow we are going to go over planning for Reaper attacks."

"And what do you think of this girl and what has been foreseen for the Reapers. Do we think there is truth in it?"

Hannah yawned and then answered. "I highly doubt that she would have even been in that place if there weren't any truth in it. She obviously knew that the Empress was a Reaper, and I'm fairly certain that she could see the auras."

Jack agreed with her. "Yeah, she could see them. When we tried to get her to come with us she didn't want to at first, because I was there. She called me 'one of them.'"

Greg Sr. smiled. "Well, you are 'one of them,' so I don't blame her. Too bad she didn't stay with you guys." He paused and eyed all of his children carefully. "All right, we are going to discuss this tomorrow. You guys look awful." He waved them off toward the house. "I love you all, glad you're safe, now go get some rest."

The goodnights took another few minutes and then everyone headed back into the house. On the way in, as the first light began to make its way into the sky, Lucy realized that she was getting used to having her father around again. When it was time for him to cross over, it was going to be even harder than losing him the first time.

Back inside, Steph, James, Dan and Liv all said they wanted to go home to get their showers and rest, but that they would be back as soon as they could. Greg, Hannah and Ethan opted to stay, although Ethan didn't seem happy about it.

Lucy cornered him in the kitchen when Jack left her alone for a minute to use the bathroom. "Why don't you just go home if you're going to be a dick?"

"I'm not being a dick, Lucy, I'm being careful," he shot back at her.

She felt her spine straighten in defense. "What is that supposed to mean?"

"You know what it means."

"The fuck I do."

"These feelings aren't even real and your letting this guy sleep in your room for fucks sake. You don't even know him."

Their eyes were locked in confrontation and she wasn't going to back down. "Well, I want to know him, Okay. I'm an adult, Ethan … like I told you before, I can have him in my room if I want."

"Well, sorry then, I'm sticking around just in case. I don't trust him."

"Dammit, Ethan. That isn't what this is about and you know it."

"It is about that, but yeah, it's also about you and me. So fucking what?" He spread his arms wide. "Fucking sue me for caring about you."

"Ugh!" Lucy almost stomped her foot she was so frustrated with him.

"Go ahead." He stepped away from her. "Go ahead and do what you want, just don't think that I'm leaving you alone with him."

"Greg's here, I'm not alone."

He rolled his eyes. "You know what I mean."

She rolled hers back. "Yeah, I do."

He turned and started to walk out of the kitchen. "I'm going to bed. I'll be in James' room. Don't do anything I have to listen to all fucking day. I need to get some sleep." He pushed out the door.

"Well, get some ear plugs then!" she called after him as the kitchen door swung back and forth. "

She turned around and pounded a fist into the counter top. "Dammit," she whispered to herself. She hated it when Ethan's feelings were hurt. No matter what, he would always be a best friend to her … but, it seemed like he would always want her as more than a friend.

She heard a cough, like someone clearing their throat, and spun around to see who dared invade her moment of breakdown.

Jack stood there, leaning against the doorjamb, staring at her with a glint in his deep, dark eyes. "So, what is this I hear about ear plugs and not getting sleep?"

JACK
26

His red headed Keeper spun around to face him. Her eyes wide with shock and her mouth hanging open. After the surprise had passed, she gathered herself together and tucked a stray lock of hair behind her ear. "You weren't supposed to hear that."

God she was adorable.

And when the fuck did he start using the word *adorable*? "I don't know who *didn't* hear it," he told her with a smile.

"I …" Her sentence trailed off as he strode across the kitchen to where she stood at the counter.

"Don't worry," he reassured her, "I'm not taking that as an invitation." He placed his fingers under her chin and gently lifted until she was staring up at him.

"What if it is an invitation?" she boldly asked.

He lowered his head until his lips gently touched hers. Damn, her lips were so fucking soft. He stepped forward again, backing her into the edge of the counter. Her lips parted, letting his tongue graze tenderly over hers.

She moaned a little beneath his lips and wound her arms around his neck, pulling his body even closer, so that their bodies were pressed up against each other.

Oh fuck. He had to get her out of this kitchen. Right fucking now. He broke away from the kiss, breathing heavily and already feeling the intensity of how much he wanted her. He reached down and grabbed her legs, pulling her up so that she could wrap her legs around him. "Where's your room?" he whispered.

She nipped his ear and whispered back. "Out the kitchen door and up the stairs, third door on the left." She kissed him again, this time with more urgency. Somehow, he managed to get out the kitchen door while holding her *and* kissing her.

He broke away from the kiss long enough to pause in the living room and look for the stairs. Spotting them near the front door, he practically ran toward them with Lucy kissing his neck. The stairs were even harder, but he made it up those fuckers and found the third door on the right.

The door was open so he strode right in, kicked it shut behind him and then fell onto the bed, crushing her beneath him. "Tell me to stop," he asked her, his voice gravelly. "Tell me to stop and I will."

She shook her head against his lips and arched her back. "I don't want you to stop."

He couldn't get enough of her. He kissed her lips, her neck, and the exposed area of her breasts. Then, he forced himself up, kneeling before her so that he sat between her open legs, looking down at the phenomenal woman before him.

Her legs were bent at the knee and her skin was almost glowing with a sexual sheen. Her lips were parted, pink and swollen from kissing. He met her eyes and silently questioned her. She gave him a nod without hesitating.

Then, he went to work on her jeans. He pulled the button loose and lowered the zipper. She gasped and thrust her hips up, as if the mere thought of being naked before him was enough to cause an orgasm.

Taking the waistband in both hands he tried desperately not to simply rip them off of her, lowering them with excruciatingly slow movement. Once those jeans were down over her ass, it was his turn to gasp. She wore black lacy panties that stood out against her pale skin, and were fucking sexy as hell.

"Still okay with this?"

Her eyes darkened with frustration. "Stop asking me that. I want this and I am not made of glass." With that, she reached down and pulled at the bottom of her tank, revealing her perfectly soft stomach and then, as the tank went over her head, a matching black lace bra which encased the most perfect breasts he'd ever seen in his life.

Whoosh, the jeans came off … all the way.

He was on top of her again and her fingers were clawing at his pants, unbuttoning and pushing them down. With one hand, he helped her get them off, and then used his leg to kick them off all the way. His boxer briefs came off the same way.

Lucy's legs snaked up around his back and her back arched as if she were unconsciously trying to get as close to him as possible. He ran one hand up the side of her torso and over the mound of her breast. He pushed the fabric away, found her nipple and swept over it with his thumb, feeling her stiffen at his touch.

This was insane and he had no idea how it could be happening, but it was and he wasn't about to give it up for anything … unless she told him to stop.

His other hand crept around to her back and flicked the snap of her bra open. With a little bit of jiggling, which he didn't mind at all, she helped slide the bra straps down her arms.

Staring down at her, he took in every inch of bare skin, then lowered his head and began to kiss every part of her that he could get his lips on. She pushed at him, turning to the side and rolling so that their positions were switched and he was now on his back.

She looked down at him, a slight smile twitching at her lips and then began to lower her panties.

Oh, holy fuck. He hadn't thought he could get any

harder, but ... yeah, it happened. She maneuvered out of her panties and then leaned down to kiss him again, staying just far enough over him that their bodies weren't quite touching.

Holy fucking hell. He groaned and rolled his hips, wanting to be inside of her more than he'd ever wanted anyone.

She pulled her lips away from his and looked into his eyes, still panting from the sexual tension.

Suddenly, and surprisingly, he was hit with a conscience. This was the heat of the moment. What if she woke up tomorrow and regretted being with him? He had to make sure she knew what she was doing.

"I could have your soul right now," he told her. "I could take it without you even knowing I was doing it." His breathing was heavy too. But she had to know ... she had to know that he wasn't safe. He was a Reaper and she a Keeper, the two species which were born enemies.

He knew these facts, but for some reason that couldn't be explained, this woman was his and he knew it. This moment sealed his fate ... there would never be another woman for him if it wasn't her.

Her eyes didn't stray from his, not even once and she whispered, "I think you already have my soul."

That was it. He pulled her down to him and kissed her with more passion than he'd ever kissed anyone. She moaned softly and then reached down until she found the rock hard length of him. She gripped him in her hand and stroked, up and down, rubbing the tip with her thumb.

What in the hell was she doing, trying to make him come before he even got inside her. Well, fuckin' two could play at that game. He caught her around the waist and threw her off to the side, then moved over until he was the one on top. She gasped in surprise, but then relaxed against the bedding. He braced himself above her so that their bodies were several inches apart.

Slowly, he lowered his head until their lips touched. He kissed her, long and hard, trying to let her know how much he wanted her. When he broke away, he didn't take time to catch his breath, he went right to kissing her neck. Then, he moved down to her collar bone trailing his tongue over the prominent bone. Next he moved lower and found her breasts. He reached up and cupped one with his right hand, simultaneously using his tongue on the left one. He flicked her nipple gently with his tongue and then circled around it.

While he would have loved to have stayed in that spot all night, he had better, far more enjoyable plans for her.

He continued his trail of kisses down over her belly, and then down one thigh. She opened her legs wider to accommodate, so he switched back and forth between both her inner thighs, kissing his way to the sweet spot.

She had already been releasing soft moans of pleasure, but when his tongue swept over her clit, she bucked and grabbed his hair in her hand, letting out a small cry.

He fought the urge to take her then and there. He wanted her so fucking bad. Not that he wasn't enjoying the taste of her, or loving the feel of her grinding against his mouth. Oh no, he was totally enjoying that, so much that he wanted to give her even more.

He braced himself up with one elbow, not letting his mouth separate from her. With his other hand he slid a finger inside her. She let out another cry, this time a little louder and gripped his hair even tighter.

After another minute or so, he felt her pulling him upward. "Get up here," she ordered in a low, husky voice.

Yeah, she didn't have to tell him twice. He moved up and hovered over her, leaning down to kiss her. The kiss was long and hard, filled with urgency that neither of them were ready to deny anymore.

"I want you," she whispered, looking up into his

eyes.

He reached up with one hand and used his fingers to push a lock of stray hair out of her face and told her, "I want you back."

And then, keeping his gaze locked on hers, he slid into her. He groaned, feeling her so hot and slick against him. Her eyes went wide when he entered her, then she relaxed and started to move against him, setting the rhythm for the both of them.

He could have stayed with her like that forever. But, far sooner than he would have liked he felt her body tense, and her back arched beneath him. Her eyes glazed over with passion and she bit down on her lip to keep her cries from being too loud as she came.

Holy shit, no holding back now, he thought as he felt his own orgasm building.

She had climaxed and then relaxed back down into the comforter when it was over. Her arms had fallen down into the blankets above her, so he reached up and grasped her around the wrists, one in each of his hands. She gasped and rolled her hips.

"You ready?" he whispered against her ear.

She nodded. "Hell yeah."

That was the only cue he needed, he couldn't hold back any more and pumped his hips getting as deep into her as he could possibly get. She bit her lower lip again to keep herself silent, but little moans and whimpers escaped anyway.

He rocked her body, his thrusts getting harder and harder with each one, until she arched upward, her breasts lifting and he felt the molten warmth clench against his cock again. He came at the same time. Feeling the sweet release of orgasm had never felt more amazing than it did with her.

Breathing heavily, he stayed inside her until both of them stopped quaking from the aftershocks of their orgasms. Then, he lowered himself down so that he was laying flush on top of her and kissed her.

"Mmmm, thank God," she murmured when he

pulled his lips away from hers.

He chuckled and then rolled off of her. "What?"

She turned on her side and smiled. Her cheeks were flushed and pink from the sex, and it seemed like her skin was fucking glowing. "I just don't know how much longer I could have gone without doing that."

He lay on his back and laughed again. "Same here, trust me!"

She pulled the comforter that they had been on top of over their bodies and then cuddled up to him, laying her head in the crook of his arm with her cheek on his chest. "You're amazing," she told him. "I know that's sorta cliché for after sex, but I don't mean that, I mean you … everything about you is amazing."

He lifted his head and looked at her. "What? You mean the sex wasn't amazing, cause I thought it was fucking phenomenal."

She slapped at his abs. "Of course it was! You know what I mean."

He couldn't keep the grin from his face. "Yeah, I know what you meant. And for the record, *you* are the amazing one," he told her, and then rolled her over so that he could show her again just how amazing he thought she was.

LUCY

27

TWO WEEKS LATER

"Dad, I am not taking Dan wine tasting. That is an accident waiting to happen!"

Lucy crossed her arms as she argued with her father in the graveyard. He frowned at her with his shimmering and transparent face. "You need to have more than one person with you all the time, Lucy."

"I'm fine. Jack is with me and we are both prepared for anything."

He shook his head. "Nope, you're not going to Napa without protection."

Lucy looked to the heavens. "You would think out of six brothers and sisters and Ethan that *someone* would be able to go besides the town drunk. Ugh!"

Maybe she could just tell him that they were taking Dan and then go by themselves. Yeah, that would probably work.

"I don't think so Lucy Mae."

She made a face and wiped some of the sweat off her forehead. Damn it was muggy out. It only got like that in Summer Hollow when a storm was heading their way. She even had on a cute little summer dress that was loose and flowing, as well as wearing her hair up in a bun, and she was still sweating. "What?" she demanded.

"How many times do I have to tell you that it is impossible to lie to me? No, you can't tell me your taking Dan and then go without him."

"Sometimes it's awfully hard being your daughter," she told him in a flat voice.

"Well, the feeling is mutual honey, raising you hasn't exactly been a piece of cake."

Good grief, like it wasn't enough that she couldn't go to classes alone. Well, the actual classes she attended alone. But Jack and one of her siblings were always standing right outside the door when she came out.

Greg Sr. moved his gaze from her to the house where Jack stood on the porch watching them. "How is your friend doing?"

She shrugged. "I think it's been harder for him than he lets on. You know, cause he's so big and tough. But, he lost his parents and his best friend. He doesn't have a job and can't work because he's always guarding me, which I hate by the way. Aside from me, he doesn't have anything anymore."

Her father nodded. "At least he moved in, that makes it easier if he doesn't have any bills."

"Yeah, easier financially, but not for him. He doesn't like taking from us and not contributing."

He shot her a look of concern. "But, he is contributing, he is working … by helping take care of you."

"Try and tell him that." She rolled her eyes. "He doesn't consider being with me a job, so it doesn't count."

"Well, I can't say that his outlook on that disappoints me. I rather like it that he treats you like a queen."

Lucy's hands went to her face. "Oh, please don't use that word."

Her father didn't say anything more, he knew she was talking about the reference to the fact that Jack was a Reaper prince. Even though he renounced the title it didn't change the bloodline.

She turned. "I'd better go and *fine*, I'll take Dan."

He waved and blew her a kiss. "Have fun on your wine tasting trip. Stay in a hotel if you drink too much."

She turned and waved back at him. "Love you, Dad."

Then, she jogged the rest of the way over to the house. Jack stepped off the porch and let her run up into his arms. "You ready?" he asked, leaning down for a kiss.

When their lips separated, she inhaled deeply to catch her breath, and then nodded. "Yes, I'm ready, let's go." Then she turned and opened the back door and stuck her head in. "Dan! We're leaving," she hollered.

Ethan came out of the house before Dan did. "Hey," he greeted her and then nodded at Jack. For the first time in their lives, her relationship with Ethan was rocky. They had made up, sort of ... but, they mostly walked on eggshells around each other now. He accepted Lucy being with Jack, but she knew he secretly hoped that it wouldn't last.

"Hey," she smiled, "I thought you would be at work already."

He shook his head. "Not yet, I'll be heading that way soon. I just had to swing by and pick up my tool belt."

"Oh." She didn't know what else to say.

He turned to go back in the house. "You guys have fun and be careful. I'll stop by after work."

"We will," she assured him. "See you, later."

With that he disappeared into the house. Lucy let out a sigh, wishing their relationship were on better terms.

She didn't have long to dwell on it though because Dan appeared in the doorway, wearing that god-awful trench coat even though it was a freaking sauna outside. She made a face that clearly displayed her disapproval. "Why do you insist on wearing that thing?" she asked.

He shrugged. "I like it. What do you care, anyway?"

"Because, Dan, we have to be seen with you."

"Yeah, so." He took a pair of dark tinted sunglasses out of his pocket and slid them on.

Jack laughed and Lucy stared, mouth hanging open. "Really?" she finally asked.

"It's to complete the whole look," he told her and then sauntered off to Jack's truck.

"Dumbass," Lucy muttered, following Dan down the porch steps. Jack was right behind her, laughing. "Don't laugh," she chastised. "That only encourages him."

They arrived at the truck and Jack opened the passenger door for Lucy. She grabbed the inside door handle and hauled herself up. She smiled when Jack "helped" her up by giving her ass a push.

Dan was already in the back seat, putting his ear buds in his ears and searching his playlists for a song he wanted to listen to. That was fine with her, since he was still being an asshole to Jack every chance he got. Jack slid behind the wheel and fired up the engine. She immediately pushed the button to roll down the window. The warm outside air was better than the hot air inside the truck.

"I'll have the air conditioner going in a few minutes," he reassured her.

She told him it was fine as they pulled out of the driveway and headed for Napa. Thinking about Napa, and grapes and vineyards, only made her think about being kidnapped by the Empress.

They had never heard from Emily, not that they had expected to, but everyone had agreed that she probably had information they might need. So, they were going to start searching for her.

"Hey," she said, getting Jack's attention.

"Hmmm."

"You heard from Aiden at all?" she asked in a low voice.

He shook his head. "Nah, and I don't expect to." I think I'm going to have to call that a loss. "Besides.

He can't call me anyway, my phone is disconnected."

"I gave you a phone," Lucy pointed out.

"Yeah, but he doesn't have the number. Damn, what … do you want me to talk to him or something?"

She leaned back in the seat, knowing that the topic irritated him. "No … I don't know." He had told her how close he and Aiden were growing up, so what happened over her and the whole deal with the Empress was pretty fucked up. But still, she felt bad that her man had lost his best friend. That shouldn't happen to anyone.

"Well, I'm not going to try and contact him. That only puts you in more danger."

"Jack, he knows where we live."

"I don't want to talk about it anymore. We are supposed to be having fun today." He took his eyes off the road for a second to catch her eye. "Well, more fun. This morning was pretty fun."

"Okay, I can hear you, mother fucker," Dan chimed in from the back seat. "Don't ever talk about sex with my sister in front of me again unless you want your ass beat."

Jack chuckled. "Keeper, you threaten to beat my ass about six times a day."

"I mean it this time."

Lucy shut her eyes and shook her head. "Knock it off guys." She scooted closer to Jack and leaned on his shoulder while he drove.

The first stop on their day of wine tasting was the Beringer House, one of the oldest and largest wineries in the area. Lucy had seen pictures before, but seeing it in person put the photos to shame. No photo would ever do justice to the beautiful architecture of the historical building.

They took the tour of the Beringer House first. Jack and Lucy walked together, holding hands while Dan tagged along behind them. He still had his sunglasses on and earbuds in. Geez, people probably thought he was some wannabe secret service agent or something.

Good grief. Lucy tried to ignore the fact that he was there at all.

After the tour they had a short break and sat down at one of the tables on the grounds. Lucy felt the air cool just a tad and looked up into the sky. It had completely clouded over while they were getting the tour of the house. "Damn," she said, feeling the first drop on her shoulder. "It's raining."

"We need it," Jack pointed out.

She frowned. "Yeah, but the one day we get to go do this and it freaking rains. Not a good sign at all."

"We're still having fun. Looking at all this historical shit couldn't be more up my alley."

She smiled. "You are such an ass."

After the break they went over to the Old Winery for wine and chocolate pairing.

"I still think this is for chicks," Jack told her during the tasting. "Wine, I can do, but wine and chocolate together … just get me a package of tampons and I'm good to go."

"Shut up," she scolded. "You wanted to come too."

He nodded. "Yeah, I did and I'm actually having a good time, only because you're here." He looked around. "Can you imagine trying to do this by yourself? How boring."

They wrapped up the wine and chocolate pairing and headed into town for some lunch. Since it had only sprinkled a little bit, Lucy chose a nice little restaurant where they could sit on the patio. The patio was like those you see in commercials or ads for trips to Greece. A lattice work with grape vines woven into it shaded the entire patio. The tables were iron, with glass tops and cushions on the chairs.

Made her feel super classy, sitting there with her big ass, fancy water glass.

Jack looked around the place and didn't seem fazed. Yeah, he'd probably been to places like it all the time, growing up the way he did. Dan kept to himself, which was fine, and ordered light, which was better. What made her happiest was that Dan was actually keeping his mouth shut and letting Lucy and Jack have their day. She would have to thank him for that later.

Just as her food was coming, a crack of thunder sounded and the sky opened up its fury on the Napa Valley.

"Shit!" Lucy cursed. "I really wanted to eat out here." She stood and grabbed her purse. Then, she heard her phone ring inside the damn thing. "Ugh, hold on," she told Jack and Dan, who were already heading for the inside of the restaurant. Luckily, most of the rain wasn't getting through the patio cover of grapevines, but even a little bit was still enough to make you want to eat inside.

She pulled her phone out of the bag and saw Hannah's face on the screen. "Hello," she answered.

"Lucy?"

"Duh, you called me."

"Lucy. I need help … you guys have to get here right now."

Alarms went off inside her body as she listened to her sister's words and the frightened waver in her voice. "Hannah, what happened?"

"Luce, I killed a Reaper. I need help *right now*."

"I'm coming … we're coming. Call the others," Lucy ordered, already heading out the door.

Jack and Dan were right on her heels as she ran out the door. "What's going on?" Jack asked at the same time Dan wanted to know "What happened?"

The wind and rain whipped at her, soaking her skin and clothes as she pulled the door of the truck open and looked over at Jack. "New mission, this time we are going to save my sister."

READ AN EXCERPT OF SAVIOR

A FULL-LENGTH NOVEL
BY JENNIFER MALONE WRIGHT

Sweltering heat emanated from the searing flames. Alex ignored his blistered skin and burnt clothes. He plunged both arms into the blazing orange inferno without a second thought for his own well-being. His hands frantically flailed until he found what he searched for. He pulled the charred remains up and hugged them to his chest before he gave a desperate glance toward the others.

Smoke curled into his mouth and nose and made it nearly impossible to breathe.

"Hurry, hurry. Get out now," a gentle voice whispered into his ears. "You must go right now if you want to live."

However, he couldn't leave them behind.

"Go now," the voice whispered more urgently.

Sparks flew when a giant log broke in half and fell from the ceiling. It crashed onto the floor less than two feet from where Alex stood. Flames engulfed the fallen wood and created yet another obstacle.

The voice tried again, crying out, "Hurry, Alex!"

Alex knew he needed to move if he wanted to live, but he paused for a moment to question whether he even wanted to bother. The flames grew while Alex stood motionless, undecided. Suddenly, a great push from behind thrust him forward toward a wall of fire.

Alex stirred in his mahogany coffin, one of the best money could buy. He felt the soft, white velvet lining rub against his cheek, but it didn't comfort him. He panted like a thirsty dog and writhed helplessly inside the narrow wooden box.

His eyes snapped open. First, he checked his hands for burns, but he found none. He groaned while he became more aware, and realized he'd had another nightmare.

He sighed, wondering if the recurring dreams were going to last forever. He reached up and unlatched the locks he'd installed for his own safety, or at least his peace of mind. He pushed open the lid and sat upright. His gaze wandered across the room while his mind tried to fight off the feeling of dread he had about the night ahead.

In the center of a large stone room that was buried deep beneath his house, his coffin rested on a massive stone slab with Egyptian hieroglyphic carvings around its edges. The carvings read, 'Death is not but eternal life.' The slab and coffin were the focus of the room, with the only other items being his slippers and a small table that held a candelabra and a box of wooden matches.

Alex lit a match and touched it to the candle wicks. A soft glow lit the room and let him safely climb out of his coffin. When he slammed the lid shut, the hollow sound reverberated off the stone walls and quickly died. He wedged his large feet into his slippers, padded to the wide steel door and punched a series of numbers into an electronic keypad. The door emitted a soft whooshing sound when the lock released.

Yawning, he stepped through the door and into a maze of tunnels that worked their way into deadly traps scattered throughout his underground chamber. Another whoosh signaled the door locking behind him. With the candelabra in his right hand, Alex moved through the maze and watched the flickering shadows play on the walls.

Alex stopped short and blinked. He saw what he thought was Malcolm's face, shining menacingly in the light ahead. He held the candles out toward the face, but the image wavered in the candlelight and disappeared.

Hmmmm, he thought, *perhaps the night ahead will prove eventful after all.*

Except for his echoing footsteps, the tunnels were deadly silent. Once he reached the end of the tunnels, he faced yet another heavy steel door with an electronic lock. Again, Alex entered a code on a keypad and exited the tunnels into a small closet.

Finally, he came to a thick oak door that simply needed a key. He removed the key from the pocket of his pajama shirt. Alex unlocked the door, entered the actual bedroom of his house, and relocked the entryway to the tunnels like he always did.

More out of habit than concern, Alex scanned the room with all his senses. Despite popular legend, the many mirrors in the room reflected his image off each other.

Alex gazed longingly at the four poster bed in which he never slept. The thick mattress was clothed in burgundy blankets with piles of decorative pillows scattered across the head of the bed. Burgundy and black dominated the color scheme: black carpet, burgundy walls, and sheer black curtains shading the windows.

Preferring the softer light of candles, he bypassed the light switch and went to the dressing table. He placed the candelabra on the table and picked up a candle that stood in a golden holder with biblical carvings on its base. Each time he lit the candle he was reminded of his time in Rome. The things there were so beautiful he couldn't resist bringing something home for himself.

Alex knew his hobby of decorating bordered on obsessive. He brought back things from his journeys all over the world to put in his main house in Reno. But his house was finished.

On top of that, his casinos practically ran themselves.

His place on the Higher Collective only occupied him every now and then.

He found it an awful feeling, having no purpose.

He tried to ignore the weakness that plagued his body with pain, indicating it was time to feed again. Glancing at his nightstand, he noticed the blinking red message light on his cellphone. Pushing back the pangs of hunger, he checked the messages.

Damion's smooth voice came through the earpiece. "Hey Alex, I've set a Collective meeting for tonight. Something is going down with Malcolm ... I really don't like the feel of it. I think we all need to get together to talk about this one. Eleven, conference room."

Clicking his phone shut and throwing it on the bed, Alex went to his closet and rummaged through his clothes. With exacting care, he chose a black Armani suit, complemented by a dark red dress shirt. Dark red was his power color, and he loved to feel powerful.

In the connecting bathroom he stripped out of his pajamas. The reflection staring back at him was one that would never change. Until the end of his existence, each time he looked in the mirror, he would see a twenty-eight-year-old man. His harsh Russian features would forever remain without wrinkles, and his coal black hair would never gray. His eyes, though, told the story of his age, and even he could see the stories in them.

His bare arms and chest still held the large muscles of the hardworking man he had been as a mortal. Although, his chest now bore the one mark he had allowed himself to get. He ran his fingers over the red longevity symbol. He had chosen longevity as a marker for being immortal. Like it was yesterday he remembered China and the tattoo shop where he had received the tattoo. As a last minute decision he asked the artist to add the three koi fish in a circle around the longevity symbol because the koi fish were associated with life-long good luck. And he felt like he sure need some of that.

Alex continued to think about China and its rare beauty while he carefully applied a dark, skin-colored foundation to his face and hands to cover his paleness. It was worth the effort to prevent mortals from questioning his light skin. After checking himself in the mirror again, Alex donned his black leather overcoat, a long flowing garment that swept the floor.

He allowed himself one last approving glance in the mirror, grabbed his briefcase off his dresser, and left the room.

He opened the garage door and sighed with pride. The room glimmered with glossy paint and shiny chrome from the many vehicles. He chose his orange '69 Mustang, because he wanted to stop at the church before the meeting, but he didn't have much time to spare. He slipped into the driver's seat, set his briefcase on the seat beside him, and then, with the turn of the key, the car came to life. After he backed out of the garage, he shut the doors with a remote and roared his way out of the long driveway.

At that hour of night, the pine-tree-lined streets were deserted. Alex liked that. Living outside the city, between Reno and Lake Tahoe, gave him more privacy. Although it was raining, he opened his window halfway to let in the fresh scent of the rain-washed earth.

When he approached the city, he took in the view of the lights. For Alex, each time was like the first time. The lights were like beacons, calling to him, enticing him. For that matter, he thought the lights were like vampires, deceivingly beautiful, alluring, and full of promise.

Until you're bitten, he thought.

Unable to help himself, he chuckled and continued the drive into the city. Traffic there was crazy compared to the lonely streets near his home. Among the multitude of hotels and casinos dominating the city, he kept his focus on the Lucas Hotels and Casinos—

the massive towers stood tall and proud—while he drew closer to them.

He passed the exit and kept going for a few miles until he came to a stop in front of a large brick church. He parked the car, ran through the rain, and ascended the cement stairway. Alex found the church deserted and locked, as it always was that time of night.

Taking out his set of lock picks, he thought about the old days when churches were never locked. They were always open for the public whenever someone needed to be close to God.

Upon entering, he felt a presence; not God, but something else.

Danielle.

She had always had a habit of following him when she was invisible. Although he knew she was there, he rarely let on. He couldn't think of any reason why she would want to keep herself secret from him, since she knew he would tell her anything she wanted to know. Besides, she could read minds.

Although the bricks muffled the sound of the rain, its presence was evident. It drizzled down the outside of the multicolored stained glass windows.

It's like they are melting, Alex thought as he stared at them.

An aisle separated two sets of pews, and at the far end of the church, behind the podium and the large choir section, was the baptismal area.

Following his usual ritual, Alex knelt in front of the podium at a short wooden table that, without fail, held a fresh flower arrangement. It also held a large leather-bound Bible, always opened to the same verse: John 3:16.

Alex lowered his head and spoke aloud to the empty church, his voice echoing in the darkness. "Lord, forgive me. I have sinned. I live a life of sin. Yet, you let me live. Again and again, I ask how that can be. How is it that you could let something as evil and corrupt as I live on this earth and walk with the humans you created?"

He dropped his head lower.

"I still don't understand a lot of things you have shown me, Lord. I'm depressed. I've never asked for anything from except guidance and strength, but it's time I humbly ask, just this once, for you to bless me with something to give me the will to go on."

A clap of thunder shook the walls of the church.

"This depression has become too great. I can barely rise from sleep when the sun sets. None of the hobbies that previously occupied me so well interest me anymore."

Alex paused and took in a deep, shuddering breath.

"I would never try to bargain with or demand anything from you. I would never be so bold as to assume I'm owed anything. All I ask is for some kind of meaning to this life, or after-life; whatever you wish to call it.

"I need a reason to persevere. After all, I no longer have a family. The only thing I have, besides a few friends, is the everlasting torment of being one of the most unholy creatures to walk this earth.

"Please hear me and consider the needs of one of your servants. Thank you. Thank you so much for everything you have given me. I would do anything for you. I am yours in all ways, and I am yours in everything.

"In Jesus's precious name, Amen."

When Alex rose from his knees, contentment flowed through his veins and filled him up. He felt the same every time he prayed.

A moment later, he rushed out the door, stopping only to relock it like he always respectfully did.

"Do you think he's ready?" Damion asked.

"He's past ready," Danielle murmured while she

slipped off her perch on the railing that separated the choir area from the rest of the church. "Damion, his depression has to end."

She felt Damion follow her to the front pew, on the right side of the aisle. She wanted to sit so she could see the altar.

He sat next to her. "I know Alex was chosen for this, but how do we know it will cure his depression? It could end this present situation, but begin another lengthy and dangerous one. How do we know this will not be the straw that breaks the camel's back?"

Danielle smiled. "I have known Alex for almost four hundred years. Even though he thinks he is dammed, he keeps his faith in God, and *that*, my dear friend, is the strongest kind of faith there is."

"So he'll do it?"

"He has yet to decide."

"I hope it goes the way we've planned."

"So do I, Damion, so do I."

"Why do you always come here to watch him pray? Don't you think that's like invasion of privacy or something?"

"I am his guardian."

"You *were*, when he was a human. He hasn't been mortal for a long time. I know enough to know you aren't required to be with him at all times."

"That's true, but his prayers are a most important time for me to be with him."

"Why?"

"He's convinced God doesn't hear his prayers. That's why he comes here almost every night. He could go on living a sinful life, believing he is dammed anyway, but he doesn't. It's vital he has some reinforcement of his faith in God. I know he feels me here."

Damion shook his head. "We'd better get to the meeting. I'll see you there."

Damion left. Danielle didn't want to leave the church. She looked up at the large cross on the wall above the baptismal. "Come on, Big Guy. His time to shine is finally here, so let's show him how much you really have in store for him."

She reluctantly stood, walked back down the aisle, and moved transparently through the tightly locked doors.

 ABOUT JENNIFER MALONE WRIGHT

JENNIFER MALONE WRIGHT resides in the beautiful mountains of northern Idaho with her husband and five children where she practices preparing for the zombie apocalypse. Just kidding!

But seriously, between the craziness of taking care of her children, Jennifer has little time left for herself. The time she does have left, usually leading far into the night, is spent working on her beloved fiction or chatting with her equally crazy friends.

Jennifer also loves coffee, has a passionate affair with red bull, wishes the sushi were better where she lives and dances while she cleans.

Please visit Jennifer's website at:
www.jennifermalonewright.com